GW00634523

Into the Blue

Into the Blue

Christina Green

ROBERT HALE · LONDON

ISBN 978-0-7090-9117-2

Robert Hale Limited
Clerkenwell House
Clerkenwell Green
London EC1R 0HT

www.halebooks.com

2 4 6 8 10 9 7 5 3 1

Typeset in 10½/14pt Classical Garamond
by Derek Doyle & Associates, Shaw Heath
Printed in Great Britain by the MPG Books Group, Bodmin and King's Lynn

AUTHOR'S NOTES

The idea for this book was sparked off by reading some of the accounts of the Victorian adventurers – men and women – who travelled the world searching for new and exotic plants. The diaries of Marianne North and Amelia Edwards showed me how highly Victorian women were beginning to value their freedom, and so my characters Hester and Ruby were born.

I am grateful to all my writing friends who listened and encouraged and particularly to Monica Hazell, who so generously allowed me access to her journal, written on a visit to the Dolomite Mountains in northern Italy in 1996.

CHAPTER ONE

Hester dipped her brush into the paint mixed on the palette and then added the last shading to the flower painting on the page in front of her. She looked at it keenly.

Germander speedwell (veronica chamoedris).

Not bad. Could be better, but she was improving. She would take the blue flower home and put it in water. It mustn't die. Father would be sure to say, 'What's that weed?', and she would tell him that it was a wild flower, growing everywhere around them, in the lanes, fields, and even in his own garden. He would harrumph and frown and pull his mouth down in disapproval but she didn't care. Flowers must be cherished.

Packing up her paints, easel and brushes, she thought how lucky she was to attend Mr Flynn's class in the Reading Room in Newton Abbot. She would continue with the lessons even though Father complained when he saw her setting out, ready to catch the omnibus into town.

It was her father's sister, Aunt Jacquetta Hirst, who had persuaded – ordered, thought Hester, wryly – Father to allow her to join this class.

'The girl has always painted, Arthur, and shown talent. We mustn't stand in her way. If you agree to pay the omnibus fare I will deal with the charges for the lessons. Joseph Flynn, I hear, although possibly a bit of a rogue socially, is a good teacher as well as a recognized artist. Hester could do no better than learn from him.'

'And where is this *talent* of hers' – Father had sniffed hard, the usual sign of annoyance – 'going to get her? I need my daughter at home here, not chasing all over the country painting flowers.'

Aunt Jacks had given him one of her pitying looks. 'My dear Arthur, times are changing. The old queen is on her last legs and women are becoming liberated. And about time, too. Why, I myself am thinking of starting a school for women gardeners. We are gaining freedom – at last. So stop moithering on about keeping your daughter at home. She needs to flex her wings.'

Hester had listened while Father and Stepmother continued to protest, but Aunt Jacks had won in the end, and here she was at the art class, hungry for a word or two of praise from the teacher, although nervously expecting something far more realistic.

Joseph Flynn looked down at her painting and she knew at once that his downturned mouth and critical expression indicated displeasure. 'Last leaf slightly too dark; veins too emphatic. Colour isn't quite right – Sap Green could do with a touch of Oxide of Chromium to calm it down a bit.' A hint of a smile lit his rugged face. 'But you're trying, you're working well. I like that tiny caterpillar. In fact. . . .' He was on the move already, stepping towards the next easel, the next nervous student. His voice drifted back to Hester and she leaned forward eagerly to catch each word. 'You might start working towards something, Miss Redding, a project, a career, even. Commercial art, lots of women doing it, think about it.' His voice rumbled away as he bent over the next canvas.

Hester breathed in deeply. At least his comments on her work were helpful, even slightly complimentary. Excitement grew. Yes, she would go on working. A project, he'd said; something warm began to glow inside her.

A career?

Joseph Flynn smiled as he held open the door for her, the last to leave the cold, bright room which served as a studio. 'Keep working,' he told her brusquely.

'I will, Mr Flynn, oh, I will. Thank you.'

She left the room, almost falling down the stairs as ambitious dreams filled her mind, arriving at the omnibus station just as the horses were moving. Extravagant thoughts continued to confuse her but, once arriving in Chudleigh, she found walking down the lane to

Oak House helped clear her mind. Determination said yes, she would step out into the world and play her part there. But then the confusion grew. To be truthful, being Father's dutiful daughter and showing unwilling affection for her stepmother brought little joy, except that she loved and respected Father and would always do so – but oh, for freedom.

To find my way through life, using my strength and ideas. It's hard to be a woman with all this male dictation, even arrogance, running the world. I will have a life that's all my own.

Her mind was full of suddenly delirious new ideas. Painting might just help her find freedom! Those wonderful flowers that she loved copying onto paper, with magical colours miraculously showing them alive and bright on the page.

Chrome Yellow. Crimson Lake. Cerulean Blue. Green Oxide of Chromium.

The late April countryside was shining with colour, vibrant with life. A chaffinch sang and a robin in the hedge looked at her with a bright eye. She stooped down, picked a budding dandelion and some leaves, and started arranging a woodland scene in her mind. This afternoon, when Father napped and Stepmother had gone visiting, she would make a start. And she would remember that Mr Flynn was particular about which green she used.

Walking up the drive of Oak House, she saw Aunt Jack's trap waiting by the front door, with the pony tethered. She heard voices in the drawing room: Aunt Jacks spoke in a commanding tone and Hester thought that Father's curt reply sounded annoyed.

Aunt Jacks was in full flood. 'Very foolish to take in a girl you don't know. She could have come from anywhere, and no reference, you say?'

Now it was Stepmother's softer voice. 'But we do know, Jacquetta, dear – Cook says this girl is well behaved and biddable, the daughter of a friend of hers. And so, surely, we need no other reference?'

Silence for a long moment, save for a snort from Aunt Jacks, and then Father saying sharply, 'We'll soon see how the girl behaves, and what sort of a worker she is. No need for you to fuss, Jacks. Emma and I are quite capable of managing our own servants, thank you.'

Time to make an entrance and bring some peace to the

proceedings: Hester went into the room, smiling at the three faces turning to look at her. 'I'm back, and it's time for luncheon. Aunt Jacks, I do hope you'll stay and eat with us?'

The small erect woman got to her feet, nodded briefly at Arthur and Emma, and hurriedly came to Hester's side. 'No, thank you,' she said. 'I have too much to do in my own home and garden. Can't waste time. But—' Her voice dropped. 'A word with you, Hester, if you please. . . .'

In the hall, Hester shut the drawing-room door behind her She looked at her aunt, resplendent in what were probably her gardening clothes – drab tweed skirt with pulled threads, a jacket of dark green that had seen far better days, and her customary shabby, out-of-shape black felt hat pulled tightly over the wisps of still bright red hair that refused to grow old and grey. Hester wondered, yet again, how Father could be so grumpy and remote while Aunt Jacks was full of life, indeed, almost bubbling over with energy.

Aunt Jacks turned and looked up into Hester's enquiring face. 'Your parents,' she said rapidly, 'and particularly your stepmother are far too soft. This new maid they're taking on – she could be anybody. Never mind Cook knowing her mother – I advise you to keep an eye on her, Hester. I don't trust servant girls – they don't know their place these days. Now I must go. Don't bother to see me out – I can manage, thank you. Goodbye.' She was off through the open front doorway, untying the tether, climbing into the trap, and then, clicking encouragingly at Duchess, rattling down the drive and out into the lane.

Hester watched until she was out of sight, then closed the door and walked back through the hall towards the drawing room. She had no idea what Aunt Jacks had been saying, apart from the fact that a new maid had been engaged. Mrs Caunter, their cook general, had been bewailing that Katy had left to get married, so this girl, whatever she was called, was surely the answer. Things would settle down very soon. Father hated disturbance and Stepmother was happy to agree with his every thought, so things would sort themselves out.

But she would watch the new girl. Aunt Jacks was observant and sensitive to other people's behaviour. Then Hester forgot domesticity and instead thought of Mr Flynn and his amazing suggestion. She would speak to Father. See how he was after his nap, and then gauge whether this was the right moment. She went into the drawing room for the customary pre-luncheon glass of sherry with a smile, aware that life had suddenly become extremely interesting.

After helping clear the table – Katy had left yesterday – Hester was ready to go upstairs to her small studio, but Stepmother had other ideas.

'Hester, dear, will you please tell Hoskins to bring the carriage round in half an hour's time? You haven't forgotten that we are going to call on Mrs Marchant this afternoon, have you?' Emma's face wore its usual patient expression, and at once Hester felt something stir inside her. Visiting – or work?

'No, I'm sorry, Stepmother, I have some painting to do. Yes, of course, I'll tell Hoskins – but please give my apologies, will you? Perhaps another day.'

Emma's voice rose. 'But Mrs Marchant is expecting us and there was talk of tennis next weekend when Hugh comes down from university. Really, Hester, I don't know what your father will say – he expects you to accompany me on calls.'

Hester tightened her lips. 'I'm sorry. But I prefer not to come.' Her mind was suddenly cluttered with new thoughts, new resolution, new aims in life. She looked at the ageing woman in front of her, whose pale eyes were full of astonishment, and knew this was just the first step in an ongoing battle which hopefully would end – *must* end, she promised herself fiercely – in freedom.

'I'll see about the carriage.' She turned away and went into the stable yard.

From upstairs, in the boxroom adjoining her bedroom – her so-called studio – she heard the rattle of harness and hooves coming around to the front door. She set up her easel by the window, then emptied out the bag of paints and brushes and the palette, but something disturbed her. A glance from the window saw Hoskins returning into the yard and untacking the horse. So, no visiting today. Guilt arose then as she guessed at once that Stepmother had been too upset to carry out her plan alone.

No doubt she had returned to her bedroom to give way to blaming thoughts and easy tears. Hester sighed as she picked up the dandelion and its leaves and set them on the small table beside her. She knew Father would hear about his daughter's unseemly and rude behaviour once he had awoken from his afternoon nap. Tea, she thought wearily, would be an unpleasant meal.

But determination, and the pleasure which arose from arranging the small flower and then mixing paints and beginning to outline stems and leaves on a fresh piece of thick paper, soon banished such thoughts. From flowers, stems and leaves, she moved on to sections of flyaway seeds. Botanical paintings required every minute detail to be shown and she was lost in her world as she worked. The light illumined every petal of the dandelion which she was looking at so keenly – the colours flowed, the shapes created themselves – and then, reluctantly, she heard sounds from the outside world intruding.

Below, Hoskins was cutting the grass with the newfangled machine Father had bought recently; Frank Bartley's heavy voice shouted at his cows as he herded them from the pasture, down the lane towards the farm and the milking shed. A dog barked, and then quietness returned. She stared at her painting.

A sense of peace contained her, and she felt she was in a dream. The brush had worked smoothly, the colours were true, the light was wonderful, and she knew she was doing something that she was meant to do. Mr Flynn's rough voice was a background song echoing quietly in her mind, and the resolution to paint, and somehow to escape, grew large and fulfilling. Teatime came without her knowing, until Stepmother's thin voice called up the stairs.

'Hester, are you there? Your father wishes to speak to you.'

The drawing room was shaded by drawn curtains and Hester could only just make out the figure of her father sitting in his big leather chair beside the fireplace. 'Shall I draw the curtains?' she said, hoping that her cheerful tone would cancel whatever brooding thoughts her father was having.

But his voice, clipped as usual, was hardly friendly. 'Hester, your mother has told me about your refusal to accompany her on her visits.'

A whirlwind of feelings swept through her and she said, 'Emma isn't my mother, she's my stepmother,' and then stopped, horrified at the unkindness of her words. She took a step nearer to his chair and looked down into Arthur Redding's narrowed eyes. 'I'm sorry, Father – I didn't mean to be rude or hurtful.'

She watched him struggling to sit up straight, the afflicted leg slowly stretching out in front of him. Saw his mouth tighten, a grimace of pain almost hiding his eyes, and wished with all her heart that she could take back what she had just said.

Kneeling beside him, she put her hand on his arm and whispered, 'Please forget it, Father – forgive me. I'm fond of Stepmother, of course I am, but sometimes I remember Mother and then. . . .'

Arthur Redding leaned back again and briefly laid his hand on hers, where it rested on his arm. He sighed, a deep painful breath, that Hester sensed took him back to those dark days sixteen years ago when Mother had died in her sleep after her weak chest had failed to survive the winter storms.

Slowly he nodded, and allowed a stiff smile to relax his thin face. 'Never mind.' His voice was as strong as ever but Hester knew that, for once, he had allowed emotion to get the better of him and was now regretting it.

She patted his arm, then moved across the room to sit in Emma's wing chair. 'Father, please can we talk it over? I know I'm too immoderate in my thinking to please either you or Stepmother, but I can't help it.' She leaned forward, suddenly eager to explain, to gain his understanding. 'It's the age we live in, Father – nearly into a new century with such amazing and exciting ideas, inventions and huge steps forward. Can you blame me for wanting to go into the world and sample some of it?'

Arthur Redding made no reply, but she saw he was listening and not contradicting her. Hope surged. 'So, you see, I haven't got time to go making calls on people with Stepmother – I have my painting to do, my plans for the future to sort out.' She stopped. So far so good, but this, as she well knew, was the barrier that she feared would never be overcome. Her future. Her plans.

Smile fading, hands locking in her lap, she waited for the usual condemnation of all she had just said. It came after a pause in which Arthur Redding again stretched his leg before resettling himself.

His voice was sharp. 'You've always been inclined to want more than you need, Hester. When you were a small child I remonstrated

13

with your mother when she allowed you unnecessary freedoms. And now you seem to think you can walk away from the duties to which you are heir, as a girl of good breeding and upbringing. Isn't it enough for you to run the house? Entertain our friends? Look after your parents who, let's face it, have given you the means of a good life with no hardships?'

She had no answer, bowed her head, and looked down at her hands, waiting for the next familiar words. She knew them by heart. For years he had repeated this unwelcome mantra.

'I have hoped that you would settle down, enjoy a social life and find a suitable man who will offer you marriage and his care for the rest of your life. Isn't that enough for you, Hester?'

His stare was steady. Hester breathed deeply, intent on finding some way of making him understand. Her voice was uneven, trying to control the passion surging inside her. 'Father, I understand what you want. And of course I wish I could live as you expect – but I can't. You must' – she tightened her lips – 'you must let me go. Let me do what I want.' This was terrible. She was hurting and disappointing him. But freedom was vital. 'Please, let me go.'

They looked at each other and she knew that it was no good. He would never give in. He loved her, just as she loved him, but he had no understanding of all her passionate needs.

Rapid, desperate words rushed out. 'I want a career. I've been told I could become a commercial artist if I work hard enough. I want to do it, Father, I want to use my painting to earn my living.'

Silence. A log in the fire crumbled. Outside in the garden a blackbird sang. And then, 'You cannot do that, Hester, without my consent.'

Her stomach knotted: that same old authority.

Continuing, his voice was even more determined. 'You're still under age and under my control. When you are twenty-one perhaps things may be different. You may even have decided on marriage instead of this rackety sort of bohemian life you seem to be dreaming of. But until then I hope you will have the goodness of heart to bear in mind that your stepmother and I are growing older and need your loving and helpful presence here at home.'

'Yes, Father. Of course. And I'm sorry. So sorry. But—'

The door opened and Emma looked into the room. 'May I come in? It's nearly tea time and, Hester, if you wouldn't mind, Mrs Caunter needs help to bring in the trays.'

It was over and there was no happy outcome. Hester got up and went down to the kitchen. Trays of sandwiches, sponge cake oozing with jam, a pot of China tea for Father and one of Indian for herself and Stepmother, just as yesterday.

Just as last year. And the year before that. Just as it would be for ever.

She had to get away.

CHAPTER TWO

Leaving the house, a heavy shadow fell from her shoulders. Breathing in the soft evening air, Hester felt thankful for her love of nature. The high hedges, winding along beside her, were sturdy walls of green foliage, and looking upwards to the oak trees, she saw them pushing out their enormous branches to form a tunnel above her head. The joy of her passion for all this rose inside her like a bird about to take wing. Gone was the tension of knowing that her parents would never agree to her leaving home and finding a place for herself in a world which they thought of as vulgar, dangerous and quite unacceptable.

She knew strongly that she was right in aiming her life in a new direction. Somehow freedom would come. She had no idea how, but believed her instinct telling her that life was pulling her and so she must follow.

As the valley flattened out, she reached Brook Cottage and opened the gate into Aunt Jacks' garden. She walked up the brick path towards the front door, taking in every flower that blossomed in the narrow beds edging the path. Pink and white daisies, purple larkspur and towering blue delphiniums that swayed in the breeze. She paused, smelling the fragrance of the honeysuckle sprawling against a couple of old lilac bushes. Aunt Jacks' garden always banished care and doubtful thoughts. Hester smiled as she knocked at the half-open door and then walked into the cottage. 'Aunt Jacks?'

'Hester, how nice. I'm in here, in the kitchen. This is the best place for my sketches and plans. Not enough light in the sitting room. Come in, my dear.'

Aunt Jacks sat at the table, which was spread with large pieces of paper. She seemed even smaller as she leaned forward in the wooden chair, pencil in her hand, spectacles on the end of her nose. Her eyes were dark, shining with energy.

Instantly at home, Hester slipped into a chair on the opposite side of the table, looking down at the plans before her. 'So, Aunt, what are you planning? Digging up the roses and growing vegetables?'

'Don't be ridiculous. My roses are the best in the county. No, I've had this idea for years and this is the time to bring it to fruition. I shall turn the barn into a room where gardeners can meet and discuss their problems.'

'Which you, of course, will resolve for them?' Hester chuckled.

Aunt Jacks put down her pencil and sat back, straight and upright. 'Naturally. I have more experience than many so-called experts. And I shall bring in other knowledgeable people. Gardening is a popular hobby these days, and I have a mission to educate those in need. We will grow seeds, prick out plants, prune shrubs, keep lawns looking immaculate, and, most importantly, learn about using manure to help the blessed earth to keep its fertility and health.' She took a long breath, and looked across the table. 'What do you think of all that?'

'I think it's a wonderful idea. And I would love to help.'

'I don't see why not. If I included a class for flower painting you could take that for me.' Her eyes were sharp. 'How are you getting on with Joseph Flynn?'

Hester heard again his rough voice uttering those magic words and her reply came out in a rush. 'He thinks I might be good enough to become a commercial artist.'

'Splendid! I always said you had talent. Have you told your father of your plans?'

Suddenly the joy inside Hester somersaulted and she felt the same dismay she had encountered in the drawing room before tea. 'He said it's out of the question. I must stay at home and behave like a lady. I'm legally a minor and under his control. So there can be no running off to a possible career. . . .' Her voice died and she saw her aunt's face tighten.

'The old fool! My brother was always a fuddy-duddy, no idea about living a real life apart from his dusty old legal papers and court appearances. Now, my child, buck up and make some plans. You'll soon be of age and then you can do what you like.' Aunt Jacks rapped the table with a tiny, hard fist. 'And in the meantime you must start creating your own flora – a collection of the wild flowers in the village. Now, look at this sketch of the barn and tell me what you think.'

Hester walked home in the twilight, knowing she must be there to help Mrs Caunter dish up and serve the dinner, but her earlier resentment had receded. Yes, she would keep painting. And, like Aunt Jacks, she would make some plans. In early autumn she would be twenty-one and by then she would know exactly what she planned to do with her life.

Returning to Oak House, she decided that two things could be done already, without Father's knowledge: start painting her flora, and ask Mr Flynn to advise her about a possible career. Words began to arrange themselves. *'Mr Flynn, could you please tell me where I could go to study botanical painting?'* Then, hair brushed and neatly arranged around her head, green dress rustling as she ran downstairs, she went kitchenwards with a new feeling of anticipation, of excitement, and helped Mrs Caunter arrange dishes on the inevitable trays.

Thinking about Katy leaving, she asked, 'When is the new maid coming?' and Cook stopped stirring the gravy to turn and answer.

'Tomorrow morning, Miss Hester. Ruby Jones, she's called. Hope she'll fit in here and work proper.'

'Of course she will, Mrs Caunter.' But Hester's thoughts were elsewhere, and she was thinking about painting as she carried the first of the trays into the dining room where Father and Stepmother were already seated.

Ruby Jones shouted a sharp rejoinder to the driver's saucy comment as she got off the omnibus in Chudleigh, put down her carpet bag and stared around her. What a quiet village, not the busy town she was used to in Newton Abbot. But she mustn't grumble. She had every reason in the world to be glad of the new situation at Oak House. And she had a secret.

Confidently, she asked a woman coming down the street, 'Where's Oak House, then?'

The woman looked her up and down. 'Past that pub on the corner, then turn into the lane and it's halfway up the hill.' Curiosity filled her face. 'New job, is it, eh?'

Ruby scowled. 'Mind yer own, can't yer?' She picked up her bag and marched off in the direction the woman pointed.

The lane was a rough track with grass growing down the middle. Such high hedges – Ruby couldn't see what was going on all around. Cows were mooing; she frowned and hoped they wouldn't appear. The country was a new sort of place, and they might be savage. She'd seen a picture of one, big and threatening.

Suddenly a sound behind her made her stop, nearly falling into the hedge to get out of the way of a horse and cart. It rattled closer and closer, bringing with it a smell of manure that was almost overpowering. She clutched her bag to her chest and shrieked at the boy who seemed to have no control over his huge, puffing black horse.

'Watch it! Get off – I'll give you what fer if you hit me!'

The boy, mousy haired with untidy curls framing his tanned face, grinned down at her and waved his stick, nearly touching her nose. 'Keep yer hair on, Miss! Prince won't hurt no one – jest keep out of the way, see?'

Ruby scowled. 'Mind yerself, you great mump'ead.' She tossed her head, watching him continue on and then smiled. She had no time for impudent farm boys. Her sights were set on better, richer things. She lifted her head an extra inch, finding herself at a gate that told her she had reached Oak House, and then walked up the long, imposing gravel drive towards the house.

The shrub-lined drive opened into a circle in front of a tall, splendid-looking house with large windows and an imposing dark brown front door. Ruby paused on the steps leading to the door and thought hard.

'Mind as you go down to the kitchen entrance, Rube,' her landlady, Mrs Beer had said when she left her lodgings this morning, but now Ruby decided on the spur of the moment to tackle this enormous building with all the confidence and courage she could muster. The secret, always at the back of her mind, produced fresh strength, and she walked up the steps, put down her bag, took the bell-pull in her right hand, and tugged – hard.

She heard the deep clang echoing into the silence of the house and felt a moment of fear. It was all so unknown. Was she really doing the right thing coming here? Then footsteps approached, the door opened, and she took a deep breath as a woman appeared, looking at her with decidedly critical eyes.

Hester saw a slender girl in shabby but clean clothes, with fair hair knotted back under a straw boater decorated with a bright ribbon. Her first impression was agreeable. Could this be the new maid? Well, she looked as if she might suit. But presenting herself here, at the front door? Aunt Jacks' words rang in her mind – *servants don't know their places any longer* – and she had to conceal the smile trying to spread across her face. 'Good morning,' she said crisply. 'Can I help you?'

The girl fidgeted but held her glance. 'I'm Ruby Jones, I've come to fill the empty situation. My landlady, Mrs Beer, knows Mrs Caunter.'

Hester heard determination in the burred Devon voice, saw almost insolent intent in the green-grey eyes, and felt herself react very sharply. 'Then you must go round to the back door and tell Mrs Caunter that you have arrived, Ruby,' she said calmly. 'The kitchen is in the stable yard. Knock and Mrs Caunter will take you in.'

They looked at each other for what Hester thought was an unseemly few seconds before the new maid nodded, picked up her carpet bag, went down the steps and disappeared around the side of the house. No thanks. No expected bobbing at receiving her orders. Hester closed the door and went into the morning room to find Stepmother and tell her about Ruby's arrival.

Strangely, she felt as if something explosive had made its way into the house. Foolish, of course, for Ruby Jones was just a servant and would soon learn the manners and duties expected of her. But there had been a very unsettling expression in those bright eyes.

Waiting for Stepmother to finish writing her letter, Hester sat down by the window and cleared her mind. This afternoon she would take the first step towards her new career, picking flowers and grasses to paint and so create her own flora. Every botanical artist she had ever read about always created a flora. And so would she.

It was such joy, wandering the lanes in the afternoon sunshine, walking through Mr Bartley's field where the footpath skirted the growing corn before it reached the woodland. As she went, she picked dandelions, and the last of the primroses. On the edges of the pasture she found cowslips, and red dead nettle, while along the damp part of the wood ladies' smocks grew in a pale pink blanket. A tendril of honeysuckle completed her specimens, and then, putting them carefully into her basket and reluctantly looking at her fob watch, she knew she must get home for tea.

The house was cool and quiet and she went up to her room, wondering what Stepmother had thought of the new maid's appearance at luncheon. Ruby, in a dull but neat print dress, a white cap on her blonde hair, had served the dishes in silence, keeping her eyes down, nodding when Stepmother had said, 'We'll have coffee in the drawing room,' and carrying the tray out to the kitchen. But, passing Hester, Ruby had looked up, and those keen eyes had seemed to interrogate her in some odd way. Hester returned the brief stare, and then banished the girl from her thoughts, for the idea of the flora was taking precedence over everything else.

She painted until the light began to dim, then laid the flowers on a large sheet of blotting paper, well out of the sunlight streaming through the open window, filling the desktop as she spread them out. Once painted, they would dry here until they could be arranged in sheets of thick paper, forming a slowly growing book.

My flora. I'll tell Mr Flynn next week.

At teatime, Emma, fresh from an afternoon nap, said pleasantly, 'The new maid appears to know her duties. I told Mrs Caunter we were pleased with her.' She hesitated, then looked nervously at Hester. 'I hope I did right?'

It was strange, thought Hester, that although Stepmother was Father's wife and in charge of the household, most small problems were passed to her to resolve. But she stifled her annoyance, saying, 'Yes, Stepmother, of course,' and then looked at Ruby, who came in with the first of the tea trays.

She wore a dark dress and a small white apron tied with a big bow, while a little white cap decorated her tightly knotted hair. Streamers drifted down at the back of her head when she moved, and Hester, watching, saw the girl deliberately flick a glance at herself in the gilt-edged mirror over the fireplace as she placed a tray on the table in front of Emma. Hester's mouth tightened and she gave Ruby a hard look as she said, 'Thank you, that will be all,' after the last tray had been unloaded.

Teatime was filled with details of Mrs Marchant's invitation to a tennis party. Stepmother was full of it. 'Hugh will be home – such a nice boy, and doing so well with his studies – and then the two Misses Wellington from Bovey will be there. And no doubt some other young people – and of course you, Hester. I'm sure that Hugh will be delighted to see you again.'

Stepmother caught Father's glance, nodding with a purposeful smile, and Hester knew exactly what thoughts were passing between them. Hugh Marchant, whom she had known since their childhood days of sharing a governess, was being proposed as a likely suitor. Indeed, a husband. Marrying into the Marchant family, with all their gentrified relatives and financial connections with the retailing world of the town, would be a good catch for someone who was being unseemly in her thoughts of escaping domesticity and living a vulgar, common life away from the family home.

Hester felt the trap being loaded and put down her cup with a clatter, which made both Father and Stepmother stare at her. Rapidly she said, 'I may not have time to accept the invitation. I am starting on a new project, creating a flora, a collection of the wild flowers that grow in the village. Mr Flynn' – she stopped briefly, crossing her fingers at the white lie, and praying she might be forgiven – 'has said this is what I should be doing.'

Stepmother looked anxiously at Arthur Redding, who crumbled the last slice of his cake and sniffed. 'It would be most impolite to refuse Mrs Marchant's kind invitation,' he said. 'Of course you will go. This flora – whatever it is – must be fitted in when you have spare time. Please write a note of acceptance today and let Hoskins deliver it tomorrow.' He looked at Stepmother. 'Another cup of tea, if you please, Emma.'

Silence filled the room until Hester allowed the knot in her stomach to untie as she realized what was expected of her – good manners and a loving respect for her parents. Somehow she forced aside the rebellious thoughts and said quietly, 'I'll do that directly after tea, Father.'

Cups were refilled and second slices of cake appeared on Father's plate, and hastily she changed the subject. 'I think the new maid is going to be suitable. She served luncheon and tea nicely, and she looks neat and tidy. Mrs Caunter has said that she is willing, and indeed quite capable of every duty that she's asked to perform.' She forced a smile. 'And so I shall no longer have to carry trays, shall I?'

Stepmother smiled sweetly, sat back in her chair, and looked at Father with a contented expression on her face. Hester tightened her lips. She would never turn into someone like this, a quiet, domesticated woman, allowing a man to run her life. An odd thought came into her mind then: would the flora help take her out of this imprisoning world?

Arthur Redding said, matter of factly, 'Yes, the girl seems competent. What's her name?'

'Ruby Jones,' said Hester.

Stepmother looked pensive. 'Such a pretty name. Surely far too pretty for a servant, don't you think?'

Hester imagined that she heard a note of surprise in her father's deep voice.

'Ruby,' he muttered, and then, sniffing, fumbled for the evening newspaper. She looked at him curiously, but his expression showed no reason for the repetition of the name. 'Yes,' he said between crackles of opening paper, 'She'll be getting ideas with a name like that. We'll call her something else.' He glanced over the top of the paper. 'What do you think, my dear?'

Stepmother was happy to concur. 'Well, I once had a maid called Gertrude – such a nice girl. Let's call this one Gertrude, shall we?'

'No!' Hester said quickly. 'You can't just change a woman's name because you don't like the real one.'

'But,' said Stepmother, quite forcibly, 'every woman, on marriage, is honoured to take on the name of her dear husband.' She looked at Hester with shocked eyes.

There was a moment of unpleasant reaction. Stepmother's face grew bright pink, Father hid behind a page of advertisements and sniffed even harder, and Hester felt every ounce of rebellion again rising inside her.

She got to her feet. 'Well, I shan't be doing that,' she said. 'Please excuse me. I must go and write that note.'

Hurriedly she left the room, closing the door behind her with a resounding – and enjoyable – bang. Her thoughts raced. *Gertrude! And then probably Gertie – that's awful.* She slammed the bedroom door loudly, delighted to hear its echo wafting downstairs – into the drawing room, she hoped.

Opening her pad of writing paper she was still thinking about Ruby. 'Dear Mrs Marchant', she wrote, but her mind went in another direction.

Even if Ruby is a bit of a miss, I won't let her be called Gertie. She shall keep the name her parents gave her. Definitely.

CHAPTER THREE

'I think creating a flora is an excellent idea, Miss Redding. Let me see it as it progresses. And before the plants dry out, you must record their details so that you have the true colours in your mind for future work.' Joseph Flynn smiled and Hester felt a glow of enthusiasm.

Collecting her bag, she moved towards the door, aware of him following closely behind her. Turning to look at him, she said, 'Thank you for your advice. I shall certainly follow it, Mr Flynn.' A pause, and then. 'And may I ask your advice about something else?'

'I'm in a hurry, Miss Redding.' He frowned. 'What is it?'

She said rapidly, 'I want to enter a school of art – do you know of a suitable place?'

For a moment Joseph Flynn was silent. He pursed his lips and then, carefully, he said, 'Of course, Miss Redding, I can give you details of many institutions where you might enrol, but perhaps for a young woman on her own it would be better to stay here, in your own locality. In which case' – he smiled – 'I could offer you private classes in my home. At a very competitive price.'

She stared in amazement, and he added, 'Your family would probably prefer you to study with someone you already know, rather than going somewhere amongst strangers.' He watched, seeing her astonishment slowly become consideration, and then growing enthusiasm. He slid her another smile. 'Perhaps your mother would like to come and meet my wife and inspect my studio, Miss Redding?' He put his hand on her arm, moving her into the passage. 'We shall get locked up by the caretaker if we stay any longer,' he said wryly. 'I'll escort you downstairs, Miss Redding.'

Standing beside him in the entrance lobby, Hester tried to find sensible words. 'May I give you my reply next week, Mr Flynn? After I've spoken to my father?'

'Of course, Miss Redding.' Raising his hat, he watched her walk away towards the omnibus station. Then, smiling thoughtfully, he made his own way home.

Hester's excitement died as she saw the waiting omnibus start to move. That brief conversation had taken precious moments, and she began running, one hand to her hat, the other carrying the bag of painting equipment. She reached the corner of Halcyon Road, only to see the horses being whipped up and the conveyance swaying and rattling away from her. 'Oh no!' How could she have been so foolish?

And then someone called, 'Hester!'

Turning, she saw Hugh Marchant reining in his pony and trap, halting by the pavement at her side, gesturing to her to stop.

'Hugh! What are you doing here?'

'Taking you home. Give me your bag – that's it – now, in you get.'

His face was full of welcome and instantly Hester forgot Mr Flynn's amazing suggestion and her anxiety about telling Father.

'Good to see you again, Hester. Hold on to your hat – we'll be home before you know it. Let's race the bus, shall we?'

'Must we? I'd prefer to get home in one piece, please.' She was laughing, gripping her hat as the pony trotted on. How lovely being with Hugh again: the old friendship easily established, and the knowledge that she could say whatever she liked, for he would understand.

'Don't you trust me?' Swerving past a lumbering coal cart, he slid her a wicked grin.

'Of course I do.'

Trust. The word lingered for a second and she frowned – was it something to do with Mr Flynn? But then it was gone.

As they drove along the Newton Road she asked, 'How did you know where I was?'

'I called in to see your parents. They said you were doing some sort of class at the Reading Room and I had an errand to do myself, so here I am.' He looked at her over his shoulder. 'Painting, are you? You were always good at it. Remember your sketches of the family picnics?'

Hester let her mind wander. Memories flashed of those picnics, with Mother, Father, Katy unpacking food hampers . . . a time of no worries. For some reason, she sighed. 'Happy days,' she said very quietly, but he heard and looked at her with a frown.

'What's wrong with life today? Surely not unhappy, is it?'

Thoughts of Father's ultimatum swept through her mind, followed by embarrassment. Did Hugh have any idea that she was being prepared to become his chosen bride? And then, what if he didn't want her? Suddenly she was laughing and clutching his arm as he performed another tricky swerve around the irritatingly slow carriage ahead of them.

'No, Hugh, not unhappy. Confused, perhaps. But let's talk about something else. What about the tennis party on Thursday – who else is coming?'

'Oh, Fanny and Norah Wellington, I suppose, and perhaps another friend or two. We should make up a foursome and a couple of pairs.' His brown eyes locked on to hers and his voice deepened. 'I intend to partner you, Hester, so don't let anyone else get a look in, will you?'

She smiled back. Life was good. Hugh was back and, even if she had no intention of marrying him, he was excellent company – for a while. Yes, she would allow him to partner her, and perhaps even tell him about her painting, how she was creating a flora, and possibly going to study at Mr Flynn's studio. Perhaps. But at the moment she just wanted him to go on talking.

Hugh drove the trap up to the front door of Oak House and made an excuse for not staying any longer. 'Mater's got a luncheon party on and wants me to host it for her as Father is otherwise occupied. I'll come and pick you up on Thursday – bring your racquet and be prepared for some fast games. Goodbye, Hester.' He turned the pony on flying gravel and saluted with his whip. Giving her a warm last smile, he rattled out onto the lane.

Hester sighed. Hugh was fun, he was easy to talk to, he seemed to enjoy her company and certainly she enjoyed his. She made her way upstairs to take off her hat and to tidy herself ready for luncheon, almost looking forward to being with Father and Stepmother again. And then something made her step into the little boxroom where she kept her painting materials and where the wild flowers she had painted had been laid out on the desk top, drying.

Just an empty space now. A bare desktop, blotting paper neatly pushed to one side. Her flowers had gone.

Ruby was slowly getting used to service in Oak House. Mrs Caunter was an old dragon, but she cooked lovely meals and already Ruby could feel the waist of her dress getting tighter. Her bedroom wasn't bad, small and square up in the attic, reached by a flight of wooden stairs which creaked with every step, reaching a tiny space between her and Mrs Caunter's room. The wallpaper was decorated with cherries, and there was a washbasin and a chest with drawers, one of them a good hiding place for the secret paper. A chair stood beside a window looking out over green trees and a distant view of Dartmoor, all blue and grey in the mist. The iron bedstead had a pillow, clean sheets and a good wool blanket topped by a colourful patchwork counterpane.

Ruby wondered who had sewn this and where the many squares of cotton had come from. Perhaps someone in the household – a nanny, a governess? – had spent their evenings cutting and pinning and sewing. She quite liked the idea of all that work going into her bedcover. It was a satisfying bit of work which added up to being useful and part of a busy life. She began to dream. She would like to sew something – it would make her feel a real part of the house.

She thought she would be happy here. Mr and Mrs Redding were old and wrapped up in their own lives. She had to make sure she was polite and bob a curtsey when they expected it, because she needed them to like her. And Hoskins, the groom and gardener, was all right. Not much to say, but he gave her a lovely flower yesterday. 'Here you are, maid. Buttercup. Put it under yer chin and see if you likes butter. . . .'

Remembering, Ruby giggled as she went downstairs, having dusted and polished the bedrooms and cleaned the bathroom and landing. She was taking all the rubbish out to the bin, where Hoskins had a weekly bonfire. This was mostly dust, cobwebs, bits of unwanted paper, hair combings (poor Mrs Redding was thin on top, under her cap) and today there were the weeds that Miss Hester had forgotten to throw away, leaving them on the desk in the room next to her bedroom.

Ruby tipped the rubbish, then returned to the house and found herself thinking about Miss Hester as she did so. Miss Hester was tall, very upright and pretty, with deep brown hair which she rolled up around her head. A few curls always fell down her neck and sometimes on her cheeks. She had a lovely voice – Ruby thought about trying to imitate the way she spoke – and was polite but seemed to live in a different world.

'Why isn't Miss Hester married?' Ruby asked Mrs Caunter. 'Hasn't she got a beau?'

Mrs Caunter glared. 'Don't you say things about Miss Hester, my gal. She's a lady, different from us. Ladies take as long as they wants to marry. And yes, o' course she's got a young man. Mr Hugh Marchant is keen on her and I wouldn't be surprised. . . .' And here Mrs Caunter gave a huge wink and changed the subject. 'None of our business. Go and get some parsley for these potatoes, Ruby. And don't stop out there talking to Hoskins.'

So Miss Hester would soon get married. That meant she would leave here. Good. Ruby, handing over the parsley, started laying the luncheon tray and thought about her secret.

Always there at the back of her mind, the old paper upstairs, a nice warm glow making the worst household jobs bearable because she knew that in the end everything would work out. Not yet, of course. She had to live here much longer before the plan could start to happen. But then there was Miss Hester.

'Ruby!' Mrs Caunter broke into her thoughts. 'Hurry up, gal, you haven't laid the table yet – dreamin' again, I dunno.'

Ruby pouted, shrugged and got on with the work. She had plenty of time to learn what sort of person Miss Hester was.

Hester was ablaze with anger. It must be Ruby who had thrown her precious plants away! No one else ever came into her studio. Or perhaps the wind was to blame? No, the day was calm and balmy without even a breeze, so yes, it had to be Ruby. Hester went downstairs into the basement kitchen, where Mrs Caunter, red faced, stood over the stove with Ruby beside her, holding vegetable dishes.

'I want to speak to you, Ruby – please come outside for a minute.'

Mrs Caunter's voice overrode hers. 'Beg pardon, Miss Hester, but she can't, not right now. I'm dishing up and I don't want it to get cold, so if you don't mind—'

Guiltily, Hester withdrew. She would corner Ruby after luncheon.

The parents were, as usual, in the drawing room, sipping their sherry. They looked up and Emma smiled. 'Hester, I fear you missed Hugh Marchant this morning. He called, but of course you were at your class.'

'I did see him, Stepmother. He found me coming out of the Reading Room and brought me home.' Hester refused the offer of sherry and sat on the chesterfield between her parents. She wanted to get on with the meal and then talk to Ruby. But of course, in Oak House, nothing could be hurried.

Arthur Redding put down his glass and said, with a stiff smile lifting his mouth but not reaching his eyes, 'And how was Hugh?'

'He seemed very well.' Hester's impatience began to mount.

'And have you arranged about the Marchants' tennis party? What will you wear, Hester?' Emma's face lit up and she beamed across the room. 'You should wear white, as they do at Wimbledon – and I expect your tennis racquet will need oiling or whatever it is they require. . . .'

'I shall do what needs to be done, Stepmother. And I will wear the tennis clothes I wore last year and the year before that.' Hester instantly regretted the tone of her voice. She should be grateful that Emma was interested enough to make suggestions, foolish though they were. 'I beg your pardon,'she said hastily. 'I didn't mean to be rude. It's just that—' She stopped, wondering whether they needed to know about the loss of her plants and then decided to continue. After all, she had to tell them about Mr Flynn and his exciting suggestion, so this might be an easy introduction. 'Something has annoyed me,' she said, smiling and choosing her words carefully, 'because the flowers I have painted and now want to dry for my flora have disappeared. I imagine the maid cleared them off my desk.'

'Just as well.' Arthur Redding's voice was short. 'This flora business seems to be merely an excuse to fill in time that should properly be spent on caring for your parents.' He looked at her coldly and Hester felt rage swelling inside her.

She heard the stridency in her voice as she said, 'I'm sorry you think that, Father, but I'm determined to continue my flora. And another thing – this morning I had an offer from my painting tutor to give me private lessons which I've decided to accept.' She waited, before adding firmly, 'I have a little money saved.'

There was a sudden silence. Emma caught her breath, and Arthur Redding sat up straighter in his chair, hands at once going down to rub his painful leg.

'Certainly not!' He stared at Hester who defiantly looked back. His voice became deeper, sharp with rising anger. 'You forget you can make no decisions for yourself without my consent, and I will not hear of you chasing off to study with some artistic nobody whom I have never met, and never wish to. You will kindly forget the whole idea.'

Hester's thoughts were full of anger and frustration, but out in the hall the luncheon gong sounded and the tense moment was broken.

Emma rose, smoothed her dress and looked at Arthur Redding. 'Come along,' she said, her voice childlike and placating. 'Time for luncheon. And let's forget all about this, shall we?' She walked towards Arthur, who was carefully getting to his feet. 'We can talk about it later, can't we? Now, dear, take my arm. . . .'

Struggling to control herself, Hester went to the door and opened it, then stood back, allowing her parents to slowly cross the room and make their way into the dining room, where Ruby waited, eyes cast down, neat and obedient. Hester felt her anger change direction. She couldn't rage at Father, but—

This afternoon, Ruby, she thought grimly, and took her seat at the dining table in silence.

They faced each other in the shadowy passage below the staircase leading down to the basement kitchen. Firmly, Hester shut the kitchen door, and looked into Ruby's sharp green eyes.

'You threw away my flowers,' she said icily.

Ruby stared. 'What, those ole weeds? Yes, I did, miss. Thought they was dead, see.'

Hester drew in a deep breath. 'Miss *Hester*, please, Ruby.'

'Sorry, Miss. Miss *Hester*.'

31

Was that a flicker of an insolent smile breaking the expressionless young face?

Hester swallowed, giving herself time to gain self-control. 'Perhaps you thought they were dead weeds, Ruby, but they were actually living flowers I was leaving there to dry. I am an artist, you see, and I am painting all the wild flowers that grow in this village. When I have painted them, they must be dried so that they can be preserved in a book. Do you understand?'

'Oh yes, Miss . . . *Hester*.' Again that hint of a quickly hidden grin.

Hester heard Mrs Caunter poking the fire in the kitchen, the noise echoing down the long bare passage. She watched Ruby reacting, turning away, and then looking back, almost impatiently, as if asking permission to go. She sighed. What good had this done? The girl was not yet used to service and there would probably be other mistakes before she settled down. But that smile had suggested that her mistress telling her off was just a joke.

Without thinking more, Hester said sharply, 'And please behave a little better, Ruby. We expect our staff to be polite as well as obedient.'

'But I haven't done nothin' wrong.' The uneducated voice rose shrilly. 'I don't see why you're goin' on about those ole weeds. Just a mistake, that's all.'

Hester gasped. So she was right – the girl was insolent and must be shown her place. Sharply she said, 'Don't speak to me like that. Apologize at once,' and then waited.

Ruby's small face coloured and her sea-green eyes glared through the shadowy passage. 'I'm not sayin' sorry just for a few ole weeds. You got it all wrong, miss .'

Hester tightened her lips, staring back in amazement, waiting.

Ruby lifted her head, returning the stare, slowly put up a hand to neaten her cap, and then muttered, 'Miss *Hester*.' A few seconds' silence brought the tension to breaking point, and then she said sullenly, 'Can I go now? I've got work to do in there else Mrs Caunter'll be on at me. And I don't want to have two rows in one day, do I?'

Hester could think of no reply. Shocked, unused to such anarchic talk, she nodded, and watched Ruby march down the passage and disappear into the kitchen.

Very slowly, and suddenly remembering that her first thoughts of Ruby had been of an explosive entity coming into the household, she went upstairs to sit by the window in her bedroom, looking sightlessly into the garden and thinking about the many problems that seemed to hedge her in these days.

A happier thought arrived and her tension faded: Aunt Jacks. She would go and see dear Aunt Jacks and learn what was happening about the proposed gardening school. As she left the house and walked quickly down the lane towards Brook Cottage, it dawned on her that leaving Oak House and its vexatious problems behind her was highly beneficial, each step edging her into a more relaxed mood. Freedom, she thought, and then smiled.

When she arrived at the wicket gate she was expecting the best to happen. Aunt Jacks would discuss her plans and Hester could ask what she thought of the idea of studying with Mr Flynn and how to persuade Father to change his mind. She entered the cottage, calling her aunt's name and then stopped. Voices were humming in the kitchen. Hester knocked on the door and said, 'Can I come in?' as she entered.

Aunt Jacks sat at her usual place at the long table, and beside her sat a tall man, who at once got to his feet, looked at Hester and smiled.

Vivid eyes, ultramarine blue, or perhaps paler cerulean blue. Hester caught her breath as the paint names flashed through her mind and hardly heard her aunt make the introductions. 'Hester, this is Nicholas Thorne, who, with his father, runs the Hayward Nursery in town. Nicholas, Hester Redding is my niece. Come and sit down, child.'

CHAPTER FOUR

He was tall, heavy shouldered, right arm in a sling. Hester noticed a dark suit and white shirt but was more concerned with the blue eyes looking at her.

He offered his left hand. 'Good day, Miss Redding. I'm delighted to meet you. I understand you are an artist.'

A deep voice, with an edge of sweetness. A hint of a Devon accent, clearly a working man. How intriguing. She liked the strength of his hand. His words hung in the air and she said, 'I'm only an amateur, but I do love to paint.'

He nodded, his thin, suntanned face showing a quick, brief smile. 'I look forward to seeing your work, Miss Redding.'

'Yes, well,' Aunt Jacks broke in. 'Nicholas is only here for an hour or so, Hester, and we are planning the programme of talks for my garden day.' She tapped the table impatiently.

Hester realized that she had come at the wrong time. She said quietly, 'I'll come back again, Aunt, when Mr Thorne has gone.' She turned to leave, but his undamaged hand reached out and touched her shoulder.

'Don't go on my account, Miss Redding.'

His smile was warm and Hester forgave the slip of behaviour. 'Very well,' she said, 'I'll stay, but I won't be a nuisance. I'll go into the garden.'

'Stay here, Miss Redding. I promise not to divide my attention.' That flash of a smile and then he drew out a chair for her, sitting at her side. He stretched his long legs under the table, turning to Aunt Jacks.

'Yes, Mrs Jacks, I'm ready to talk about your plans. And I promise that I won't let Miss Redding divert me.' There was mischief in the last words and Hester was surprised at his familiarity in calling her aunt Mrs Jacks and not Mrs Hurst. She looked down at the table quickly as Aunt Jacks'mouth tightened, her small hand picking up a pencil. 'Very well, Nicholas. So get out your diary and we'll arrange the timing for your talk.'

Hester listened to what they said but was too aware of the man sitting next to her to take in much of it. She found him attractive, but his behaviour, although charming, was unconventional. Father would have no time for Nicholas Thorne, and she wondered if she had time for him, either. Not the sort of man she was used to meeting. So very different from Hugh Marchant.

But those eyes, with their intent, direct gaze. And that voice. And had she been wrong in hearing an unsaid invitation in his seemingly harmless words? She made herself concentrate.

As she wrote and then put down her pencil, Aunt Jacks said, 'It's possible that Miss Watson, the traveller, may be able to come down to my garden day. I've written to invite her – and reminding her that we met as young women. I know she's living in England again and has some wonderful paintings to prepare for showing.'

'Yes,' said Nicholas. 'Emily Watson would be a speaker in a million. And she's a delightful lady, too. I met her when I joined her expedition to Italy last year: she impressed me with her courage and commitment.' He looked at Hester, about to rise.

'As an artist yourself, Miss Redding, you might benefit from meeting Miss Watson.'

Hester felt ill informed. 'Emily Watson?'

'Yes, she is following in the footsteps of the legendary Marianne North, another brave and famous lady painter who travels from continent to continent, painting the weird and wonderful new plant species she finds there.' Nicholas was on his feet, smiling at her. 'How would you like that, Miss Redding? Travelling miles up the mountains, across rivers and flimsy bridges, sleeping where you could and eating native food?'

Hester shook her head. 'Not very much. The wild waste of Dartmoor is quite enough for me sometimes. I like my comforts, you see.' But even as the words left her lips, she wondered if she was being truthful. What about adventure? Freedom?

Had he expected better of her? She was glad to turn away, saying, 'Shall I make some tea, Aunt? Why don't you and Mr Thorne sit in the garden while I get it ready?'

Aunt Jacks got up, adjusted her hat, tucking in a red curl, and said, 'What a good idea. Come along, Nicholas. We'll sit in the summerhouse and carry on talking.'

'You can sit there, Mrs Jacks. I shall help Miss Redding with the tea.'

In the kitchen, Hester moved across to the black range, aware of her aunt disappearing into the garden. She felt awkward about Nicholas Thorne remaining in the house, but why should she be embarrassed by him? Pushing the kettle closer to the flames, she turned and met his steady gaze.

'One of the farm girls comes in every morning, tidies up for Aunt Jacks and cooks for her. There's probably a cake somewhere.' At the dresser, she took down cups and saucers, adding casually, 'Have a look in the larder, will you, Mr Thorne?'

As she poured boiling water into the teapot he came back, carrying a large plate. 'Looks good,' he said, and put it on the table. 'A pound cake, if I'm right. When I was a boy and always hungry, my stepfather used to make one on a Sunday. One piece, that was it, and just the taste of it having to last until next time.'

Hester heard warmth in the deep voice and turned to look at his face, full now of a softness she hadn't seen before. 'Always hungry?' she queried. 'Were you working?'

Nicholas nodded, opening the table drawers and finding knives and spoons to put on the tray. 'From six years old I helped my stepfather with odd jobs in the nursery, and then I was properly employed as a garden boy when I was ten,' he said, suddenly looking up and meeting her gaze. 'I was well looked after, but the work was hard. And I was a skinny little urchin.'

He wasn't very different now, Hester thought, thin and tall but muscular. She saw him blink, as if wiping away memories. And then he laughed. 'Which is why I'm partial to cakes now. . . .' More laughter, and a new brightness in the eyes regarding her so intently.

'It sounds as if you deserve them.' She felt herself warming to the hidden glimpse of a past, which she sensed would be fascinating to hear more of.

'I'll carry the tray. You bring the cake.' He was ordering her, but she nodded obediently and preceded him into the garden. Something about him. Someone who was so different. Someone she instinctively wanted to know better.

The summerhouse was enclosed by the sloping garden, facing south-west and with an open view of everything that grew in the half-acre space. Hester had always loved coming here. Even the spiders with their dangling webs, which hung around the stone walls, capturing adventurous insects, held interest for her. She was always on the alert to free the struggling, minuscule captive, for even as a child she had seen freedom as a vital part of life.

Now she and Aunt Jacks sat on the two shabby cane chairs while Nicholas folded himself onto the bench seating running the width of the summerhouse. Fragrance from the white rose climbing just outside filled the air, and Hester heard a cuckoo calling down in the pasture.

They talked for nearly an hour, Aunt Jacks clearly relaxed at having Nicholas at her tea table, and asking questions about the nursery.

'We're doing quite well, Mrs Jacks. The new plants are growing – the old man is hoping for great things this summer.'

Aunt Jacks saw the curiosity on Hester's face and smiled as she explained. 'Edward Hayward agreed to Nicholas going to north Italy last year with Emily Watson to collect new species of plants. All the nurseries are doing it these days. He came back with some particularly fine alpines which Edward is very pleased with.'

'And about which he's writing a book. He's keen to tell the world about these new plants.' Nicholas grinned.

'New plants? How exciting.' She felt a glow of curiosity.

He nodded. 'Exciting indeed, Miss Redding. A plant-hunting expedition is certainly that, but dangerous.' His left hand reached out to touch the damaged arm and a grim expression slid across his face. 'This cracked shoulder was the result of a fracas among my native helpers which I tried to stop. Doing so, I was thrown against a rock.' A flash of a smile. 'A particularly large, hard rock. And only last week

37

I had the bad luck to strain the healing joint. Hence the sling.'

Hester could only stare, images suddenly vivid. Difficult porters, snow and huge mountains. Exotic plants, brought back to England, to the nursery where Nicholas worked. How fascinating and exciting.

She looked at her aunt. 'Why are such expeditions being sent if it's so dangerous?'

'Because all our landowners and London merchants want to show off their wealth, dear child. To have wonderful new plants in one's garden is the thing these days.' Aunt Jacks pulled a wry face. 'As if we haven't got enough marvellous native plants in England. And this is why I am starting my gardening school – to make gardeners aware of our own beautiful flora.'

She looked at Nicholas, her smile warm. 'Which you also are enthusiastic about, Nicholas. Why' – her smile broadened – 'I remember how our friendship started when I came to the nursery with Frank, my late husband, and you showed us around the wild flower beds because your father was indisposed. We got on well – we still do.'

He nodded, laughing with her, and Hester was intrigued by the warmth of their unlikely friendship.

'Will you be going abroad again, Mr Thorne?' she asked.

Nicholas edged back on his seat. When he spoke Hester heard an unexpected note of hardness in his deep voice and wondered at the care with which he chose his words. 'Probably, Miss Redding, but not yet. I'm not fit enough at the moment. Although I agree that we must continue searching for unknown plants; we are part of these adventurous times and so we must continue to search for new treasures.'

Hester listened, absorbed by this fascinating information and, wondering at Nicholas's past, dared to ask, 'After your spell as a garden boy, what did you do next, Mr Thorne?'

He looked at her. 'Left my father's nursery, wanting more varied work. And eventually I became head gardener on Lord Daley's estate in Cornwall, but then Father recalled me as he grew older, and I've been here at the nursery ever since.'

Aunt Jacks sat back in her chair, stirred her cup of tea and smiled nostalgically into the distance. 'And we've been friends, haven't we,

Nicholas, always chatting about plants and how to grow them?'

'We certainly have, Mrs Jacks.' His eyes met hers and Hester thought how clear it was that they shared both their knowledge and pleasure in working with plants, with flowers. Hester felt, deep inside and not yet ready to venture out, her own longing to share in that pleasure.

Flowers. She must go home and paint.

At last Aunt Jacks looked at her fob watch and said firmly, 'Time for you to go back, Nicholas, I know how busy the nursery is these days.' She rose, dark eyes smiling as he got to his feet, tall at her side, looking down at her with what Hester knew instinctively was fondness.

'No, Mrs Jacks, I mustn't delay any longer. Because of this sore arm, I've left young Jim Dawkins, our apprentice, to help Father in the nursery for a couple of days, to see how he'll get on, so I can be here again tomorrow morning, if I may take up more of your time? I could do some weeding for you, if necessary. One hand out of action doesn't mean I'm quite useless, you know.'

Hester saw understanding in her aunt's face and wondered again at this unlikely friendship. As Nicholas bowed, making his farewell, she said spontaneously, 'Perhaps I can come and help with the weeding tomorrow? Three hands might be better than one, Mr Thorne – what do you think?'

He laughed, his face opening into almost mischievous warmth. Reaching out, his hand touched hers and then dropped. 'I think I'm looking forward to it, Miss Redding. Let's see what we can do between us!'

He refused the offer of a lift into town, saying three miles to Newton Abbot was nothing to an explorer like himself. Then she and Aunt Jacks watched him leave, closing the gate behind him and saluting as he strode rapidly up the lane and out of their sight.

'Where does he live, Aunt?'

'In their old home at the nursery, a rather decrepit building, but his father is more involved with plants than repairs.' She looked at Hester very directly, adding, 'Nicholas is very much his own man; yes, he's just a professional gardener, but he has excellent and sensitive manners and would never embarrass either you or me. In fact, he is what I call a natural gentleman. Now, child, what was it you wanted to talk to me about?'

Hester stared at her aunt as they returned to the kitchen. Indeed, what had she come here for? Meeting Nicholas Thorne had thrown everything else out of her mind.

Ruby cleared away the tea tray and then opened the front door to Miss Chatters and the little girls who came from the village school every Tuesday afternoon to show Mrs Redding their sewing. Occasionally they were told to unpick their ugly stitches and start again, but Emma was more inclined to encourage than to admonish.

The children stood awkwardly around the dining-room table while Emma greeted Miss Chatters and then were told to sit down and show her their work. Ruby loitered in the passage outside the dining room, listening to the voices and suddenly aware of a wonderful idea; a step in the direction that she wanted to take. She went back to the kitchen, washed up the tea things and then asked Mrs Caunter, drowsing by the fire, 'Is it all right if I ask Mrs Redding something?'

Mrs Caunter opened her eyes, yawning ferociously. 'Course not. You don't speak to Madam 'less she speaks first.'

'Oh,' said Ruby, turning away and polishing a saucepan lid with her apron. 'All right, then. Can I go in the garden for five minutes? 'Tis awful hot in here.' She smiled sweetly at Cook and, having received a grudging nod, disappeared from the kitchen. But not to go into the garden, instead tiptoeing up the stairs and standing outside the dining room, thinking, planning. And then, after a quick knock on the door, she went inside, keeping her eyes down and standing quietly beside Emma, who was telling a small girl that she must try and make her stitches neater and not prick her fingers so much.

'You don't want bloodstains on your sewing, do you, Sarah?'

'No, M'm,' whispered the child.

Emma looked aside. 'Yes, Ruby, what is it?'

Ruby took a deep breath and said very politely, 'Can I ask you about my sewing, Madam, seein' as how you're helpin' these girls with theirs?'

A moment's pause while Miss Chatters and Emma exchanged glances but then Emma smiled. 'I didn't know you were a seamstress,

Ruby. What are you sewing?'

'Haven't started yet, madam, but I wants to do some patchwork, like the lovely counterpane on me bed. I'd like to do that.' Ruby dared to meet her employer's surprised eyes. Was it going to work? Had she gone too far?

But Emma's sweet smile surfaced and she said, 'What a good idea. Yes, Ruby, you can come with the children every week. Would you like that?'

'Oh yes, madam, thank you ever so. I'll do that. But—' She fidgeted from one leg to the other and added, 'But I can't really start till I got some pieces, you know, squares and bits which I can start sewing together. Do you think. . . ?'

Emma fell for it. 'Of course. Have a look in the rag bag that Miss Hester keeps and help yourself to a few pieces of material. And come next Tuesday and show me what you've done.' Delighted that she had the opportunity to educate this new maid, who might well learn to deal with household linen needing repairs, her smile grew. She would ask Hester to produce the rag bag and let Ruby have her pick.

Hester was in her room changing for dinner when Ruby knocked at the door. ' 'Scuse me, Miss Hester—'

'What is it, Ruby?' Hester frowned, pinning her mother's pearl brooch on to her dress. She wasn't sure about this new maid and at the moment her thoughts were far away. Collecting plants in the mountains. Playing tennis with Hugh on Thursday.

'The rag bag, Miss Hester. Madam said as I can take bits from it. For me sewing, you see. Patchwork, an' Madam's going to help me.'

Hester stared. What a strange little creature Ruby was. Patchwork? And Stepmother agreeing to help her? Concealing a smile, she nodded. 'Very well. It's hanging in the broom cupboard on the landing. Take what you want, but be sure and put the bag back.' She watched the girl turn to the door and noticed the smile on the small, cat-shaped face and for a few seconds wondered why Ruby should look like that simply because she had access to the household rag bag. But then, with a bob, Ruby went out of the room, and Hester dismissed the matter from her mind.

Downstairs she joined her parents in the drawing room, planning

41

how she would tell them about Aunt Jacks' guest. Tell them about Nicholas Thorne, whose smile and voice she was finding so hard to dismiss from her mind.

And then, pushing aside the appealing images and musical sounds, another thought flew in, even more exciting than anything else. *Flowers*. In the garden, around the village, through the fields and woodlands. *Painting*. Mr Flynn and his suggestion of private classes. Stronger now came the certain instinctive knowledge that this way lay her freedom.

She hurried into the drawing room, saw the filled sherry glasses and smiled lovingly, full of expectancy and warmth, only to feel a shadow falling on her when her father's gruff voice said disapprovingly, 'You look very flushed, Hester. Not at all becoming. Sit down at once.'

CHAPTER FIVE

The evening passed quietly without Hester saying anything about Nicholas Thorne, and although her father's immediate dismissal of the idea of studying with Mr Flynn still shadowed her mind, she had been overtaken by a new awareness.

Since the longing to get on with her painting had grown stronger, occupying all thoughts, she realized that she had outgrown the need for the quietness and comfort of Oak House. But – and here the bleakness of filial responsibility grew powerful – she accepted that Father and Stepmother enjoyed her presence, needed it, and would never willingly let her go. She was all they had in their increasing old age, so surely she must stay here with them. Irritation churned as her own need for freedom challenged the guilt she felt.

The routine of going to bed as the hall clock struck ten o'clock forced her into smiling stiffly and saying, 'It's late, isn't it? I hope you both sleep well,' and then watching them climb the stairs to their bedroom.

Dutiful thoughts returned. One day she too would be old, immersed in memories and doubts of the future. Who would care for her? And she knew then that she must devote to her parents all the time and loving consideration they needed.

Yet dreams of that elusive freedom still stayed; she longed for it, thought about it even as her responsibilities made sense and weighed her down.

In bed she lay awake, listening to night sounds before finally sleeping. Dreams came and went. Mr Flynn was demanding a reply. Nicholas Thorne sailing away to a foreign land. Hester's fingers flexed as she prepared paper, took up brushes, selected her paints and tried to create a beautiful flower but all she painted was a dark blob with no shape or structure. Beside her, Ruby gave a sly smile, took away the paper and tore it in half. Mr Flynn muttered that her painting was a disgrace and she was thankful when dawn awoke her, hearing the Bartley dog barking.

She got up, weary and confused. *What shall I do?*

Ruby was settling down nicely. She knew now how to deal with Mrs Caunter's rages and imprecations, turning them aside with a joke. Carefully she watched Mr and Mrs Redding and soon discovered how to please them without pushing herself too much.

For instance, Mrs Redding often came down late to breakfast, her legs slow as she descended the stairs. So to be on the landing as this happened was easy; a suggestion of 'Can I help, Madam?' and the offer of a strong arm brought a smile and a nod of gratitude.

Oh yes, thought Ruby, hurrying away to make beds, dust rooms, clean the bathroom and water closet and then help to prepare luncheon, I'm glad I'm here. One day it'll all work out proper, I'll tell 'em and then. . . . Her quick smile was triumphant. Time would help and the paper upstairs was safe. But one lurking feeling of unease stayed. What about Miss Hester? Not soft like her stepma. What would she make of it all, when she knew?

Going into the grey-walled scullery to wash pans left from breakfast, Ruby thought. I must get to know Miss Hester better.

And then, as a demand trumpeted out from the kitchen, she dried her hands, muttering 'All right, I'm coming,' before adding silently, 'Mrs C., you're an ole cow. Jest you wait till I come into me own.'

After breakfast Hester went to her room. She must paint. Only that would calm her restlessness. Some painting, and then she would go to Brook Cottage. Nicholas Thorne would be there. A smile touched her lips, but firmly she concentrated on finishing the painting of the dandelions she had started last week. Some more shading. Some light and emphasis on the strong, tooth-shaped leaves.

Slowly, her confused thoughts relaxed. She knew this was her panacea, a talent she must be grateful for and develop. And in that moment the fateful decision was made: she would accept Mr Flynn's suggestion of private classes. How she would attend them she was not sure. But she would find a way.

I must.

Aunt Jacks was already in the garden, picking a bunch of fragrant white pinks that lolled over the path between the borders. She straightened up as Hester approached.

'Good morning, Hester. You can give a bunch of these Mrs Sinkins to your stepmother.'

'She'll love them, Aunt. Don't they smell wonderful? May I have a couple to paint?'

'Certainly.' Aunt Jacks looked at her keenly. 'You never did tell me what it was you wanted to discuss yesterday.'

Hester hesitated, and then said, 'I just wanted to tell you I am going to study painting privately with Mr Flynn.'

'That sounds a good idea.' Aunt Jacks paused, but only for a second. 'And what does your father say?'

'He was extremely angry and forbade me to do so, but it's something I must do. Mr Flynn is encouraging me to work towards a career but Father has said he won't let me do that.' Hester's voice slowed as she remembered his stern words and her subsequent frustration.

'A career – how splendid.' Aunt Jacks smiled. 'Women must be true to themselves. No more kowtowing to our dictatorial menfolk. Well, I will certainly try and help you in this plan, Hester. Give me a little time and I will think of an idea to get you away from your father's eagle eye and off to do your studying. Now I must go and put these flowers into water.'

Hester watched her aunt disappear into the cottage. Those determined words rang in her ears and she smiled again, wandering down the border, taking in the loveliness of the flowers filling it. Dignified blue delphiniums, rich scarlet snapdragons, and tiny pink and white mop-heads of daisies made a blur of colour, a background to her more positive thoughts.

To study she must get out of the house on some pretext. Then walk up to the village, catch the omnibus into town and on to where Mr

Flynn lived. Yes, she would do it. And then, a sudden, brilliant idea – perhaps Hugh could help her. They would play tennis on Thursday, and afterwards she would ask him if—

'Miss Redding, good morning.' The deep voice snatched her back from plans and deceptions and she turned quickly.

'Good morning, Mr Thorne – yes, it's a beautiful one.' Her smile mirrored his and she stood still as he came down the path, holding something in his left hand.

'I found this in the hedge on my way here.' His expression was thoughtful. 'Will it be useful? Your aunt told me you are painting your flora.'

With the small white and delicately marked flower in her hands, she looked at it closely. 'Bastard balm – not very common. How kind of you. Oh yes, I'll include it in the flora.'

Looking at each other, she thought their minds were at one because of the bond of flowers. And something else, perhaps, which she didn't recognize, but which filled her with an exciting and guilty disturbance. She felt close to this tall, strong man, this gardener, this adventurer, who worked for his living among plants and made dangerous expeditions in search of new ones.

Then an extraordinary thought came: she felt closer to Nicholas than she had ever felt to Hugh, friend though he had been for most of her life. She knew it was ridiculous and impossible that she and Nicholas might become friends. But – a quick breath – why not? The world was changing, and attitudes and prejudices, too. A quick vision flashed of herself introducing Nicholas to Father and Stepmother, and then she was almost laughing at the thought.

Lightness of heart swept through her, until she blinked, recalling the conventions of her upbringing, and she stepped away from his side, ashamed of the feelings running through her. *I'm out of my depth. What am I thinking of? Perhaps I should go home.*

'I'm sorry, Mr Thorne,' she said unevenly. 'I-I can't stay, I'm afraid. I-I have to go now. . . .'

His smile died. Did she see disappointment? Her emotions raged.

The low voice was alarmingly persuasive. 'But you are going to help with the weeding, because my one hand can't manage alone.' He took the single flower from her and walked towards the stream at the bottom of the garden. 'I'll put this here while we get to work. It mustn't die before you can paint it.'

Turning, he looked back at her and she wondered if he was feeling the same thing that so disturbed her. That warm instinctive flash of attraction, and then the cold, imperative need to banish it? Of course not. Nicholas Thorne was merely expecting her to carry out the offer of help which she had made yesterday. And of course she would stay. She was a woman, not a gauche child.

'Thank you. I'll collect it when I go home.' The strange feeling had gone now and she smiled cheerfully. 'And I suppose you're relying on me to clear Aunt Jacks' border?' Her voice was light, but a certain anticipation remained.

'I certainly am.' Laughter gleamed in his eyes. 'Where shall we start? At the far ends? I'll find you a kneeler and a hand fork. Watch out for nettles, won't you, Miss Redding? I wouldn't want those painting fingers to get stung.'

She watched him stride away to the garden shed at the back of the cottage, emerging again with the tools, a couple of baskets and a well-supported kneeler which, slightly awkwardly and using only his uninjured arm, he loaded into the wheelbarrow. As he approached, she acknowledged that this was an unexpected, slightly disturbing experience. But then her thoughts strove for balance. Why shouldn't she work alongside him? He seemed more than just a gardener, even though that was all he was. A man whom Aunt Jacks clearly thought of very highly and with trust – treating him almost like a son. He had a certain charm about him, and seemed to be offering easy friendship, which Hester knew she would like to accept. But what would everybody say?

Father would rant about class differences, Stepmother would be terribly shocked, even Aunt Jacks might suggest this wasn't quite right. And Hugh? Hugh, with his Cambridge colleagues, his degree in law and his gentrified family – would he be angry and shocked too? But, as Hester accepted the small fork handed to her, she decided that there was no need for Hugh to know about Nicholas.

Pulling aside her skirt and kneeling down, she wondered what Nicholas himself was feeling. Opposing ideas pulled her thoughts apart. Her feelings were clear enough, but what must it be like for him to try and offer friendship to a well-bred girl with middle-class values?

Difficult. Yet perhaps appealing? His smile had been very friendly.

For a moment they looked at each other. Then he moved away, took the wheelbarrow to the far end of the border and began his own work while Hester stared down at the weeds which were clogging the mauve scabious and the Canterbury bells in front of her, and began forking them out. She felt very happy. Would that life could stay just like this.

Aunt Jacks offered sandwiches and soup for a light luncheon, but Hester said she must go home, and Nicholas also had to leave. 'I can't be away from the nursery for too long – who knows what young Jim will get up to when I'm not there to boss him around.' He smiled at Aunt Jacks as he washed and dried his left hand free of garden soil and then glanced at Hester, standing by the door, the pinks and the bastard balm safely in her basket.

'I hope we meet again before too long, Miss Redding.'

She saw the twitch of the straight lips and wondered if the polite words hinted at something closer. But she knew Aunt Jacks listened and watched so her voice was cool when she replied. 'I hope so, too, Mr Thorne.'

They left the cottage together, and walked up the lane in silence, she turning off at the entrance to Oak House while he continued on into the village, and then to Newton Abbot.

'Goodbye, Miss Redding. It's been a pleasure working with you.'

Warmth spread through her, but she merely nodded her head and gave him a controlled smile. 'Yes, we dealt with a few weeds between us, didn't we? I hope your arm improves.' She stopped. Were the clear blue eyes telling her something? Really, she was being quite ridiculous. Briskly she said goodbye, and then walked away, up the curving drive. She didn't turn back to see if he watched – that would be common, flirtatious behaviour and not worthy of her, but an emptiness suddenly filled her, striving to turn away all the pleasure of the morning.

Entering the quiet house, with strength of mind she banished the extraordinary thoughts Nicholas Thorne had engendered and went to her room to get ready for luncheon with her family Her attention was on the flowers in the basket as she went upstairs and onto the first-floor landing; this afternoon she would paint the balm.

Her door was ajar, and she thought she heard a sound as she neared it. Entering the room, she stopped. Ruby stood by the dressing table, hand reaching out to touch something. For a long moment neither spoke. Hester felt her heartbeat quicken, recalling what Aunt Jacks had warned her about, and stared at Ruby, whose small face coloured and then quickly widened into a grin.

'Lost me duster, Miss Hester. Looked everywhere, an' here it was.' She produced the duster from the shadowy space between Hester's jewel box and the silver-plated hairbrush, bright eyes at once looking at the basket Hester carried.

'Oh, what lovely flowers. Shall I put them in a vase, Miss Hester?' Her smile was infectious, and despite her suspicions, Hester could only join her. What a child Ruby was; and how foolish and unpleasantly judgmental she was to think badly of her.

'Thank you, Ruby. A small vase for the wild flower – this one. Bring it back up here, and take the other scented flowers into Mrs Redding's room.'

'She'll be pleased, Miss Hester. Oh, they smells lovely. . . .' Ruby buried her nose in the pinks before leaving the room, closing the door quietly behind her.

Hester looked into the mirror at her reflection and said questioningly, 'There's something not quite right. But she seems very willing. Too familiar, but she'll soon learn.'

Soon there was a tap at the door and Ruby reappeared, holding a vase with the bastard balm in it. She giggled. 'Cook says it's got a rude name, Miss Hester, did you know? Beginning with a B.' The giggles grew louder and Hester frowned. Ruby put a hand to her mouth. 'Sorry, Miss Hester, shouldn't 'ave said that.' And then she was gone and Hester was left looking at the innocent wild flower, frowning, and wondering why.

She turned her mind again to her painting, and then her glance fell on the small carved, sandalwood box which held the few pieces of jewellery left to her by her grandmother and her mother The pearl brooch, a gold bracelet, emerald earbobs, various other brooches and tiepins, a set of matching rubies and the beautiful blue-green Venetian beads which had been an eighteenth birthday present from Aunt Jacks.

Hester smiled, remembering that day. 'My dear child, you need to wear something decorative to celebrate. Your Uncle Frank and I found these in a shop in Venice when we were on honeymoon. I hope you like them.'

Her smile died. The box lid was slightly open, sunlight touching the jewels lying inside it. Hester's expression tightened. Ruby had obviously opened the box.

Surely she hadn't taken anything? Had she?

CHAPTER SIX

Nothing was missing and Hester sighed with relief. She hadn't wanted to blame Ruby. But even so, as she went downstairs she still felt that small knot inside her that insisted Ruby must be watched.

In the dining room her father stood behind his chair at the head of the table, her stepmother, looking anxious, at the far end, her back to the window.

'I needed you this morning, Hester. Had you forgotten it's the time for us to look at the household account books together?' His voice was gruff, his expression intimidating.

Yes, she had forgotten. For a second she was back, weeding the border, odd thoughts about Nicholas Thorne filling her mind, but now she banished them. 'I'm sorry, Father – I did forget. But perhaps we might look at them this afternoon, after your rest?'

'Morning is the time for accounts, not the afternoon.' He sniffed and sat down, nodding at Emma to do the same.

Hester's mind flurried with thoughts. Father was almost like a gaoler. Surely he could look at the accounts without her? She looked at him. 'I was visiting Aunt Jacks this morning – only for an hour or so.' Resentment welled up and she added sharply, 'You treat me almost like a prisoner, Father.'

Silence spread through the room, broken only when Ruby came in and put the tureen of soup on the table. Hester, watching, thought distractedly how well the girl managed the serving of the soup into the bowls placed before them. In a flash of unexpected bitter humour, she wondered what Ruby must think of the Redding family. Silences, raised voices occasionally, words broken off when she appeared. She must have realized that discontent lurked; and did she know why? Had she worked out that Hester's strong will was the problem? That freedom called to Hester and could not be taken because of the family conventions? A last thought: did the girl, in fact, know anything at all about personal freedom?

As Ruby left the room, Hester said, 'I will help with the accounts later this afternoon, Father.' She saw his hand shaking as he wiped his whiskers after the first spoonful of soup and felt the usual guilt. Father was old; she was young and didn't understand how he thought. Slowly, her mind simmered down and again she looked at him. 'I shall be at the Marchants' tomorrow morning, Father. And in the afternoon I will accompany Stepmother on a visit. I know that's what you expect of me and I'll try and be more helpful. Please forgive me for what I said.'

He gave her a long look but made no response. Gathering her courage, she said slowly, picking each word very carefully, 'But in return I ask for your permission for me to study with Mr Flynn.' She breathed deeply, aware of the disapproval on the two elderly faces. 'Aunt Jacks is in favour of my doing this, so perhaps you might consider—'

'Jacks is a meddler!' Arthur Redding's spoon fell with a splash into the bowl, sending soup cascading over the tablecloth. Emma whispered, 'Oh dear,' as he leaned back in his chair, eyes narrowed, dark with anger. 'She always has been. *Always*. And she has no right to interfere in our affairs. Kindly keep away from her in future, Hester.'

They stared at each other. Hester rose, went to the fireplace, pulled the bell tie, turned to look back at him. She didn't want another argument, but something inside her was too powerful to resist. 'I can't do that, Father. Aunt Jacks is helping me with my painting, my flora. She knows about plants, and I need to know, too.'

Ruby came in, saw what had happened and silently went out again, returning with a cloth, a tray and a fresh bowl which she refilled with soup.

Arthur Redding motioned her away. 'No more,' he said gruffly and rose. 'Bring my luncheon to my study.' He waited until she had left the room and then glared at Hester. 'I don't wish to stay in your company any longer if these unpleasant arguments are to continue. You know my feelings, so give them further thought before you speak to me again. No, Emma—' He frowned. 'Stay here. I wish to be alone.'

'Oh dear.' Emma clutched her napkin and watched as he walked out of the room. 'Oh Hester, upsetting your poor dear father like this! It's so unkind when you must surely know he's only doing what he thinks is the best for you. And I can't stay here, either.' Painfully, she rose, walking towards the door, turning at the last moment to say, 'I couldn't eat a thing. But I might manage a cup of tea – in the drawing room.'

Hester's heartbeat quietened as again she summoned Ruby. Her father's anger had hurt her, made her question her reason for being so defiant. Feeling exhausted and confused, she told Ruby to take a tray of tea to Mrs Redding and then to serve her own luncheon here. Standing by the fireplace, she tried to control her thoughts.

The room had never seemed so silent. Walking to the window, she looked out into the walled garden below. The pear trees were full of blossom and the first green leaves. Yes, there would be a good harvest this year. And those iris in the little rockery beds were just showing rich purple buds. All so lovely, and yet here, in this house, there would never be peace unless she and Father could agree.

Ruby's voice fell into her chaotic thoughts. 'Here's your fish, Miss Hester. And the veg. Anything else you want?'

Turning slowly, Hester brought herself back to the present. She said wearily, 'No, thank you.' She thought she saw condemnation on the girl's face, and abruptly her mind leaped. Even Ruby is against me. *Am I really so selfish and cruel? I must be concerned about other people's feelings, but what about my own? Does no one think about how I feel? About what I want so desperately?*

Pulling her feelings into tight control, she nodded at the maid. 'Tell Mrs Caunter, please, that we mustn't waste what isn't eaten today. Perhaps she can use it tomorrow.' She returned to the table, sitting down and looking from Father's abandoned chair to that of Stepmother. A desolate feeling of loneliness hit her, and it was almost impossible to eat her luncheon, wondering what would happen next.

*

Ruby couldn't wait to tell Mrs Caunter. 'Soup all over the tablecloth – have to soak and boil it to get the stain out, you know what egg yolks is. And Master and Madam going off and Miss Hester staying there alone. What a carry on! They're all goin' to eat in different rooms. Wonder why?'

Mrs Caunter turned down her mouth. 'Never you mind. Nothin' to do with us.' She looked over her shoulder at Ruby, saw her grin, and frowned. 'So get on and do it. An' take that grin off yer face. Remember, there's no accountin' for what the gentry gets up to.'

Ruby carried the master's tray to the study, returning to the kitchen to prepare the tea tray which she took to the drawing room, knocking and then entering. Poor ole souls, she thought, even as she kept her eyes down; Master had been red in the face and staring out of the window, and now Madam was in tears, dabbing at her face and making funny little moans.

As she put down the tea tray, Ruby's thoughts wandered into the future. If she had her way, she'd tell Master not to worry about that unkind daughter of his, and then comfort poor Madam with an arm round her shoulder, even adding a drop of something strong to her teacup. But of course the future wasn't here, not yet. So today all she could do was offer Madam a smile, asking quietly, 'Can I get you anything else, Madam?'

A watery look and a shake of the head was her only answer. Ruby returned to the kitchen, grinning, but carefully removing it before Mrs Caunter could notice. Things were moving. And in the right direction. How exciting it was.

In her studio, Hester forced herself to concentrate on painting rather than going over the unpleasant lunchtime upset. The bastard balm flower was delightful to paint and she felt it was going right: a pale wash to colour the paper, leaving space to provide white where necessary, the stem curving at an angle that showed off the open flower and the leaves delicately framing the whole picture. She looked intently at her work, trying to see what Mr Flynn might see, should she manage to attend his private class. Shape, texture, colour, the whole picture on the page: so many details to bring the painting to life. But she was pleased with what she saw, and it drifted into her mind that she wished Nicholas Thorne could see this painting of the flower he had given her.

Suddenly, noises downstairs and Aunt Jacks' clear voice echoing up the stairwell. Hester put away her paints and went onto the landing, wondering if she should go down.

'Well, Arthur, I'm glad that you've seen sense.' Aunt Jacks and Father had come out of the study and were in the hall. 'So I shall call for Hester next Wednesday morning and after we leave the botany class at the Reading Room she can do some shopping – or something – while I attend the meeting of the Flower Society. We'll be back in time for luncheon. Don't change your mind about the class, will you? Hester will be a great help to me once her knowledge of botany improves. No, I can't stay for tea, thank you – I am meeting someone who is interested in my gardening school. I know you think that's rubbish, but to me it's my *raison d'être*. I can't stop. Goodbye, Arthur.'

Hester saw her aunt wave as she left the house, and then heard the trap clatter down the drive. She felt inexpressible relief as the meaning of all that she had overheard started to make sense.

Botany class – yes, she and Aunt Jacks had discussed attending that – and presumably the so-called 'shopping or something' – could be spent at Mr Flynn's studio. It was deceitful, but she must seize the opportunity. Still at the top of the stairs, her body relaxed. She knew that this was the moment to see Father and apologize; to thank him for meeting her halfway and, she hoped fervently, to resume the old fond relationship which had split so painfully earlier today.

He was crossing the hall as she ran down the stairs. 'Father?'

He stopped, standing beside the drawing-room door. 'Hester.'

She thought his voice was softer, and saw a lift to his lips heralding a smile. It was all right. Things would be back to normal, and he had agreed to her wish to paint and study. 'Father,' she said again, at his side, smiling, putting out a hand and hoping that he would respond in the same loving way.

'I apologize for everything, Father. I was rude, unkind, and I'm sorry.' She paused, looking into the eyes that met hers with an unfamiliar show of affection. 'I heard what Aunt Jacks said – that I can go with her and attend the botany class.'

Arthur Redding sighed and looked at the longcase clock in the hallway. 'Teatime. Your stepmother will be down in a minute. Ruby will be coming up with the tray.' He took her hand in his and looked deeply into her eyes. 'So we have this moment together. You are my beloved daughter, and I was hurt – offended – by your unthinking words. But time has made me consider the truth of what you said, and I understand that you are of an age when you need to venture out into the world. So I agreed when your aunt suggested this plan of studying botany together.'

Clasping his hand, Hester felt tears behind her eyes. 'Thank you, Father. Dear Father.' Her voice was unsteady. 'You know I love you.'

'As I love you.' But the familiar harsh note was back in his voice and he pulled his hand away. 'Of course I do. But I expect you to behave as a young lady should do. Don't press me further, Hester – you have upset your stepmother, and I wish to forget the whole unpleasant incident.' He opened the drawing-room door and she went in, knowing that although this was a small victory, it did not open the way to unconditional freedom, the dream of which still filled her mind, even as she smiled and prepared the table for tea.

The next morning was fresh and sweet scented and Hester found herself looking forward enormously to meeting Hugh and some old friends. Tennis, conversation and laughter would be enjoyable, the last few days having been so unhappy. She found her racquet, dusted it down and felt for sagging strings, hopeful that it would last just one more summer. A disturbing thought struck: would she still be here next year, playing tennis, immersed in mind-searing domesticity and still hating every moment of it?

At breakfast the atmosphere was sober and quiet, and she did not engage either Father or Stepmother in conversation. Enough that they both looked happier than yesterday, she thought.

Stepmother, finishing her toast, looked up and said, 'I suppose Hugh will be here soon. And will you stay at the Marchants' for luncheon?' Her pale face managed a smile and Hester returned it.

'I don't know, Stepmother. It might be best not to expect me.'

Emma blinked. 'I see. But you'll be back in time to come with me when we go to tea with Vicar's wife, of course?'

Hester sucked in a breath. 'Yes, Stepmother. I'll be here.'

Hester's faded blue linen dress was then carefully inspected by Emma, who murmured, 'It must be difficult to play with a bustle bouncing up and down at your back. And have you pinned your hat on securely?'

'Yes, Stepmother.' Hester adjusted the small, brimmed straw hat and ran a hand down her tightly waisted dress. She wished that the modern decision to remove corsets from feminine fashion would soon have results: in the exciting future that lay ahead women must throw out such tight and uncomfortable manifestations of men's dictatorship. With Nicholas Thorne's words about the amazing lady adventurers echoing in her head, she wondered whether they wore something easier and looser as they travelled, and she had to hide the laughter bubbling up as she remembered. Corsets in the jungle would surely be very restrictive indeed.

At ten o'clock precisely there was a knock at the door and Hugh stood there, his smile broadening as he looked at her. 'Good morning, Hester. My word, you look ready for anything. I predict we shall win all our matches this morning.' Taking her racquet, he held out a hand to lead her into the pony trap at the bottom of the steps. 'Up you get. And now – where would you like to go for luncheon?' The pony moved down the drive and then, as Hugh flicked the whip over its back, trotted up the lane and away from Oak House.

Away from home. Hester took a long, deep, enjoyable breath, realizing that life was blooming all around her. Away from home, a meeting with old friends and some exciting games of tennis. She smiled at Hugh. 'What a good idea. All of us, going off on the spree?'

'No.' He sounded authoritative, and his expression was intense enough to make something flicker inside her. 'Just you and me. I think we're old enough friends to allow our families to accept we need to be alone sometimes. Your parents don't expect you back too soon, do they?'

She shook her head. 'I said I might be back at lunchtime, but they won't worry if I'm not.'

'Well done.' His grin was approving. 'So think about where you'd like to go.'

As they turned into the main road, Hester looked around her, saw the inviting blue-grey hazy outline of Dartmoor a few miles away and said impulsively, 'Let's go up on the moor. We'll find an inn. Oh, what fun!' And then she heard the ambiguous sound of her words and knew she was perhaps encouraging him to imagine more than she really meant. Alone, together on the moor, he would think she was taking one step nearer in their courtship.

The worrying thoughts stayed in her mind until they turned in at the large gateway of Court Hill House on the outskirts of Bovey Tracey, and then she switched them off. She was free to enjoy herself, to savour a suddenly fresh life, and she would make the most of it. So she took Hugh's hand as he helped her off the trap and, walking beside him, smiled across the stretching lawn at the group of people waiting for them by the tennis court, racquets in hand, voices chattering and laughing.

Yes, life was suddenly very good.

CHAPTER SEVEN

Ruby, after making the beds and dusting around, heard the knock at the front door, and then a man's voice. Was this Miss Hester's beau? What was he called, Hugh somebody? Hidden as she leant against the landing banisters, she listened intently; Miss Hester sounding happy for once. She scurried into Miss Hester's room as the front door closed and the trap began crunching the gravel. Leaning out of the window, she could just see it moving. Miss Hester wore a blue dress, carried a racquet and was clearly enjoying going out with Mr Hugh. How lucky to have such a nice, handsome man beside her. For a second envy hit Ruby hard, but not for long. After all, her future was here, a path in front of her. And she was making steps every day.

She loitered in Miss Hester's bedroom, opening the wardrobe and looking at the clothes inside it. Nothing very interesting, no satin ballgowns like she'd seen once in a magazine. Ordinary clothes, she thought, until she looked at them closely and realized they were made with expensive cloth – silk, velvet, gabardine, tweed – and sewn with tiny stitches, trimmed stylishly, all looking elegant and gentrified. This was what made Miss Hester look so attractive. Something clicked in Ruby's mind. One day she would have clothes like these.

She closed the wardrobe and went to the dressing table, fingers reaching out to stroke the sandalwood jewel box. The top was carved with dragons and flowers and inside were all Miss Hester's jewels. Ruby paused; no one about. Cook was cutting up a rabbit, Mr Redding in the garden with Hoskins, and Mrs Redding writing letters at her desk. Ruby smiled. What would she look like, decked out with jewels? She took out the brooches and pendants, put aside the rope of pale moonstones, tried on the gold bracelet, and then, with an intake of delighted breath, picked up the green-blue glass beads and fastened them around her small, warm neck. Probably not precious like the other stuff but, oh, didn't they suit her? A lovely shining bluey green, making her own green eyes all the brighter. Ruby swallowed the lump forming in her throat and suddenly knew the heat and force of desire.

'Ruby? Are you upstairs? Come down, please.'

Mrs Redding. Hurriedly Ruby took off the necklace, pushed everything back into the box and closed the lid. She left the room and made sure she was heard running down the stairs. 'Coming, Madam. Just giving the windows an extra shine – this sun shows up all the dust, it does.'

Mrs Redding stood by her desk in the dining room, holding out two letters. 'For Hoskins to post, please, Ruby. And you've done the windows? Well done – you think of everything.' She smiled approvingly.

Ruby took the letters, bobbed a curtsey, and said meekly, 'It's the least I can do, Madam, living here in this nice house, with nice employers.' She left the room, smiling to herself. Madam was a real old softie. No problem in making a friend out of her. But when the time came, would Master be so easy?

'Ruby!'

Mrs Caunter's voice was loud and Ruby's smile died as she went down to the kitchen.

The sun shone on the immaculate lawn at Court Hill House and the sagging tennis net had been adjusted. Fanny and Norah Wellington, in cotton muslin dresses with floaty flounces and with small hats perched on their half-hidden rebelliously curly hair, decided they would play together. Fanny, always the speaker, giggled. 'We haven't practised since last year, so don't expect too much, will you, Hester?'

'I'm just as rusty as you are, Fanny. Anyway, this isn't Wimbledon, so let's just enjoy playing, shall we?' She and Hugh walked to the far end of the court and Hugh grinned at her, taking his place behind the line. 'Stay by the net, Hester, you play well there. We'll show those two how tennis should be played.'

Love all, deuce, 'van in, 'van out, and then, 'Oh dear, Hester, you and Hugh have won – Norah and I are so slow. I knew you would!'

All the activity made a rest necessary. Deckchairs were arranged beside the summerhouse and Hugh said, as Hester sat down beside the two puffing and giggling sisters, 'Like me to teach you how to serve overarm? It makes a much stronger game.'

Fanny blew out her breath, rubbed her ankle, adjusted her misplaced hat and looked at Hester mischievously. 'Doesn't sound very feminine,' she murmured, while, beside her, Norah laughed aloud. 'But let's see you try, Hester.'

After they had drunk glasses of lemonade and nibbled at ratafia biscuits, Hugh got up, took Hester's hand and said, with a sideways grin at the two chattering sisters, 'I think Fanny is challenging you, Hester – let's show her, shall we? Believe me, there's nothing about serving overarm that should shock anyone. Come on, over here, where your audience can enjoy the performance.'

No shock? Hester knew he was being untruthful from the moment he came up behind her, putting his arm around her to take her right hand, swinging her arm back over her head. She felt a flush spread through her and pulled away.

But Hugh was intent on the lesson. 'See?' he said. 'That's the movement – easy. Try it on your own.'

His arm dropped away and she knew at once that he was teasing her; it didn't matter whether she could serve overarm. It simply meant that he was enjoying her nearness – hand touching her body, feeling her pulling away from him.

She wouldn't let him see her disturbance. Throwing up a ball, she copied the movement he had shown her and felt a thrill of satisfaction as the racquet connected, sending the ball sailing over the net, to land just within the double lines of the court.

Turning, she smiled proudly at the girls sitting by the summerhouse. 'Why don't you clap? I'm a champion in the making!' But, returning to the chair and another glass of lemonade, she still felt Hugh's touch and she knew she was looking forward to their promised trip to Dartmoor.

Excuses made for not staying for luncheon, they were soon on the road heading for the moor. As they drove up the hilly track over Trendlebere Down towards Manaton, she felt the wind on her face, slipped her shawl down and took off her hat, giving herself to this new, refreshing world.

Outings to the moor had been childhood treats. If Father had been away on business, Mother and Aunt Jacks had made the day into something wonderful to savour. Hester's feel of the short stubby turf under her boots had been memorable. And the fact that it was studded with yellow flowers was equally exciting.

'Tormentil.' Aunt Jacks had picked one small specimen and put it carefully inside the brown paper bag she always carried in her pocket on these outings. 'Hester, at home you must look up the Latin name and repeat it to me tomorrow.'

'I will, Aunt Jacks. I will.' And so she had. *Potentilla erecta*. Now the name flashed through Hester's mind and she repeated it silently, feeling again the urge to learn, to paint, to create her flora – to live her life far beyond the domestic cage of her home.

Those outings and Aunt Jacks' encouragement had been the start of her passion for wild flowers, and Aunt Jacks was still helping her in the development of that passion. She realized how lucky she was to have such loving help. And then she had a fleeting image of Nicholas Thorne, holding out the single flower he had brought her.

Hugh halted the trap outside the farm at the bottom of the hill leading up to Hay Tor and, suddenly confused at the pleasure that the unexpected image brought, she was glad when his voice cut into her thoughts.

'Hold the reins, Hester – I'll go and find Daniel and ask him to stable Prince here for a while. I thought you'd like a walk?'

'I'd love it. Shall we go up to the tors?'

He nodded, disappeared into the house and then came out accompanied by an elderly man with beard and whiskers who took off his hat and bowed politely to Hester. 'Pony'll be all right here, Miss Redding. Enjoy your walk – good views today. 'Tis clear and lovely.'

She smiled and watched the old man leading the pony into a shed beside the house. Hugh said, 'Daniel was our groom, he's retired now. Prince will be fine for a while. Come on, Hester. I only hope you're wearing sensible shoes.'

She watched, surprised, as he took a covered basket from the trap, and latched it over his arm. 'Luncheon. Not at an inn, but somewhere up there, in the sun. Yes?'

'Wonderful! What a marvellous thought.'

They began the uphill walk over the heather-dotted turf leading to the huge tors ahead of them. The shadows faded from Hester's mind as she paused, looking around her. The boundless landscape made her heart leap. Golden sunshine, and in the distance indigo shadows, grey, fresh green and many blues.

If only she'd brought her sketchbook. She longed to pin it down on paper. 'I can see for miles. There's Teignmouth – and oh, ponies!' A small herd of brown ponies came trotting across the track; mares with last year's foals still at heel, all long legs and awkward gangling movements, and the stallion, rough, wild eyed and possessive, rushing his family along.

'Want a ride?' Hugh was laughing.

'No thanks – and anyway we're supposed to be walking, not riding. Come on, let's get to the top.'

He pulled at her arm, drawing her to a halt. 'Not while this basket is so full, thank you. Let's find a comfortable rock and sit down and eat – that one over there.'

It was large enough to shelter them from the fresh wind that sneaked around the tors, and provided a good picnic place. Hester sat down after inspecting the turf for sheep droppings and adders. 'Why didn't you tell me you were planning this?' She looked at him, opening the basket and spreading its contents on a ledge in the rock beside them.

'As a conventionally well-brought-up young lady, I knew you would have looked shocked and said no. Alone, with a handsome male?' He laughed. 'Of course I didn't tell you. That would have spoilt everything.' He looked into her amused eyes, then held out a sandwich. 'Salmon and cucumber.'

Such pleasure in eating in the open air. Hester's appetite had never been so good. A pair of ravens croaked overhead and the landscape opened wide before her. She thought about his words, and then said, 'But I'm not really conventional, Hugh.'

'No?'

She saw his eyes narrow, looking at her intently.

Gathering her courage, she said slowly, 'I want to be free. I hate those fussy old conventions. I can't live my life like that.'

He frowned. 'You're not one of those suffragist women, are you, Hester? Such nuisances, decrying all the virtues of decent womanhood.'

'No, I'm just a girl who wants to live a freer life.'

She couldn't stop the laughter bubbling up at his mystified expression and then tried to explain. 'I'm planning to have a career. I'm going to leave home and take my ability to paint flowers into a situation where I can earn my own living.'

Hugh put down his half-eaten sandwich and sat back against the rock. He stared, thoughtful eyes intent on hers, his face suddenly touched with what she sensed was unexpected deep feeling.

She held her breath. Was he going to rant like Father? Or had he the freedom of thought that, even in their brief meeting last week, she had sensed Nicholas Thorne possessed? Then, suddenly, the ponies appeared again, on their way to new feeding grounds, and the moment lengthened.

He put out his hand and took hers. 'Hester—' His voice was low, his lips beneath the tawny moustache lifting into the hint of a smile. 'You never cease to amaze me. Overarm serves, no feminine twitterings about this damned wind, and now you're off to make a living from painting. I can't believe it.'

She smiled triumphantly. 'But you must. Because it's what I'm going to do. Somehow.'

His thumb stroked her hand and curiosity spread over his face. 'Somehow? That sounds as if difficulties are already appearing. Tell me.'

She breathed deeply and turned away, looking into the distance, searching for the right words. 'I accept my responsibilities to my parents.' She looked back at him and her voice rose. 'But surely I have some of my own? To live my life as fully as I can? To step out into the world which is so exciting and full of extraordinary opportunities.' She met his steady gaze. 'Hugh, don't blame me for wanting this one thing. After all, it's so little – not fame, or riches, but just a chance to see what I can do with the talent I've been given.'

He said nothing but kept looking at her and she felt her cheeks colouring, a sense of unease spreading through her. 'Well,' she said sharply, 'tell me what you think.' Slowly he finished the half-eaten sandwich, offered her another, and she shook her head impatiently. 'Of course you don't think I can do it. So come on, tell me.'

His voice was quiet. 'We've been friends for so long, Hester, and, to be honest, I've always hoped we might go deeper.'

She caught her breath, but he was leaning towards her, his face suddenly tightened by what she saw was a new seriousness.

'Well, you've got your plans, foolish as they sound and I've got mine. But I want you to change your mind. You see, now that I've got my degree I am going into the family firm – a junior partnership to start with. Believe me' – his eyes widened, grew brighter – 'with younger blood the old business will soon develop. This is a potentially prosperous time and the old firm is already well established.' He laughed. 'So I see myself as an up-and-coming tycoon! What do you think of that?'

She hesitated, reaching out to the open basket and taking another sandwich. 'I didn't realize you were so ambitious, Hugh. Are you quite sure that this is what you really want to do? And do you truly think that a small law firm will catapult you to the top?' Biting into the sandwich, she gave him a mocking smile. 'And what if you're not tycoon material? You like to have fun in life. Are you serious enough to become a businessman?'

He leaned towards her, drawing back her hand as she raised it, and said, with a new sober note in his voice, 'I'm serious enough about one thing, Hester, and that's you.'

Her breath caught as, at once, she knew what he meant. Stepmother's voice echoed with its hopes of courtship and marriage. But Hugh was taking things too fast. She wasn't ready for him to declare that he loved her. She must play for time. 'Hugh, what ever do you mean?'

His lips lifted into a wide smile. 'Just what I said. I want to have you at my side when I'm a successful businessman because you'll be a good hostess. You'll charm my dinner guests. You'll make my big, expensive house – when I buy it – the attraction of the county and keep it well run. And you'll be there when I come home, tired or worried about a difficult case. You'll calm me, comfort me.' He lifted his hand, ran a finger down her cheek. 'Keep me going through my hectic and ambitious life.'

They stared at each other and Hester felt herself suddenly chilled. Stumbling for words, her thoughts in chaos, she said slowly, 'I don't know what to say, Hugh. You've, well, shocked me. Your business, the big house, marriage?' Her voice was low. 'But not a word about being fond of me.'

He shrugged, sat back against the rock and looked at her with an expression that she found hard to understand. Gone was the lightheartedness and the humour. This was a new Hugh. She listened to his crisp words and realized abruptly that he was a man in search of his future and planning to ensure that it would be a successful one.

'Of course I'm fond of you, Hester. We've been friends for all our lives. But a marriage is principally about property and status. You must know that?'

Bleakly, she nodded. Yes, she did. What had Stepmother told her? And she understood Hugh's plan, but it seemed an empty, cold sort of plan to make. Shouldn't love be there somewhere?

As if he read her thoughts, Hugh said, almost casually, 'Well, if you're waiting for those three little words, of course I can say them.'

'And mean them?' She met his gaze, felt her face stiffen and tried to tell herself to keep control of the emotions suddenly thrusting through her.

'Love?' His voice was light, his smile more amused than emotional. 'But that comes later, you silly girl. Once we've learned to live together and make a good partnership, then perhaps we'll love each other. Love can wait – everybody knows that.'

'I don't.'

The smile vanished. 'Hester, for heaven's sake, I don't have to make it any plainer, do I? I'm suggesting you should be my wife.'

She shook her head, feeling an enormous weight pulling her down. This lovely, friendly time together here on the moor was turning into a turmoil of uncomfortable emotions. What could she say to him? That she was very fond of him, but would prefer to marry someone whom she truly loved? How he would laugh! And supposing, just supposing – the extraordinary thought flew into her confusion, hardly believable but strong enough to widen her eyes – that she did marry him, where would the time be for her painting?

She shook her head. 'I'm sorry,' was all she could say. And then again, watching his face tighten, his eyes narrow. 'I'm sorry.'

They sat in silence, bodies carefully not touching, Hester's thoughts whirling and coming to no useful conclusions. She looked again at the colours of the stretching landscape and felt herself slowly easing back into normality.

Such colours. My painting.

The vital question: if she married him, would she have time to paint? Would she have that freedom she craved? *He doesn't love me. Would he ever understand my needs?*

Suddenly she remembered Oak House and Stepmother awaiting her return. Breathing in a draught of cold moorland air, she scrambled to her feet, glanced at her watch and said as casually as she could manage, 'Goodness, it's really late. I must go home, Hugh – my stepmother is expecting me to accompany her on afternoon calls.'

He rose, repacked the basket, and then, suddenly turning to her, pulled her roughly towards him. 'Hester. . . .' His eyes were dark, his voice rough. 'Think about my proposal. It could be an excellent partnership. Don't turn me down at once. After all, you and I both know that your dream of painting and so forth is just that – a dream.' He gave her a little shake. 'Wake up, Hester. You know how fond I am of you – think of all the fun we can have together. Like this. . . .'

She was drawn into his arms, her face so close to his that she felt his warm breath on her cheek. Something softened through her body; she looked at the half-open lips, recognized his intent, and, even as she longed to give in, knew she must not. His touch this morning had been exciting and she knew his kisses would be sweet, but she pulled away.

'No,' she said. 'I mean – not yet, if ever.' She walked rapidly down the hill.

'Hester!' He was following, calling after her, but she took no notice. Eyes on the turf at her feet, she stopped abruptly as a small blue flower drew her attention. Stooping, she picked it, examined it, put it carefully into her skirt pocket, wishing she had one of Aunt Jacks' brown paper bags, and continued walking back to the cottage and the pony trap. Hugh's unlikely proposal was now only half filling her mind, for here was another flower which she would paint tomorrow morning when she had time to return to her flora.

She looked again at the moorland stretching around, complete and impersonal in its beauty, took in the colours and the age-old, primitive freedom, then heard Hugh following her down to the road, and realized the decision had made itself.

'Devil's-bit scabious,' she whispered to herself, and then smiled, remembering all that Aunt Jacks had taught her. *Flowers dark blue purple, rounded heads, in damp grassy places. Succisa pratensis.*

Already she could see the blue shades mixing on her palette.

CHAPTER EIGHT

The Hayward Nursery was always busy. A narrow plot of land stretching beside the main road from Newton Abbot, which Edward, son of the founder, had inherited, it was a plantsman's business of excellent reputation and increasing growth.

Glasshouses gleamed in the sunshine, the shelves of terracotta pots home to innumerable small plants now in the full beauty of vivid flowering, with outside beds of greenery filling the remainder of the plot. Bothy, office, tool and packing sheds were discreetly hidden behind a tall macrocarpa hedge, the nursery itself presenting a weedless, unblemished front to the passers-by and to the wealthy customers who drove their carriages into the waste field beside the nursery. From sun up to sun down, Hayward's was busy, with orders being prepared for delivery, and the everyday work never stopping. The garden boys kept up their ceaseless duties, Edward inspected his plants, talked to customers and in his spare moments thought about the monograph he was writing on primulas, while Nicholas and his apprentice dealt with any problems, and so the whole nursery seemed like a beehive, with every worker carrying out his prescribed duty.

On this May morning, Nicholas Thorne, son of Edward's wife Maude, but not of Edward, walked through the glasshouses in the wake of his adoptive father. Such inspections never varied. Edward, in grey flannel suit and matching soft hat, led the way, talking over his shoulder to Nicholas. He listened, remembering his early days here, when, a boy of ten, Edward had told him his duties. 'Polish the door handles of the glasshouses till they shine. Customers must never see dirty handles. Get on, lad, use some elbow grease.'

And then later had come a hope of something more exciting. 'Fill those buckets and bring them here.' Carrying the water from the butts beneath the staging, Nicholas wondered if he would be allowed to actually pour the precious stuff onto the plants. Hopes were dashed. Edward's fading sandy brows frowned at him. 'Pour it into the watering can, up to the top – go on, lift that bucket, what's the matter with you, boy?'

Now Nicholas followed Edward up and down the rows, reaching out to turn a leaf there – pests? Surely not here at Hayward's – and twitching aside a stem to reveal new shoots, giving it more air, ensuring its growth; willing it to multiply. His lean, suntanned face creased as he watched, before turning back to his own work. His adoptive father would never stop this daily inspection, as necessary to him as the breath that powered his ageing, slight frame. Would Edward ever retire? wondered Nicholas, and knew the answer before it came. *Never.*

Back in the first greenhouse he began his own work, but for once his mind was not concentrated on the small vivid flowers colouring the shelves running down the narrow building. He thought of Jacquetta Hirst and her forthcoming garden day. He was to give a lecture there. Should he write up his notes in advance? Or would it be better to speak freely and without plan, simply talking about last year's trip to the Dolomite Mountains? Of course, he would take specimens to show them, some of the new plants he'd brought back with him – primulas, hellebores, miniature iris, and a few splendid gentians – but should he also tell them of the dangers – indeed, the horrors – of the expedition? Would enthusiastic amateur gardeners want to know that the plants they so admired and bought with such alacrity these days were collected at the expense of broken limbs and even, on occasion, accidental deaths?

Removing a dead leaf from a burgeoning plant, he thought grimly, No of course not. Keep all that to himself, where it already lodged; in a mind that daily recognized the obsession to find new plants but was reluctant to strike out on a further expedition.

Edward did not share his passion. If Nicholas went again, his stepfather would insist – having told him so many times – that he must search for the few plants particularly named and wanted; for the primulas that were making up the long-awaited monograph. He must certainly not waste time and money wandering about just 'looking and getting into trouble', as Edward put it darkly.

Nicholas straightened his long back and stared at the window in front of him, his mind unexpectedly sparking an image of pleasure other than his beloved flowers. Thoughts of Mrs Jacks had brought Hester Redding into his mind and he smiled, remembering her pouring tea from a brown pot and listening as he told her about the small, hungry urchin eating pound cake. They had, he thought now, been at one for those few moments. What was it about her that had stayed in his mind? He had no time for women in his busy, passionate life, but she had put herself there.

Quickly, frowning, he banished her and returned to his work. But her tall, attractive figure, mobile face and rich brown hair refused to disappear completely. He saw her behind each plant he touched, walking around every corner he approached, heard her pleasant voice behind Edward's breathy, impatient instructions. And the knowledge that he would surely see her at Mrs Jacks' garden day stayed with him, striking when he had time to remember, even waiting for him at the day's end. In the evenings, in the shabby home he shared with his stepfather, he allowed that indulgence of remembered pleasure to overtake the day's weariness. Beyond the stress of planning ahead, dealing with difficult customers, dreaming of new discoveries waiting somewhere in the world, complex financial arrangements and the problems of working with elderly, dogmatic Edward, he saw her floating image and was amazed at the way it stayed just there, on the edge of his vision.

Women, thought Nicholas, picking up a new catalogue from a competitive nursery up country, had no place in his life; he had no time for them. He couldn't be tied down. There was no room in his mind to consider a future that included marriage and all the subsequent obstacles. How could he travel if he married? No, better to remain single and just enjoy any unplanned pleasures that might come his way.

He looked at the catalogue. Time soon to update Hayward's catalogue. After the garden day he would tackle the task properly. He needed to concentrate; to work out details, prices, offers. One must never stop building on a business. Other nurseries were sending collectors abroad all the time these day and so pleasure must give way to the sterner stuff.

He went to his bedroom with a head full of memories. In sleep, dreams came and went: towering Italian peaks glinting down on the rocks and ravines below tiny jewel-like brilliant flowers pushing through the snow. But in the background the dark shadow of Jonathon West's accident turned his dream into a nightmare.

Waking, one thought came. Soon – *soon* – he must go out there again.

Hester delighted in painting under Mr Flynn's tutelage. This was the third week she had managed to escape parental control with Aunt Jacks' help. But the hour allotted to the study was all too short and it was hard, arriving back at Oak House, to contain her excitement and satisfaction. She guessed that Arthur Redding put down her mounting *joie de vivre* to the botany class which, of course, had been the purpose of the visit into town. At least he didn't upbraid her.

In fact, he seemed more agreeable than usual. 'And are you learning well? Tell me what you learned today, Hester.'

She saw a gleam of interest in his dark eyes and responded quickly. 'The Latin names of the wild flowers that I find in the lanes, Father. For, in the botanical world, every plant must have a name that is known in every country, despite differences in languages. And we learned the various shapes of flowers, their processes of propagation and seeding and. . . .'

But the interest faded, and thank goodness for the luncheon gong and Stepmother demanding assistance to walk into the dining room. Hester listened to small complaints, suggested remedies, and then, with the changing courses, became increasingly aware of Ruby's growing familiarity.

'Cook's made a nice veal dish today, Madam. Looks tender and lovely. Shall I give you some more gravy?'

And Stepmother smiling and nodding, and glancing at Father as if to say, 'What a good girl Ruby is.' And nothing had been mentioned about turning Ruby into Gertie, thought Hester, drily. Somehow the girl had established herself – and her fancy name.

She ate her luncheon in aware silence, recognizing that new forces were at work in the house. Ruby brought in the coffee, poured out for each member of the family, and then produced the box of Bentinck mints from the sideboard without any order.

'Your favourite, Master. . . .' Her smile was almost flirtatious, thought Hester, suddenly tight-lipped. Why were the parents allowing this unseemly and unwanted friendliness?

Leaving the dining room, she mentioned it to Stepmother, but Emma frowned and said sharply, 'Don't be so critical, Hester, the girl is working very well, and I don't want to upset her. We're lucky to have such a good maid.'

Hester retreated to her room for the quiet hour after luncheon, when Father napped in his chair and Stepmother rested before dressing up and then visiting friends. Hester told herself crossly that Ruby didn't matter at all, because one day quite soon she would be leaving Oak House and leaving everything behind her.

In the studio, intent on her painting, a new serenity fell upon her, and she suddenly knew that the house meant nothing to her these days. Just a shelter, somewhere to while away the tedious hours when she couldn't paint and was unable to go into the outside world where things happened, where people talked and argued and very often complained, but also made plans. Plans to live more interesting lives.

Now, putting the last touches to the picture of the dandelions, she thought how sad it was not to love her home any longer. For a second, memories of childhood swamped her, until she forcefully pushed them away. She must fight for her career, and old sentimental memories were not part of that fight.

Instead she thought about Mr Flynn's words this morning as she left his studio. His rough voice had softened into something approaching approval.

'You're improving, Miss Redding. Time for you to tackle something more professional. A poster? An entry for a competition? Your flowers are coming along well, you should do something with them. I'll make a few enquiries.'

Now warmth spread through her and she felt a new optimism filling her. Until, as Mr Flynn suggested, something more positive came along, she was happy to work at her flora. Its pages were mounting up, as was her botanical knowledge, and Aunt Jacks' recent comments had been complimentary.

'Such confident colours, my dear. You're doing well. Bring it along next week to my garden day – I'm sure people will be interested.'

Aunt Jacks had invited several local gardeners, as well as Miss Emily Watson from London, who had last year returned from a painting tour of the Dolomite Mountains in northern Italy and had agreed to talk about her work. Hester read the names of the other speakers and suddenly stopped. Nicholas Thorne was going to speak about his trip to the Dolomites last year. Of course, he had said he had been there with Miss Watson.

She looked up, staring at the summer border stretching the length of the garden; they had weeded it between them and now it looked abundantly beautiful and full of colour. Scabious, lupins, big white daisies with butterflies hovering over them. She smiled to herself, it would be good to see him again. The smile became a silent chuckle: Aunt Jacks must be reminded to order a pound cake from the farm.

The garden day dawned hazy, veiling a pale half-hidden sky that promised to surprise everyone with later heat and brilliance. Up early, Hester wondered what to wear for the occasion, quickly deciding on a dark green linen skirt, a high-necked white blouse and the new straw hat bought last week in town. Fashionable with its crisp boater shape and elegant ribbon decoration, she knew it suited her because Ruby had commented on it as she left the house on Monday morning.

'Nice new hat, Miss Hester. Looks lovely, it does.'

Hester had frowned and left without replying. She had no time for Ruby and her increasing familiarity.

Now, entering Brook Cottage, she was glad to leave Oak House behind; this was going to be a busy day with many people to talk to. And there would be plenty to do. Indeed, the cottage was a hive of industry. Both girls from the farm were at the kitchen table, with jars of homemade jam and great pans of clotted cream beside them.

Arthur Redding had loaned Hoskins to Aunt Jacks for a couple of hours to mow the lawn and do the last bits of tidying up before the visitors arrived. Now he had returned to Oak House to drive Father and Stepmother down the lane to the cottage.

Hester pulled up her sleeves, took orders from Sally and Mary in the kitchen and began cutting egg and cress sandwiches, while Aunt Jacks flitted from cottage to garden and back to the kitchen, supervising everybody, all the while keeping an eye open for the first arrivals, driving in from Newton Abbot in carriages and pony traps.

It was about noon when the small white gate began clicking open, allowing people to enter and walk down the path. Soon voices filled the quietness of the garden. 'How nice to see you again, Mr Hayward. And your son – good morning, Nicholas – and, oh yes, good morning, Miss Watson – I hope you had a pleasant journey down from London?' Aunt Jacks was welcoming and bright.

More voices, more visitors wandering down the path, inspecting the border, sitting in the summerhouse and being offered fresh lemonade and biscuits. Even Father and Stepmother smiling and nodding to their acquaintances.

Hester kept busy inside the kitchen until she was called outside. 'Hester – come and meet Miss Watson. And bring your flora to show her.'

Emily Watson was a plump, mature lady with greying hair and strong features. She greeted Hester with sharp, deep-set eyes. 'So you enjoy painting flowers – and this is your work?' The pages were turned and Hester held her breath, suddenly very conscious of her amateur talent. What if this professional artist thought nothing of her pictures?

'You are studying with Joseph Flynn? I understand he has the gift of enthusing his students and bringing out the best in them. Well, these paintings of yours are good. Excellent shapes, true colours and a fresh vitality bringing them alive on the paper. Well done.' The small face eased into a smile as Miss Watson returned the flora and put a firm hand on Hester's shoulder. 'You have a gift. Use it well.' And then she turned away, suddenly spying a face she knew among the small crowd of people.

Hester stood quite still, the flora clasped to her breast, her face alight with surprise and excitement. A feeling of elation and resolution spread through her. *Use it well*. Miss Watson could not have said anything better or more encouraging. At last she knew that her life was leading her in the right direction. Whatever happened at home, whatever Father thought of her becoming an artist, she knew she must move on. She must grasp the gift she had been given and use it to the best of her ability.

When a man's voice cut into her thoughts she took a moment to return to reality. Turning, she saw a strong, tanned face, a shock of dark hair with matching brows, and brilliant eyes looking into hers.

Her breath paused briefly, and then, with a thrill of quick pleasure at seeing him again, she smiled back joyfully. 'Mr Thorne! How good to see you.'

He raised his hands and pressed something hard and heavy into hers. 'The pleasure is all mine, Miss Redding. I've brought you a plant. I'm sure it will enjoy growing for you.'

She looked at the flowerpot. It held a gentian, its bud just starting to open, cushioned in green leaves. Smiling, wondering, she looked back at him and saw that the blue flower was the same colour as his eyes.

CHAPTER NINE

Hester had no words. She looked down at the small plant, then up at Nicholas. For a moment neither of them spoke. He raised an eyebrow. 'Perhaps you don't like gentians? I could have brought something else. Would harebells have been more acceptable?'

She shook her head and smiled, feeling foolish. 'No, of course not. I'm sorry, Mr Thorne – I was so surprised. I never expected. . . .'

'No. But I wanted to give you something different from the wild flowers you said you were painting. And gentians are so beautiful.' He paused, then added, 'They're my favourite of all the mountain flowers.'

Her manners had returned, and she said politely, 'I'm delighted with it. Thank you.' She stroked a leaf and the word *mountain* resonated through her mind. 'Should it go in a greenhouse? Is it very tender?'

His smile broadened. 'I don't think it's fussy, after living on a mountainside, Miss Redding. Put it where you can see it and don't let the rain spoil it. It's part of the stock collected in China a few years ago, but I saw them in the Dolomites last spring.'

She kept looking at it, her thoughts suddenly flying. This small, spectacular blue flower, growing on a mountain among snow and ice – now to be cherished here, in her garden. And he had seen them when he was there. Frustration struck her. How free men were. The old yearning swept through her. She looked at him curiously. 'Don't you long to go back there, Mr Thorne?'

She thought he looked surprised, even taken aback. He frowned. 'Yes, I do. Very badly.'

'And will you go?' She was asking far too personal a question, but the expression on his face intrigued her. She saw the brilliance of his eyes dim slightly and wondered why.

'Perhaps.' But his voice had flattened and he was turning his head, looking at the groups of people now walking through the garden towards the barn on the far side of the orchard. Taking the plant from her, he said briskly, 'I'll put this indoors for now, Miss Redding. And I think we should take our places to hear Miss Watson. I'll find you a seat in the barn – wait a moment, will you?'

Alone, Hester tried to sort out her muddled thoughts but the chatter of Aunt Jacks' visitors was distracting, and she was glad when he returned, offering her his undamaged arm.

'Are you still in pain?' she asked. 'It must be hard to work if you are.'

He gave her a brief sidelong smile as they went through the orchard, walking under the trees towards the barn. 'It's not the pain so much as the frustration of only having one workable hand.'

'How did it happen? Why were your porters being so difficult?' Another personal question, but she felt something needed closer investigation. He had been to the mountains, found gentians and many other beautiful plants. He held a source of information that she was unwilling to let go.

Nicholas paused beneath a full-flowering apple tree and looked up into the pink-studded branches. 'Plant-collecting expeditions aren't as pleasant as you might imagine, Miss Redding. I expect Emily Watson will have some charming tales to tell, but there is always another side.'

'Yes?'

His smile flashed down at her. 'Do you really want to know about all the dangers that abound in such a wild and lonely country?'

'Yes.' Hester searched for words that would explain her surprisingly urgent need to hear the worst of his tales. 'I-I just can't help wondering how ladies manage to cope with these dangers. After all, mountains are – well – surely not the best places to go to, alone and at the mercy of whatever happens next.'

Nicholas nodded, his eyes never leaving hers. 'What do you know of mountains, Miss Redding?' His voice was quiet, and she sensed he wanted to change the subject, but the fact only teased her, increasing her need to know more.

She thought for a minute. Then, as the images came, said, 'They're high and craggy, a sort of dark grey rock, I expect, and covered with snow on the highest peaks.'

A slowly spreading smile softened his narrow face, accentuating the brilliance of his eyes. 'You're right, grey when it rains or when fog or mist half hides them.' He paused and she knew she hadn't seen this expression on his face before. 'But when the sun shines, they're blue. A blue that you'll never forget.' His voice deepened. 'A blue that draws you on and on, wondering what you'll find when those dangerous peaks finally reach the blue sky beyond.'

She drew in a deep, wondrous breath, imagining all that he saw; and now she understood something new about him. Nicholas Thorne was passionate about mountains and the plants they nurtured. Today he was showing hidden parts of his personality that she had no inkling about. Indeed, now she knew that he was a passionate man with a damaged shoulder and some obscure reason that was hindering him from returning to those blue peaks. To the blue that she knew so well was calling him to return.

By now they had reached the barn, and Nicholas said, 'I've got you a seat in the front row. You won't want to miss any of Miss Watson's stories, I'm sure.' There was a twinkle in his eyes, and Hester understood that the moment of shared thoughts was over. Dismayed acceptance swept through her. Those few seconds of words and pictures had meant so much – but why? She could find no answer.

The barn had been tidied and prettified with swathes of greenery decorating the black timber beams overhead. A scent of hay and of the old building itself filled the air, and Hester's thoughts settled down as she took her seat.

She glanced at Nicholas beside her. He seemed relaxed, eyes on Aunt Jacks and her companion standing by the table at the far end of the barn. Perhaps he felt her gaze on him; quickly he returned her instantly hidden glance and smiled. She thought he was at ease now, no longer the inspired, even haunted man who had shared his secrets with her just a few moments ago.

Her own thoughts circled. He was good-looking and personable, exciting in some strange way, a plantsman who had offered her a gift, which was kind of him. But how ridiculous of her to think it all meant anything more. So she lifted her head an inch higher and concentrated on the two women facing the suddenly attentive audience.

Aunt Jacks' smile was broad. 'Let me introduce my friend, Emily Watson, one of the brave ladies who travels to foreign lands and paints the amazing new plants she sees there. She has some entertaining tales to tell you.'

The two women could not have been more different, Hester thought. Aunt Jacks was a small, insignificant figure in her old-fashioned dark dress and misshapen gardening hat, while Emily Watson, the picture of elegance in cream embroidered linen and a hat that was surely straight from a Paris boutique, took centre stage and looked around her audience with a self-possessed and experienced smile.

'Sitting on a wooden saddle – side-saddle, of course – with one's skirt bunched up on an obstinate mule all day in very hot weather is hardly a pleasant way to travel,' she began, 'but I have done it and will do so again before long. I will show you some paintings of the beautiful valleys that we rode through, and the mountains that we saw, on my last journey.'

Her voice was magnetic and Hester knew the audience was caught. Large oil paintings, unpacked from a portfolio, brought gasps of pleasure as exotic plants of vivid and sometimes startling forms and colours were shown.

'And there were other plants, too.' Emily displayed a smaller painting of tiny jewel-coloured flowers and Hester felt Nicholas lean forward beside her.

'Harebells, so delicate, iris with wonderful gold-trimmed petals, and of course the famous gentians, blue and eye-catching. And so many of them that it was like looking at a blue sea rising out of the snow still lying on the peaks.'

Hester closed her eyes; yes, she saw them. The towering mountains, shadowy valleys, great grey rocks and beneath them these jewel-like flowers. Opening her eyes, she looked at Nicholas.

Her voice was a whisper. 'Gentians.' He nodded, and again that brief flash of a smile warmed her.

Emily Watson continued. 'There are many other distracting

beauties in the mountains, especially butterflies, but as a painter I kept my eyes on the amazing plants that appeared with each new step my mule took.'

She talked entertainingly, with tales of rogue landlords in seedy, often uncomfortable hostelries on the way through the villages; of the misty crags and rushing rivers of north Italy. But there were stories, too, of friendly women who had cooked enormous meals and made her party most welcome.

By now Hester had built a picture of such an adventure. Not all danger, then, so why had Nicholas suggested the opposite? She imagined that his experience had been different, but how different? What had happened? And why had he not told her about the accident which had damaged his shoulder? Glancing at him, she saw his expression was taut, and felt a chill, making her edge further back on her chair.

'Rain, of course,' Emily went on, 'was a constant delayer. Not just showers, but storms, whipping up the rivers, making the cliffs and ravines dangerous to draw close to. And I mustn't forget the fauna – insects and reptiles.' She raised an eyebrow and the audience gasped again. 'One had to be careful where one trod.'

She spoke for nearly half an hour and ended with a modest suggestion that she was only one of a number of women who continued to explore, and to paint. 'We live in liberated times and we have a wonderful world to discover. I hope I have helped you to understand, and enjoy, that great gift.'

Applause rolled around the barn. Emily smiled and Hester wondered if it was her imagination, or did those deep-set eyes look particularly at her? Was she being encouraged to share this new freedom, this splendid gift of appreciation of all that surrounded them?

She kept silent as Nicholas rose and ushered her out of the barn into the orchard, and back to the garden, where a buffet luncheon had been laid out in the summerhouse and on tables beneath the shrubs and trees. As they walked, he looked at her and asked, 'Did you enjoy hearing all that?'

'I did. Yes, I did.' She nodded and smiled, glad that his taut expression had gone, his mouth now twitching at one corner, as he said, almost mischievously, 'and is your curiosity satisfied, Miss Redding? Now that you know about rushing waters, collapsing cliffs and snakes lurking behind every plant that you bend to admire?'

She laughed, suddenly feeling elation and hope spread through her. Of course, Emily Watson's work was very different from her own delicate watercolours, but now she knew for certain that she must find her place in that world of artists and free exploration. Her talent was small, but she would improve; she would indeed use it well, as Emily had ordered. Reaching the summerhouse, Hester looked at Nicholas and said, with warm spontaneity, 'I'm even more grateful now for your lovely gentian than I was when you gave it to me, Mr Thorne.'

'Nicholas.' The vibrant depth of his voice surprised her.

She stared. 'I don't think—'

He stepped away, expression at once stiff and full of regret. 'No, of course not. Forgive me, Miss Redding.' A pause, and then he frowned, brows shadowing his suddenly steely-blue eyes. 'It's just that we seemed to think alike for a moment or two . . . and I enjoyed it.' His gaze was deep, and she wondered if he could see into her mind.

She nodded, ashamed of her unthinking response, and impulsively laid a hand on his damaged arm, wondering what she was doing but knowing it was right, even if unconventional. 'I felt that, too . . . Nicholas.'

They looked at each other, hesitant and uncertain, and then Aunt Jacks was beside them, leading Hester away. 'Nicholas, you must go and get your plants ready for the talk you are to give us after luncheon – and Hester, Emily Watson wants to see you.'

Emily Watson sat in the shade of the arbour where the scented white rose sprawled in lazy drifts. She smiled. 'Come and sit down, Hester. I've had time now to look at your flora more carefully, and I feel I must do all I can to help you get on. You paint well.' She looked at Hester with a wry, enquiring expression. 'But how determined are you to succeed?'

Firmly, Hester said, 'I've made up my mind that nothing will stop me from improving my work and' – she took a deep breath – 'and having a successful career.' It was out. She had committed herself. She looked at Emily and, with relief, saw approval on her face. 'I know it will be hard. And it will upset my family. But I have to do it. . . .'

Emily put her hand on Hester's. 'You have the right attitude, my dear. If you feel passionate about your talent, then you will let nothing prevent you from working with it. Now. . . .' She removed her hand and smiled. 'The best advice I can give you is to copy the masters. Discover their techniques, develop them in your own work. And take commissions. As many as you can. Enter competitions, apply for a place in an art college. Are you prepared to travel? London would be the best place. Have you relatives who could offer you a room?'

The advice continued until Hester could hardly remember it all, but by the time luncheon was over and Emily and the other visitors had returned to the barn to hear Nicholas's talk about alpine plants, she had mapped out a plan. Find someone who would commission her as a first step. On Monday, she would ask Mr Flynn again.

She slipped into the barn, finding a seat at the back, as Nicholas began to show some of the many alpine plants already displayed on the table in front of his audience. She listened to his quiet, deep voice, watching his movements as he picked up one plant after another and talked about them, describing their habitats, their ways of growing, and finally smiling and saying, 'Perhaps this gentian is my favourite of all. Even the primulas, the saxifrages, the iris, beautiful as they are, don't hold a candle to this blue flower.'

She watched him stroke a leaf and then heard him say, as if to himself, 'There is a legend among the natives in the mountains, that somewhere a double gentian has been seen.' He looked up, raised a dark eyebrow, and flashed a smile at the listeners. 'Can you imagine anything more wonderful than to find it? To bring it back here, raise it and allow the rest of the world to enjoy its rare beauty?'

Into the moment of silence that followed, someone asked, 'And are you planning to search for it, Mr Thorne?' and she saw Nicholas's smile vanish. He replaced the plant on the table, saying crisply, 'I have no plans for further expeditions. Not at the moment.'

And then it was all over. The visitors rose, came to the table to ask questions about various plants, and then walked out into the garden. Hester went with them, needing peace and time to think about all that had happened today.

She watched her aunt seeing off her visitors, accepting their thanks and good wishes, and then saw Nicholas loading the plants into the nursery gig. He looked about him before climbing into the driving seat and she thought perhaps he wanted to say goodbye, but she stayed where she was. If he really needed to see her, he would come and look, wouldn't he? As the gig drove off down the lane and Aunt Jacks came and sank into the seat beside the summerhouse, Hester told herself to forget Nicholas and his disturbing attraction. He had much to occupy him and those few shared moments between them had been momentary pleasures in a life committed to business and the developments of his beloved plants.

The quick strike of disappointment was banished as she made herself remember all that Emily Watson had said. Yes, now she too had a committed life, one that she would take steps to develop. Tomorrow, she would tell Mr Flynn her plans.

She and Aunt Jacks shared cups of tea and then it was time to go home and join Father and Stepmother, who had left earlier. The pound cake had disappeared, and Hester hoped that Nicholas had enjoyed a slice. Taking a last wander through the garden, she saw with fresh insight and enjoyment all the beauty around her. The flowers, mixing their shades and textures, blues, purples, dusky pink and startling creamy white; the shrubs with their leafy shelter, fragrance and shadow and the trees in the deserted orchard, frothing with blossom and seeming to colour the coming dusk with a pale warmth. A blackbird sang in one of them, its song echoing down the valley like a chorister singing in a cathedral.

Hester went indoors, collected her gentian, and then looked at Aunt Jacks. 'What a wonderful day, Aunt. You must be so pleased.'

'I am, my dear. So many people and all keen to improve their gardening knowledge. Emily's talk went well, I thought – and Nicholas gave so much information about his plants.' Aunt Jacks screwed up her mouth into an ironic smile. 'Fancy him thinking that those old tales about a double gentian might hold any truth – I thought he was far too prosaic a man for that.'

'No,' Hester said, without thinking what she was saying. 'He's passionate about gentians, that's all.' She saw her aunt's surprised expression and hurried on. 'But of course he can't really believe in the tales. Just a nice idea he likes to amuse himself with, I daresay.'

Aunt Jacks looked at her with discerning eyes. 'You seem to know a lot about him.'

Hester coloured but kept her voice even. 'Not really. Just that we got on quite well – for a few moments.' She rose and brushed a rose petal from her skirt. 'I must go home, now, Aunt. Thank you for a really lovely day. And I'm so glad that Father and Stepmother came.'

'I don't think they enjoyed themselves very much, but it was good of them to make the effort.' She laughed. 'Gardening isn't their passion – not like it is for you and me.' She gave Hester a straight look. 'Keep painting, dear child, and forgive your poor father for not understanding how life is changing. He must find your commitment to your talent very hard to accept.'

'Yes.' Hester thought for a long moment. Aunt Jacks was right. She must be more understanding with Father. This evening she would talk to him about his own interests – his law books, the paper he was writing about certain fascinating court cases, his health.

Walking home down the lane, she allowed her thoughts to flow more calmly. Beauty lay everywhere, each step showing her new aspects of the countryside. Green and wild, it spread all around her. The seeded farm fields were growing well, the hedges newly sprouted, trees opening their buds and Dartmoor's outline in the purplish blue-grey distance a sharp edge to the spreading fertility.

She was enjoying her walk so much that at first she didn't hear the pony hoofs clattering down the lane towards her. Turning into the hedge for safety, she looked up at the driver of the trap and at once anxious thoughts filled her.

Hugh. What was he doing here? Her serenity fell away.

What did he want?

CHAPTER TEN

He reined in the cob beside her and smiled down. 'Told your parents I'd fetch you from your aunt's cottage. Had a busy day, have you?'

Hester was confused. What had he been doing at home? She stood beside the trap and said coldly, 'Yes, it all went very well. But Hugh, why are you here? I thought you were busy organizing yourself ready to join the family firm?'

Holding the reins, he got down to stand beside her, his smile easy and amused. 'So you remembered all that! And I hope you've remembered everything else I said to you that day.' He paused, looked into her unsmiling eyes. 'Have you, Hester? Have you thought about my plans? Have you been sensible and changed your mind?'

Hester saw determination in the jut of his chin and his intense expression. Alarm filled her, until something new swept through her mind. She was liberated, on the way to a career. No one should bully her and certainly not her old friend Hugh Marchant. So treat all that he said lightly; let him see that she had a mind and a life of her own, and that nothing he could say or do would change that.

Confidence rose. She smiled, walked around the trap, then climbed up onto the seat, twitching her skirt away from the dusty floor. 'How you do go on, Hugh. Honestly, I'm too full of thoughts of flowers and gardens and painting to have the time to consider marriage at the moment. Yes, drive me home, please – and I'm sure Father will offer you a glass of sherry if you behave properly and stop ordering me about.'

With a look of amazement he stared up at her, then slowly climbed up, sat beside her, told the cob to walk on, and they continued down the lane.

Neither of them spoke until Hester pointed out, 'You're going the wrong way.' But she wasn't really worried. Perhaps he was continuing to the next field gate where he would turn around.

'I'm taking you for a drive.' He didn't look at her, simply snapped the reins and encouraged the cob to trot.

Hester frowned and held the gentian more firmly on her lap. 'I want to go home, Hugh. Please turn around.'

No answer. They drove along the lane, finally coming into the village and the main road. She was getting a little anxious now. Why was he behaving in this unfriendly way?

'Hugh, tell me where we're going. And why. Turn around, please – I really do want to go home.'

At last he turned and looked at her, his face set and unsmiling. 'We need to talk, Hester, and we can't do that with your parents pretending they don't hear us. Give me a chance to find a secluded place and I'll stop. Don't worry, I'll get you home in time for dinner.'

Gripping the gentian, she realized that this was male domination and the very thing she was opposed to. She would not give in.

Putting a hand on his arm, she kept her voice very calm. 'Hugh, please take me home. We can talk – if you insist – another day. I need to get ready for dinner with my parents. You'll make me late and I don't want that. So please, turn around.'

He smiled then, an amused expression that exasperated her even further. 'I like it when you get cross, Hester. What spirit! It's charming.'

She tensed, somehow keeping her temper under control, knowing that anger would get her nowhere. Hugh must be persuaded.

'Yes, I have lots of spirit, Hugh. Surely you haven't forgotten all my childhood furies when you wouldn't let me win at snap or said it was your turn to ride the pony when I knew that it was mine?' She gave him what she hoped was a winning smile as he looked at her. Was that the beginning of a reluctant grin she saw? 'You were always trying to get the better of me,' she said wryly, 'but it didn't always work. And you won't do so now. Come on, Hugh, take me home and let's forget these hard words.'

Slowly he drew the trap to a halt, turning to look at her properly, and she saw she had won the day. His mouth twitched. 'Hester, you're too much for me. I can't refuse you when I remember all that – was I really such a brat?' He turned the cob in the road. 'No, don't answer. All right, we'll leave the big discussion for another day. I'll take you home, but don't expect me to stay. Your father's probably seen enough of me today. Well, here we go.' He cracked the whip and the trap rattled down the lane.

Hester sat back, congratulating herself on her firmness. But he still wanted to talk – what had he said, the big discussion? It was only as the trap turned into the drive of Oak House and he reined in the cob at the bottom of the entrance steps that an uneasy question flew into her mind.

She climbed down and looked up at him. 'Hugh, what did you want to see Father about?'

His smile as he clicked the trap forward and raised an arm to wave goodbye was hardly reassuring. 'He'll tell you.' The cob reached the gate, paused and then disappeared.

Her hand on the door-bell, Hester frowned. She had a feeling that Hugh, after all, had won something.

She rang the bell twice, heard it echoing through the house, wondered where Ruby was and why she was taking so long to open the door. When it finally opened it was Mrs Caunter who stood there, something smeared on one cheek, cap slightly awry, and wearing an expression of doom. 'Thank goodness you're back, Miss Hester. I dunno how we'll get the dinner on the table, really I don't.'

Hester entered, put the gentian on the bench inside the door, and turned. 'What's wrong, Mrs Caunter?'

'It's that Ruby, slipped on the stairs, said her heel caught on spilt candle grease, she thinks, and now she's in her bed and says as 'ow she can't move. An' I've got the veg to do and the meat to roast, an'. . . .'

Hester breathed deeply, removed her hat and said quietly, 'Where is Mrs Redding?'

'In the drawing room with Master. Sherry time, see. What'll we do 'bout bringing up the trays, Miss Hester? Me legs aren't so good these days.'

'I'll help, Mrs Caunter.' Hester put an arm on the cook's shoulder and smiled. 'Stop worrying. We'll manage between us.' Wryly she thought, heading for the drawing room, It's back to trays, is it? And that wretched Ruby in her bed.

The drawing room was airless and shadowy, the curtains on the curving bay window half drawn to keep the sun out of Arthur Redding's eyes.

'So there you are, Hester. You've been a long time coming home.' His voice was cool, his expression hardly welcoming.

'I came as fast as I could, Father. I met Hugh in the lane and we talked for a little while.'

'Ah. Yes.' Arthur Redding sipped the last of his sherry, looking at her over the rim. 'Hugh called here this afternoon. We also talked. But I'll come to that later. What is all this fuss in the kitchen? Mrs Caunter has some story of the maid – Ruby, isn't it? – having had an accident.' He looked across the room at Emma, sitting in a tense bundle in her usual chair, and shook his head. 'My dear, I don't want you trying to get up to see the girl, you couldn't manage all those stairs. Wait until she's better.'

'Yes, of course.' Emma Redding was clearly in a state of nerves. Her thin hands fidgeted with her spectacle case, and her expression was one of terrible expectation. Hester crossed the room, pulled up a stool and sat beside her, smiling reassuringly.

'Don't worry, Stepmother. I'll help Mrs Caunter with dinner and I'll see Ruby. Everything will work out. Now, shall I refill your glass?'

Dinner was twenty minutes late, and Hester carried the trays up from the kitchen and then down again when the meal was over. The uneven wooden staircase was longer than she had thought, and she began to understand how servants always complained about their legs. Which brought her back to Ruby.

After seeing that both her parents were comfortably drinking coffee, and even looking slightly drowsy, she returned to the kitchen where Mrs Caunter was making a business of having to wash all the dishes on her own.

'Jest hope as 'ow she'll be better tomorrer, I can't go on like this for ever, Miss Hester.'

'No, Mrs Caunter, and I don't expect you to. If Ruby is really indisposed I will find a replacement. But for the moment, did you put her supper in the oven to keep warm?'

Grumbling to herself, Mrs Caunter set a plate of rather dried-up roast beef on a tray. 'Ses she doesn't like my Yorkshire pudding, hmm, she's lucky to have any.'

'I'll come back and help put the dishes away, Mrs Caunter. I won't be long.'

Hester carried the tray up the three flights of stairs, having to slow down as she started up the final narrow wooden staircase leading to the two attic bedrooms. Her shoes resounded on the wood, and she wondered if Ruby heard her coming.

Ruby sat up quickly. Footsteps. Miss Hester probably, to see if she really was took bad. She shoved the battered envelope, and its precious content, under the pillow and put a weak smile on her face. Miss Hester would expect her to be helpless and sorry for herself. That shouldn't be hard to do. Even though she hadn't actually fallen down the stairs, she had misjudged the first step and yes, her heel had slipped on something greasy, and her ankle did hurt – just a bit. But to be really bad was part of the plan, so she must act it out.

'Have you brought my dinner all the way up? Oh, Miss Hester, you are good – but I don't think I can eat anything. I feel so sick. It's the pain. . . .'

She watched Miss Hester put the tray – Ruby's stomach began to rumble, she hadn't eaten since an early luncheon – on the small table, then step back, standing by the window, looking at her.

Not very friendly, Miss Hester's eyes. Neither was her voice; tighter than usual. 'What happened, Ruby? I understand you fell and hurt your leg. Which leg? Show me, please.'

Ruby's scowl swiftly became a pathetic smile. 'Yes, Miss Hester.' Pushing aside the covers she slid out a slim, unblemished leg. 'It hurts here.' She rubbed the ankle and flinched as the supposed pain stabbed. 'Oh, it doesn't half hurt. . . .'

Miss Hester ran her hands – not very large, but strong and

beautifully pale pink, Ruby saw, enviously – over the afflicted joint while Ruby moaned and twisted.

'I can't feel anything out of place, Ruby. But if you're not better in the morning, Hoskins can fetch Dr Winters from Chudleigh. For now, swallow these two pills – my stepmother takes them for her insomnia when she can't sleep – to help you through the night. And eat your supper – you need to keep your strength up.'

They looked at each other, then Hester moved towards the door. 'Hoskins must scrub down the stairs. We don't want any more accidents, do we?'

Was that a suspicious note in her voice? wondered Ruby uneasily. Things hadn't gone quite as she had planned. Covering her leg, she slumped down in the bed, saying grumpily, 'It's those bloomin' kitchen stairs that's the problem, Miss. Up and down, up and down – goodness knows how many times a day. Ought to be a lift or something, you know, put the meals on it in the kitchen, pull a rope and up it goes to the dining room. Like a dumb waiter, on'y without the waiter.' A grin replaced the scowl. 'Girl I knew once worked in a grand house with one of them, said it was ever so nice.'

Staring at Miss Hester, her thoughts plummeted. All that planning, but now Miss Hester wasn't reacting as she'd hoped. Then a new idea struck her. 'I s'pecs Madam's worried about me. Will you tell her that I'm trying to sit up and get on with my sewing, even though me ankle hurts so bad, an' I'll be down to show it to her on Tuesday?'

At the door Hester looked back at the petulant face with its sly expression. The green eyes were veiled but hid a gleam of excitement: something was going on, but her mind was too full of personal thoughts to understand exactly what. Her hand on the door latch, she breathed deeply, felt weariness slide through her. It had been a busy, emotional day and she could do without all this. And why this message to Stepmother about the sewing?

A lift? A dumb waiter? Whatever would the girl suggest next? Her lips tightened. Now she must go down and help Mrs Caunter put away the dishes. And then she must talk to Father. She sighed.

'I'll give Mrs Redding your message, Ruby. Now eat your supper and then try and sleep.'

Their eyes met. A wind rattled the window and Ruby shivered, sliding down beneath the covers.

'Good night,' said Hester closing the door behind her, looking carefully at the shadowy stairs before going down.

'Good riddance,' muttered Ruby. Damn everything. It wasn't going right. And then she realized that her dreams wouldn't come true unless she worked at them. She knew it was important to be like Miss Hester, walk like her, sound like her, because that would impress Madam and Master and make them think well of her. Sitting up again she pouted her lips and smiled, hearing Miss Hester in her mind, and trying to make her own voice sound the same. *Go-o-o-d n-i-i-i-ght.*

That was good. She repeated it, then delved beneath the pillow for the envelope and the creased document inside it. She read it yet again, her smile growing into a chuckle. It was time to get things moving now; why wait any longer? When she was up on her feet again, and Master and Mistress realized how much they had missed her, that's when she would go and show them what she held in her hand.

Hester put the last meat dish on the top shelf of the big dresser lining the kitchen wall and said wearily, 'If you can manage the breakfast, Mrs Caunter, I'll help during the day. But let's hope Ruby will be better in the morning.' She looked at the cook, sinking down into the cane chair by the hearth, and remembered Ruby's impudent suggestion. Thoughtfully she said, 'These stairs must be very tiring for you both. Perhaps my father might consider a lift. Would there be enough space for it here and in the dining room?'

'A lift? Oh, Miss Hester, now that would be lovely. Put the meals in and then pull on the ropes and up it goes. Oh yes, we could fit it in, I'm sure.' The cook's aged face lit up with a huge smile and she sat straighter in the creaking chair.

Hester nodded. 'I can't promise, but we'll see. Now I must go up – good night, Mrs Caunter.'

'Good night, miss.' A definite note of hope brightened the rough voice and as Hester climbed the stairs – *Oh my legs! Thank goodness I'm not Ruby* – she wondered whether Father would be in a good enough mood for her to suggest the installation of a lift. Perhaps not tonight. Wait until tomorrow and a new day. But she had to ask him why Hugh had come here this afternoon. Her spine was tense as she reached the top of the stairs.

The drawing-room gas spluttered and Stepmother's gentle snores made Hester close the door quietly and seat herself on the corner of the chesterfield nearest to her father.

He was sitting straight in his winged armchair, a newspaper open on his lap, polishing his spectacles with his handkerchief. His eyes followed Hester as she neared, and he nodded at her and then said, quietly, 'We must talk, Hester. As you know, Hugh Marchant called late this afternoon. Your stepmother was resting after our trip to Jacks' garden, and I have not yet told her what Hugh's call was about. She gets upset very easily, and so you must bear that in mind when you hear what I have to say. I want no arguments, no noisy recriminations. You understand?'

His gaze was fixed and Hester tensed even further. 'Yes, Father.' But she kept her voice even and watched as he folded the newspaper, put it on the table beside him and then looked back at her. 'Very well. There's no point in beating about the bush. Hugh Marchant came here to ask my permission to propose marriage to you.'

She caught her breath, felt quick rage flash through her, but said nothing. Her mind was too full, her emotions too unstable.

'Naturally, Hester, I thought the matter over very keenly. Hugh assures me that his entry into his father's law firm cannot fail – his degree was an excellent one – and I can foresee a good future for him. Although I find this new age difficult to accept, I agree that there are many more opportunities today. Hugh has a private income from a deceased godmother, and excellent prospects of his own family inheritance when – God save him, not yet, I hope – his father passes on. And he considers you will make a good, eminently suitable wife for him. He will, of course, in due time, become senior partner, and so his prospects are very acceptable.'

For an interminable moment they looked at each other. Then Arthur Redding settled himself more comfortably in his chair and narrowed his eyes. 'Well? You've said nothing. Not surprised, surely? But complimented? He's quite a catch.'

A *catch!* Hester flinched, but she could find no words to express all she was feeling How dare Hugh? *Dominating her. How dare he!*

Her father frowned impatiently. 'You know very well that this marriage is something I and your stepmother have been hoping for. You have always been friends with Hugh, and I gather the friendship continues – tennis, for instance, last week. He plans to invite you to visit his newly organised chambers very soon, when you can suggest a day.'

Deep breathing had helped to cool Hester's fury. She must summon up her strength, put aside her pent-up denial of thoughts of any marriage at all. She must keep Father appeased, for to upset him and Stepmother would do no good. But why must this happen just when it was so important to get him to agree to the new plans Emily Watson had suggested?

Go to London? Paint for a living? Father didn't even know that she was studying with Mr Flynn! Oh, what a terrible muddle life had suddenly become. How on earth was she going to resolve it?

'Father.' She inched to the edge of the chesterfield and looked at his lined, rather grey face and a chill defeated her anger. He was old. He didn't look well. Her heart paused and then rushed on. 'Did he say. . . .' She stumbled. 'Did he say that he loved me?'

'Loved you?' Arthur Redding's eyes grew deep, irritation pursing his mouth. 'My dear girl, surely you know that where marriage is concerned, it's the prospects and financial arrangements that are important?' He sniffed, reached for his handkerchief and blew his nose with a loud blast. 'Love, if that's what you want, will come later. Or not, as the case is. It's a minor detail in a marriage.'

'But you loved Mother. Don't you love Stepmother?' She couldn't help it, the words just raced out. Her face flushed, her hands knotted in her lap.

Arthur Redding's bony cheeks grew patches of red. In a low voice he said slowly and distastefully, 'That is nothing that concerns you.'

Hester couldn't leave it there. This was almost too painful to endure, yet inside her the determination grew. 'But you did love Mother – you were always smiling when she was here. You talked, Father, I remember so well, you laughed, you were happy together. And you missed her so much, I know you did.'

Arthur did not meet her eyes. A silence grew, filling the space between them, allowing the gas to emphasize its burbling, letting

Emma's heavy breathing deteriorate into snuffles and then gradual slow movements in her chair.

'There, you've woken your stepmother,' he said at last, the words full of condemnation, deep and harsh. 'And I particularly asked you not to. Hester, how can you be so extremely difficult? We'll say no more at the moment. I can only hope that by the morning you will have thought through all that I said, and be prepared to give me a sensible answer.' Painfully, he rose, refusing her offer of a hand as he straightened up from the chair.

Glancing across the room, he looked at his wife and walked very slowly towards her. 'Come, Emma, time for bed. Take my arm. We'll go up together.'

Emma blinked, opened her mouth and shut it again, finally finding a weak smile. 'Oh, Arthur – did I drop off again? How rude of me. And yes, I'm ready for bed.'

With her arm hooked through his, she moved towards the door, suddenly seeming to notice Hester standing by the chesterfield. 'Why, Hester – I haven't said anything about your aunt's garden day. Perhaps tomorrow we can have a good chat. Good night, now, my dear.'

Gardens, mountains, flowers, Nicholas. It was a long moment before Hester could reply.

'Good night, Stepmother. Good night, Father.' Then she moved quickly and opened the door for them. Arthur avoided her gaze, merely nodded his head, and led his wife towards the curving staircase. They ascended slowly, reached the top, and then the bedroom door clicked shut.

Hester went back to the dying fire and stood, looking down at it. Her mind was too full of muddling, painful, inescapable thoughts for her to focus on any one of them. She collapsed on the chesterfield and shut her eyes.

Tomorrow she must make decisions, but for the moment all she wanted was to escape from the problems that surrounded her, whichever way she looked.

And then she found herself laughing, an unfamiliar, bitter sound. The business of the lift in the kitchen had been completely forgotten. It was just one more thing to put on the list for tomorrow.

CHAPTER ELEVEN

'I think I've found my artist.'

Nicholas, at his desk in the office at the back of the house, looked around. Standing behind him Edward Hayward was smiling, the copy of his manuscript, *Primulas Around the World*, recently accepted for publication, clutched in his hand.

Nicholas prepared to listen. His father's enthusiasm was hard to ignore.

'Joe Flynn – that artist fellow – came around just now, suggested one of his students as being eager to find work, and I need to find an illustrator, so. . . .'

Sitting back, Nicholas controlled his impatience. Joe Flynn? He frowned. 'I've heard that Flynn is less than honest in his dealings – can you trust him, Father?'

Edward waved an arm. 'Rubbish. The man knows about art and that's all that matters. Anyway, this student is a relative of Jacquetta Hirst, and we can't have a better recommendation than that.'

Nicholas got to his feet, his face tightening. He met Edward's querulous stare with a frown. 'What's the student's name?'

Edward fished a piece of paper from his pocket, pushed his spectacles closer to his nose and peered at the scribbled writing. 'Miss Hester Redding.'

He looked up and met Nicholas's startled stare. 'A good solid family – and I bet the name of a local artist will help sell my book.' He leaned forward, grinning. 'So you could add her name to the advertising you're working on.'

Nicholas said slowly, 'But you know nothing about Miss Redding's work, Father. You haven't seen it. You only have Joe Flynn's words, and he could be saying anything just to get his own name acclaimed. She may. . . .' Biting off the words, he paused, then forced himself to go on. 'She may have no talent at all.' He frowned, but honesty mattered.

Edward's grin evaporated. 'We shall see,' he said testily. 'Write to her, Nicholas, say I'll see her on Thursday at eleven o'clock. Tell her to bring some work with her. Got the address, have you?'

'Yes.' Nicholas took the paper and put it on his desk.

'Good. Now, I must get on.' Edward breezed out of the office, putting on his hat, shouting for Jim and swinging his arms jauntily as he marched down the nursery.

Alone, Nicholas looked at the paper, read Joe Flynn's scribble and wondered what Hester Redding would think of working for his father. If she was good enough. His frown grew. How terrible if she were just an enthusiastic amateur without the necessary talent to take on professional work. He sat down at the desk, pulled out a sheet of paper, and allowed his thoughts to wander. If she came, where would she sit and paint? How often would she come? Or perhaps she would prefer to work at home?

The act of taking up his pen brought a brief hint of pleasure, appreciated and then dismissed. He knew it would be good, having Hester here. He wrote:

Dear Miss Redding,

Mr Flynn, your tutor, has told my father, Edward Hayward, that you might be willing to accept a professional commission illustrating his book on primulas. To that end he invites you to call at the nursery with some examples of your work. He hopes that eleven o'clock on Thursday this week will be convenient.

Yours sincerely,

The pen was poised, not touching the paper as he gazed into the whirlwind of his own thoughts. She had called him Nicholas. He had called her Hester. But this was business.

He wrote *Nicholas Thorne* in his upright, firm hand, and then read through what he had written. Folded, put in an envelope and stamped, it was done. He got up, strode out of the office and down the nursery towards the entrance, on the main road.

There was a pillar-box fifty yards away. Work must wait for this small five minutes of pleasure – communication with Hester. The letter posted, he returned to the nursery, and made himself concentrate on the crate of plants Jim was packing up, due for delivery to a local bigwig's garden this afternoon.

Briefly, images of mountains, gentians, last year's disastrous accident, Hester Redding and her warm smile flashed through his mind, but he frowned and dismissed them all. Business must go on.

Hester sat in her studio two days after Ruby's accident. The girl had appeared next morning, saying that she was better, still in pain, but of course she would do her work; mustn't let Master and Mistress down.

That had been one problem resolved, leaving Hester free to concentrate on her painting. Now, filling in the delicate, branching leaves on a slightly hairy stem of a frothing spray of cow parsley, the local names ran through her mind – Honiton Lace, Rabbit's Meat – and then, smiling, she carefully added the correct botanical name, learned from her recent studies: *Anthriscus sylvestris*. This was the next addition to her flora, to be taken to Mr Flynn for comment in a few days. Mr Flynn – she thought back to the recent conversation with her father that had got her nowhere. She still had to tell her father about studying with him. And if – *if* – she somehow found a professional commission, what on earth would Father say?

Putting the last touch of paint to the tooth-edged leaves, she sat back, considering. Things must come to a head soon. They needed to talk without any more rancour or resentment; she must explain that marriage to Hugh Marchant was not in her plans and he must realize she would soon be legally free to live how she wished.

But leave Father? Tell him that she was going away, to find work somewhere in the outside world? He would miss her, even though his dismissal of her longings was so set in stone. He loved her, as she loved him. But they had never spoken of it. Could they now?

She sighed, returning to the painting. Then there was the business of the proposed lift from the kitchen to be thought about and suggested to Father. A smile touched her lips. Yes, it was an excellent idea. She should compliment Ruby, but then decided that was foolish. The girl was sly and underhand, and Hester's thoughts slipped away to how Ruby was pushing herself into Stepmother's life.

'I'll fetch that for you, Madam. No trouble. . . .' And off Ruby would fly, a satisfied smile on her face.

I don't trust her, thought Hester. Don't know why, but I don't.

A knock at the door, and Ruby appeared, holding a letter. 'Just come, Miss Hester, afternoon post.' She stared. 'Oh, isn't that lovely, what you're painting – can I have a look?'

Hester took the envelope and put it down beside her paintbox. She would open it when Ruby had gone. 'Yes, but don't touch – the paint's still wet.'

She watched the girl's face change, saw the overfriendly expression fade, replaced by something which suddenly struck her as being sincere. 'You're clever, Miss Hester.' Ruby's voice was low, her eyes no longer sly. 'That's lovely. Why, you ought to be a proper artist, Miss, pictures in galleries and things.' She nodded emphatically. 'I'd buy one of your paintings, if I was rich. Hang it on me wall, I would.'

They looked at each other in a new way, with something almost akin to friendship. Hester frowned, surprised. Ruby was smiling, no longer smart and on the edge of insolence, but warm and understanding. Then she too smiled, taken unawares, realizing that her life was taking steps forward in many unexpected directions. She said quietly, 'I'll give you a picture, Ruby.'

'Oh, miss, oh, thank you!' Their eyes met. Green looking into golden flecked hazel, smiling, sharing the moment. Then Ruby said slowly, almost unwillingly, 'Must tell you, Miss, Madam's been ever so nice about my fall the other day. Give me some ointment, she did. And when I asked about the lift—'

Hester shot back to reality. 'You had no right to ask her, Ruby. I told you I would speak to my father.'

'Yes, but I thought if Madam agreed with me it would be good.'

'And what did she say?' The old feeling returned – the girl took too much upon herself – but Hester awaited the answer with interest.

'Said she'd speak to Master. Said what a good idea. Didn't want Cook or me to have bad legs, she said.' Ruby was back in the doorway, looking over her shoulder, grinning like a cream-filled cat, and Hester couldn't stop herself smiling back, although whether in admiration or amusement, she wasn't sure. 'All right, Ruby. We'll see what happens.'

'Yes, Miss Hester.' Another big grin and Ruby disappeared, closing the door behind her.

Hester's thoughts circled. Yes, the girl was too forward. But Stepmother liked her. And if Father could be persuaded into installing a lift, did it really matter that Ruby had engineered it all? It would be something taken off her own shoulders.

And then she remembered the letter. Opening it, she looked immediately at the signature because she didn't recognize the handwriting – black, large and very strong. And then: *Yours sincerely, Nicholas Thorne.*

She sat up straighter as she read, and a glowing smile spread over her face. An interview, her work to be assessed. The possibility of a commission. She was swelling with excitement. It was all happening. Life was opening out and the possibilities were infinite. Certainly she would go and meet Mr Hayward. Take her flora and greet Nicholas with the warmth that his letter had built inside her.

Then all the joy turned to dismay. She would have to tell Father about Mr Flynn and her plans to leave home. But even the thought of such a confrontation could not quite dismiss the feeling of elation that still floated through her. Quickly she wrote a note of acceptance to Mr Hayward, sealed and stamped it, ran down into the garden and asked Hoskins to make sure it caught the last post.

The small scree garden was calling her, the bed where she had planted the gentian Nicholas had given her. Now opening into wide, brilliant flowers, its rosette leaves spreading out into the slatey soil, she thought the low sun, reflecting on the rocks and pebbles surrounding it, brought an even brighter tone to the blue of the petals. She stood, thoughts flying to places far away, and then returned to the man who had brought this gift. She would see him when she went to the nursery. Would he be pleased to see her? Or had he forgotten her, except as a possible illustrator for his father's book?

She went back into the house, hoping that those eyes, which seemed to be as blue as the gentian flowers, would soften when he saw her. That he would smile and make her welcome.

To live.

On Wednesday she walked around to Brook Cottage with her bag of painting things, ready for Aunt Jacks to drive them into Newton Abbot to attend the botany class. Then she would be dropped at Mr Flynn's studio while Aunt Jacks passed an hour of shopping or visiting, before driving them both home.

Hester knew she was taking a new step towards freedom today. Everything looked fresh and exciting. The hedges, as she walked down the lane, were fuller and greener than yesterday. Dartmoor's long lines, with an occasional tor rising up into the sky, were misty and inviting, and she realized yet again how much the country and its flora meant to her.

When she left, she would miss this wonderful natural life. Briefly her optimism thinned. Living in a city, among thousands of other people, having to wait for a chance to visit the countryside – what would it be like?

But, as she walked into Aunt Jacks' garden, she dismissed the foolish fear.

Life would be what she made it and the country would always be there, wherever she ended up. London parks, village greens, hills and dales and rivers and meandering lanes. *Mountains*, whispered a quiet voice, and she blinked at the excitement the word engendered.

Aunt Jacks walked with her to Mr Flynn's studio. 'You mustn't rely on gaining Edward Hayward's commission tomorrow, Hester. Your work might not be quite right for him. Just be prepared to wait until the right one comes along. And tell Mr Flynn how grateful you are.'

'Yes, Aunt.' Hester watched the small upright figure march away, intent on some personal project, and thought yet again how lucky she was to have this caring woman upon whom she could try and model herself. If only Father understood as Aunt Jacks did.

Joseph Flynn smiled and she thought his manner more pleasant than usual. 'I've done my bit, Miss Redding – now it's up to you to impress Mr Hayward.'

Hester unpacked her paintbox and palette and put her picture on the sloping board already set up on the table. 'I'm very grateful to you, Mr Flynn.' She looked up, met his small, veiled eyes, and said spontaneously, 'And I'd like to show my gratitude.' Could she offer a fee? How embarrassing. But even as she stumbled over the words, his smile broadened and his usually rough voice took on a smoother tone.

'It's been a pleasure to help someone with your talent. But if you really feel you should repay me, Miss Redding, then one of your paintings will do. I like to keep a record of my students' work.'

Relieved, she said, 'Of course. Please choose which one you would like.' And then, 'Should I sign it? I don't really know—'

He cut her short. 'No need. I'm familiar with your work – quite different from my other students. Thank you. I'll look through your portfolio and choose one. Most kind.'

She passed him the large black portfolio and then turned to her work. The cow parsley was finished, but no doubt Mr Flynn would want it polished. She was right. 'A pale wash for the background would let the flower tones stand out more. But it's good. Another page of your proposed flora, I suppose. Keep working and you may well get somewhere.'

That afternoon, she sat with Stepmother in the summerhouse chatting about domestic things. 'Ruby,' said Emma brightly, 'has finished sewing her patchwork cushion and it's really very good. She has an eye for colours and the stitches are neat. I've suggested she should start on something else – a nightgown case, perhaps.' Her smile widened. 'She may well be able to deal with the household sewing. The girl is becoming such a help. I mean, her excellent idea of the lift in the kitchen – I talked to your father about it yesterday and he is thinking it over.' Emma's innocent eyes found Hester's. 'I don't know how I would get on nowadays without Ruby's helping hand. I mean, she's always here, which is so useful when you're away. . . . Oh dear, I didn't mean to scold you, or anything, please don't think that—' Her drooping cheeks grew pink and she straightened herself stiffly in her chair, looking at Hester anxiously. 'What I mean is that you have so many interests which take you out of the house these days. . . .' The thin voice died away.

Hester looked at her little stepmother and felt an onrush of guilt. Was she really so badly missed? Was she neglecting her parents? Her mind sank. Was she selfish to the degree of becoming uncaring? She said, she hoped, comfortingly, 'I'm glad you find Ruby so helpful, Stepmother.' Then she added a warmer note to her voice. 'But I'm not away all the time, you know. And I do try and accompany you on your calls quite often.'

'Yes, dear, of course.'

She watched Emma droop back into her chair, unclasp her tightly folded hands and close her eyes. 'I think I'll have a little nap.' But there was a hint of petulance in the quiet words, and Hester knew that, although the subject was closed, resentment lingered. She sat beside her dozing stepmother, looked into the peaceful garden, at the formal beds of scarlet pelargoniums, pale blue lobelia and white alyssum, and thought that perhaps Ruby being here was a good thing, after all.

How strange life was. And perhaps – her heart leaped – tomorrow would see the fruition of the first of her hopes. Would Mr Hayward commission her?

She was up early, wondering what to wear, taking first one dress from her wardrobe, then another. The lilac was too flowery, the turquoise too dressy; perhaps that pearl-grey dress with tight sleeves and a high neck? And her mother's cameo brooch to relieve the drabness, to show that she had a certain style, to emphasize her femininity despite the fact that she was setting out on a professional career.

When she left Oak House to walk to Chudleigh and catch the omnibus into Newton Abbot, she felt like a fugitive, having chosen the moment when Father went to his study and Stepmother lingered in the dining room. There was no one to see her go. She had casually mentioned at breakfast that she might be out for an hour or so during the morning, and, apart from Father's pursed lips and Stepmother's gentle sigh of resignation, no comment had been made.

Except that Ruby, busily piling up the breakfast plates, had looked at her and Hester had felt, yet again, that strange and unwanted sense of . . . what was it? Almost like a feeling of communication.

And now, walking down the drive, her hat pinned on at an elegant angle and her gloved hands carrying reticule and attaché case, Hester felt eyes watching her. She glanced around but the front door was shut and the front windows deeply curtained. Then something made her look up at her bedroom window, wide to the sunlit morning, and yes, someone was there: a figure stepping away the moment she caught sight of it.

Ruby? And if so, why? But the coming interview was too important for her to consider the matter further. She caught the bus, and was three minutes early when she arrived at the entrance gate to the Hayward Nursery, three minutes of walking up and down and wondering how to introduce herself.

As she stepped to the gate and put out a hand to open it, Nicholas Thorne appeared. His smile was a welcome and his deep voice saying, 'Good morning, Miss Redding. Do come in,' banished all the polite words she had been juggling with.

'Nicholas – how good to see you.' The unthinking use of his name confused her, made her fumble with her attaché case, drop it, and, then, bending to pick it up, found him far too close to her as he also bent down, eyes brilliant and full of amusement.

'Let me help, Hester.'

They stood up and looked at each other. 'Thank you, Mr Thorne.' She wouldn't use his Christian name again. What must he be thinking of such forward behaviour? Yet he had used hers.

But clearly he was thinking of other things. He stepped away and gestured for her to walk towards the house. 'My father is waiting. I'll introduce you.'

They walked up the path and she was only dimly aware of the shrubs, full, leafy and covered with blossom, edging the entrance of the house. She could only think of Nicholas beside her, of his tall body clad in dull gardening browns and greens, a flash of excitement firing inside her, quite unsuitable to the occasion. Sternly she clung to the thought that she was here on business. As they reached the open door she had control of her feelings again and heard the steadiness in her voice with a sense of triumph. 'I believe your father is a specialist in alpine primulas, Mr Thorne, but my paintings are only of native wild flowers, so I don't know whether he will like what I've brought to show him.'

Nicholas led her towards a back room leading off the shadowy hallway, saying over his shoulder, 'Don't underrate yourself. My father will soon decide if your talent suits his requirements.' Then he turned, looking at the man standing behind the desk in the untidy, cluttered little room. 'This is my father, Edward Hayward. Father, this is Miss Hester Redding. Shall we ask her to open her case and show us samples of her work?' He pulled out a chair, cleared it of a pile of papers, then smiled as he took the case from her and laid it on the desk, long, earth-stained fingers lifting out the pile of paintings which he placed before Edward Hayward, now seated in his chair, an expression of intense interest on his ageing face.

Opposite him, Hester sat on the hard-backed chair, mind ablaze as she awaited his verdict. She was aware of Nicholas standing beside his father, looking down as page after page of her paintings were picked up, scrutinized, then laid aside in a neat pile.

The sun glared through the window and she felt half dazed by the light and the mind-sapping anxiety that suddenly shot through her. This was an important moment – so important, her whole future life depended upon it.

Nicholas looked up, met her eyes, shook his head very slightly, and gave her that remembered brief flash of a smile. 'Stop worrying,' he said, the words hardly loud enough to hear. Certainly Edward Hayward did not hear them, but she did, wondering at his awareness, and at once his encouragement made her breathe more smoothly, lower her taut shoulders, and return the smile. After all, what did it matter if this first interview was a failure? Aunt Jacks had suggested it might be and if it was, then she would just wait for Mr Flynn to produce another one.

Slowly she relaxed, watching her paintings move from one pile to another, saw Nicholas's hands reach out, take one and raise it for further inspection. Gratefully she smelled the fragrance of a shrub outside the open window, felt the sun as a blessing, and then was able to sit back on the uncomfortable chair, waiting for Edward Hayward to give her his decision.

CHAPTER TWELVE

'When can you start?' Edward Hayward's voice was eager. He tapped his desk and leaned over, smiling at her. 'Your work is excellent. Delicate and full of vitality, Miss Redding. Yes, I can well imagine how you will portray my primulas.'

He looked up at Nicholas. 'You agree?'

'I do.'

Hester thought she heard a clear note of relief in the spontaneous reply.

'Miss Redding's paintings are beautifully detailed.' He smiled at her, that remembered quick flash of warmth and brilliance. 'And, as you say, Father, full of life. I'm sure your book will be all the better for her help.' He paused; looked intently at her. 'You have great talent.' Spoken very low, the words were clearly meant for her alone.

She sat back on her chair and felt a great wash of joy, like a seventh wave crashing up the beach, engulfing her in pleasure and relief. For a moment she couldn't speak. So many thoughts ran around in her mind: this first step, professional work, the excitement and challenge of illustrating Mr Hayward's book. And then suddenly, a stab of something else, unfamiliar but stirring; she would be working here, with Nicholas not far away.

Then she became aware of the two men and all the thoughts vanished with the need to show her gratitude, to agree to whatever conditions were demanded of her.

'Thank you,' was all she could say, looking into Edward Hayward's impatient eyes. 'Thank you. I'll do my very best, Mr Hayward. And I can start whenever you wish.' Father would have to be told, but even if he disagreed, she would still accept the commission. She must! This was the chance she had been dreaming about, and now the path ahead looked clearer. She told herself determinedly that the parents would – must – accept her news; she would catch the omnibus every morning, and she would work hard.

She ventured a glance at Nicholas and returned his smile but could think of nothing to say. He was looking at her with such an intense expression that for a moment she felt a stab of unease. Perhaps he didn't want her here, in his nursery. Was he one of those men who didn't think women should be free – like Father, like Hugh? Her smile died and she got up, to collect the paintings scattered over the desk, to avoid the watching eyes. Coldness hit her as abruptly another shocking idea came: if Nicholas didn't want her here, half the joy of the work would be gone. She wanted to share his company. She felt a strange excitement whenever she saw him. What was happening to her? Where was her well-bred self-control? Why did she feel this way about Nicholas and not Hugh?

Edward Hayward's voice cut into her churning thoughts, offering her a remuneration far higher than she had dared to hope. 'Is that acceptable, Miss Redding?'

'Yes, thank you, Mr Hayward.' Her voice was unsteady, her hands clumsy as she put the paintings into the attaché case and closed it.

'Good. And if you can start tomorrow, that will suit me very well. We'll have a corner of the room cleared, a table brought in, perhaps, and no doubt you'll bring your own painting slope, or do you prefer an easel?'

The reality of his expectation helped to banish the wild thoughts. She picked up her reticule and the attaché case, hoping she looked confident and reliable. 'I shall bring my slope, Mr Hayward, and yes, a table would be excellent. By the window. So – tomorrow morning. At nine o'clock, or is that too early?' In her head she heard an echo of Emily Watson's clear voice and knew she was trying to copy the same self-assurance.

'Not for us, Miss Redding – eh, Nicholas? Up with the lark, we gardeners are.' Edward's wheezy laughter filled the room and Hester smiled back at him. She took a step towards the door and glanced at Nicholas as he came to her side.

'Let me carry your case, Miss Redding. I'll come to the bus stop with you.'

She walked down the dark passage, through the open doorway and into the brilliance of the sunlit garden, aware only of his presence behind her. And suddenly it was all too much – the excitement, the knowledge that her talent was good enough to be professional, and now Nicholas wanting to walk beside her. Escape became imperative.

She turned and looked at him. 'No, please don't.' Her voice was sharp and instantly she regretted her impulsive reaction. 'I can manage. I'm used to being on my own in town. Thank you, but please don't bother.'

At the gate they stopped and he opened it, looking at her quizzically. 'It wouldn't be a bother, Hester, more a pleasure. But if you don't want—' His voice was slightly rough, his eyes alarming her with their sudden coldness. She stiffened. What had she said? What had she done? Words erupted. 'I must hurry, Mr Thorne. The bus will be waiting ... goodbye. . . .' She flew down the street, not looking back, furious with herself, with him, with the fact that she was behaving childishly and must be showing him how immature she was.

The journey back to Chudleigh helped to calm her thoughts and fears and by the time she reached Oak House she was almost her usual self again, already rehearsing the conversation she must now have with her father.

Nicholas watched her walking away and stayed in the gateway, thinking. So she would be here tomorow, which was a pleasant thought. But clearly she had no use for him. He took in a long breath and then expelled it, returning to the nursery and the work awaiting him. Hester Redding's rude dismissal suited him: he had no time for dallying with her, however attractive and intelligent she was. Plants, he thought wryly, were far easier to deal with than an ambitious young woman with her mind so obviously focused on her potential career.

And then a last thought dared to surface: yes, he had been looking forward to her arrival this morning but now – narrowing his eyes he squinted into the sun, and pulled his hat further down over his brow – she was just the artist who would be coming to illustrate his father's book and he wouldn't need to give her any attention.

A pity. But better that way.

He walked towards the glasshouse. 'Jim, have you done the spraying?' And then he pushed aside all thoughts of the attractive young woman whose presence tomorrow would conspire to divert his attention. After inspecting the apprentice's work, he went back to the office and sat down at his desk.

Time to deal with the morning's post. A packet addressed in Emily Watson's familiar handwriting. Opening it, something fell out, something so familiar, so charged with emotion and foreboding, that for a few seconds he had to wait for his heart to stop racing. A pale blue leather book, scuffed and dotted with mud: Jonathon West's journal.

For a moment he was back there in the Dolomite Mountains, along with Jonathon, and other members of Emily Watson's party, feeling the rain, the wind, hearing the porters arguing about the packs they were carrying, demanding more money and causing Jon to lose his temper. Cursing them, he had stepped forward quickly to help Nicholas, who, dodging a blow from a raised staff, had overbalanced and fallen, hitting his shoulder on a rock.

Nicholas sat back, remembering the passion of that moment. He had recovered, standing upright again, rubbing his shoulder, telling Jon to watch out for the slippery, moss-edged track running beside the raging river. And now, eyes closed, Nicholas saw again the terrifying waters; in his mind he feared the rocks that struck upward through the current, sending white water surging along in powerful waves.

Then the final image and sound. Jon's voice shouting for help as he slipped and fell; his shouts growing weaker and weaker as he was rapidly swept out of sight, away from all attempts of rescue. Nicholas knew he would never forget. Never forgive himself for not, somehow, rescuing his friend.

He forced himself to open his eyes again but knew that the sight of Jon disappearing in the swirling water would haunt him for the rest of his life. He hadn't saved him and the consequent guilt had been a dark, threatening shadow ever since, always present.

Slowly, he fought for self-control, and read Emily's accompanying letter.

This has just come to light in Jon's effects, sent to me by his grieving family. I think you should have it but I hope the contents won't distress you too much. And, a propos of that expedition, Nicholas, I am arranging to return to the mountains in a month or two and hope that you will again accompany me.

I look forward to hearing from you soon.
Sincerely,
Emily

Nicholas opened the book, finding the last entry on a blurred, crumpled page. Jon's writing was hard to decipher, scribbled, full of misspellings and comic sketches, but in Nicholas's mind the words were deeply engraved, reminding him of that terrible day and the reason for the disaster.

Those damned porters [with a tiny sketch of a little man brandishing a staff] *are still playing up, saying the rain makes the wieght of their packs too heavy – they want more money, of course, but I refowse to pay. We agreed the amount before we started and they must do as I ordered. Hope the rain keeps off – tomorrow I must try the track which the head man spoke about, saying that's where the famous double gentian grows.*

It's probably nonsense, just a folktale, but we must try it out. Fingers crossed!

And, in the margin of the page, a hand with an index finger linked with the next one.

Very slowly, almost tenderly, Nicholas closed the book, smoothing the rough cover and still seeing that wild scene of lashing water and the small, fast-disappearing figure of Jon, arms over his head as if in supplication, white, half-submerged face taut with fear and hopelessness. And then it was gone, only the water surging down, ignoring this latest bit of flotsam as of no account.

It took moments of determined strength to convince himself that the past could not be remedied. Jon had died, and here was his journal. Nicholas kept staring at the book and very slowly felt a new hope rising from deep inside him. Yes, Jon's resolution to keep

111

searching for the double gentian must be continued. There was a scribbled map showing the almost completely obscured track leading to the supposed location. A track to be explored and searched.

Resolve hit him. He must go back to the mountains and carry on Jon's search. Perhaps there was a double gentian. And if he found it, then, by God – suddenly he stood up and smiled into the sunshine beaming through the window – he would be doing something to avenge Jon's death, and – the smile grew broader, stronger, as a great surge of determination flowed through him – he would be doing what he could to rid himself of the dark sense of guilt that haunted him and threatened to ruin his life.

He would talk to Father, explain that he must join Emily's expedition. He must plan for the future.

Hester entered the house, stowed the attaché case and her reticule in her bedroom, looked at herself in the mirror and wondered who this newly confident figure might be. Each step, going downstairs, was firm and quick, coming to a halt outside the study door where she guessed that her father would be busy.

Taking a deep breath, she knocked, heard 'Come', and went in to confront him.

Arthur Redding looked up, eyes dark, face tight. She saw he was irritated at being interrupted and so stopped just inside the door, suddenly deflated, not knowing what to say.

Leaning back in his chair, he pushed away the scattered papers on the desk and looked at her. 'What do you want, Hester?'

She blinked. She must break through this hostile non-welcome. It was important to talk – properly, warmly and without any of the old boundaries. She smiled nervously. 'Just to talk, Father.'

Frowning, he gestured at the untidy desk. 'I'm busy, as you can see. Can't it wait until after luncheon, whatever you want to say?'

Abruptly all the old annoyances, resentments and frustrations fell away and she knew exactly what to say. She stepped nearer the desk. 'No, Father, it can't wait. I have to talk to you.' She paused, saw him frowning, but continued. 'I want to tell you what I plan to do with my life.'

His expression was unwelcoming. Hester drew in a huge breath, and walked towards the chair facng the desk. 'May I sit down?'

She saw a gleam of surprise in his narrowed eyes as he nodded.

'Father. . . .' She was searching for words. They came slowly. 'Father, I have been given a private commission to illustrate a book about primulas.' She saw the change on his face from annoyance to growing surprise and anger but went on.

'Mr Flynn, the artist I have been studying with, suggested that I visit Mr Edward Hayward at his nursery in town this morning, and—'

The dark eyes were furious. He sat up in his chair. 'But I told you I wouldn't agree. . . .'

Hester rallied her courage. 'I know. And I disobeyed you – but, Father, it's wonderful that I have gained this commission.' Her voice rose and confidence grew. 'I am to do a professional piece of work for Mr Hayward, and he will pay me—'

'*Pay* you?' Quick fury flew out of the two words and Hester instinctively edged back in her chair. 'Becoming a working woman, are you? A common girl who has no idea of behaviour or of education, a woman who is out on the street and. . . .'

Arthur Redding ran out of words and breath and could only glare at her across the desk.

Hester straightened her back. She met those furious, near-black eyes and said, as steadily as she could, 'No, Father, I will not be a common girl, neither will I forget my education and upbringing. But I will, most certainly, be a working woman, and proud of the fact.'

They stared at each other. Then Hester said, her voice softer, in the hope of still persuading him, 'I just ask you, that when you've given it more thought, you will try and be proud of me, too.'

Silence. Her hopes fell. A nervous tic moved in Arthur Redding's jaw. She sat there, full of apprehension, waiting. He made no reply and, dismayed, she knew she must try and placate him. 'I'm sorry, Father, I know this is not what you want. But I can't marry Hugh. I don't want a dull, domestic life; I have this talent and I believe I must use it. And so, you see. . . .' The words faded.

Use it well.

Thank you, Emily Watson, I will, oh, I will.

New strength came. 'Father, please forgive me. Please try and understand, because I have to do this.'

113

The room was warm, stuffy, redolent of winter fires and cigars, and a welcome touch of fragrance from a vase of double white lilac. Hester sat back in her chair, watching her father's face, tight, with inner thoughts chasing across it.

For a moment her own thoughts wandered. This room, full of law books of past court cases, with watercolours of Dartmoor on the walls, was full of memories. Father's study had always been sacrosanct, never entered without permission. Here she had come for lectures on bad behaviour and sometimes, on birthdays, to be given presents, smiles and kind words.

The red patterned carpet was faded; long velvet curtains which had once been the same red and now were pale cherry colour were forever in her memory and always would be.

A shiver pricked her spine. She was leaving here but part of her, that happy, cherished childhood, would remain. She must think more positively. *Forget the memories, see it as it is.*

She got up, walked to the window and released a fluttering tortoiseshell butterfly caught in a curtainfold. Pulling down the sash she watched it fly towards the garden and envied it. This is what she must do: fly away.

She turned. 'Father, I'm not a child any longer. I'm a woman and I need your permission – and love.' The last word slipped out unbidden, and she saw his face soften.

He got to his feet, running a hand down his leg, and came to her side in the sunlit space of the big window. 'Hester. . . .'

Something in his voice renewed her hope.

'Hester, you are my daughter, my only link with your dear mother whom I grew to love. Yes—' He looked at her very intently. 'Ours was an arranged marriage, but soon we became friends – companions, I might say – and then. . . .' The pause was a long one. 'Lovers.' Silence, and then, in almost a whisper, 'I was lost, I missed her so when she went. . . .' Another pause while he looked out of the window into what Hester instinctively knew were memories. 'Yes, I missed her very much.' His voice was soft and he blinked into the sunlight.

Clearing his throat he turned and she thought she saw something warm – loving? – on his face as he looked at her. 'Come and sit down. Yes, we must talk this thing out.' Taking her hand he led her back to the chair she had just left and seated himself behind the desk. For a long moment he looked at her.

'You want me to understand your needs, but I need you to understand mine. Ours, Hester.' He nodded emphatically. 'Your stepmother is my wife now and I must care for her. So. . . .'

Hester sat upright, her body stiff, eyes glued to his face. She had no idea what he would say next. Would it be understanding or disapproving judgment? Her hands knotted in her lap.

'If you leave this house – your home, Hester – you will need to find somewhere else to live. By yourself. No servants, no parents to lay the law down.' A smile flickered briefly. 'You will earn a wage, which I can assure you will be nothing compared with the allowance I give you. Your accommodation will be poor with none of the comforts you experience here. Are you prepared for all this?'

Her mind racing, she thought hard. His words conjured up facts which she had chosen to ignore. All she had wanted was freedom. But to live alone? Her breathing slowed and she allowed a few moments to pass while the images and thoughts chased around her head. And then, at last, she knew the answer.

'Yes, Father. Thank you for pointing out to me just how hard it will be. I hadn't considered that. But now I have decided. I shall work and live apart from you and Stepmother. I need to be free.'

Slowly he nodded, eyes fixed on her face. 'Very well. Then you must go and face whatever trials lay ahead of you, alone and without any help. No good coming back, Hester, when the money runs out, when the rent is due and your commissions are not paying enough. And don't forget that you have to buy food. And clothes. And painting equipment. But you will do it, you say.'

They seemed locked in their closeness, their separate needs. Arthur Redding breathed very deeply and noisily. 'I cannot give you my blessing because I do not think you should do this. And I would remind you of something you have evidently forgotten: because of my love for you I shall live in fear of what is happening to you, but it is very clear that you have no love for me, your father, who has nurtured you through all the years of our lives together.' A distasteful expression spread across his face. 'Perhaps not the love you seek – sentimental, overflowing and effusive – but a strong sense of what is

115

the best thing to do. How to bring up my daughter; care for her; see that she has a safe life ahead of her as I grow older and more infirm. Love that says I must provide for her when I am gone.'

The room was too warm, too stuffy. Hester ordered herself to stay calm, but her thoughts ran too fast, too painfully, and she slumped in her chair.

He stared across the desk. 'No, Hester, it is plain that you are happy to forget all that, and so I have to understand, as you say, and watch you fly off, like that butterfly you've just released, into the blue, which may well cloud over in a day or two, bringing dark clouds and extreme unhappiness.'

She had not expected any of this and the slow delivery of such true and revealing thoughts was a wound to her heart. 'Father, I-I don't know what to say. Of course I know you love me, as I love you, but I have to go.'

Silence grew. Pain, resentment, frustration, a void of non-understanding, deep and ugly, lay open between them.

Then there was a step outside the door and Emma's voice came between them, splitting the emotional charge filling the room. 'Arthur, dear, are you ready for luncheon? Ruby is carrying up the trays. I have no idea where Hester is.'

It was done, finished, all over, everything said and final, inescapable boundaries laid out. Arthur Redding nodded at Hester. 'Time to go,' he said, getting to his feet, and she thought she heard irony in his unsteady, harsh voice.

CHAPTER THIRTEEN

Luncheon. Ruby grinning at Stepmother and offering assistance whether needed or not. Father grimly silent. Hester felt that the overblown emotional feelings around her were too painful to be borne. She picked at her meal while Stepmother ventured a few vapid remarks about the weather. Father grunted and kept his eyes down. And in the silence, Ruby, Hester felt, was taking it all in: wondering, guessing, hoping for something to her advantage?

Leaving the room when the meal ended, Hester escaped to her bedroom and sat on the bed, her thoughts a confusing mixture of words, ideas, places and people. Eventually she calmed and was able to think sensibly.

Tomorrow was the start of her new life. She must rise early, leaving the house without any terrible goodbyes. Catch the early omnibus in the village, reach Newton Abbot and book a room at The Globe Hotel for a few days. She would soon find more suitable and cheaper accommodation.

Before that she must sell her jewels. The sandalwood box was emptied into a chamois bag. Taking out each piece – three rings, strings of pearls and moonstones, the Venetian glass beads, Grandmother's topaz pendant and matching eardrops, the set of rubies and Mother's cameo brooch – Hester wondered if this bid for liberation would help Father to realize that she knew what she was doing; that she understood the need for careful future undertakings.

Her packing was soon done. Just enough clothes and toilet pieces in the valise, along with the bag of jewellery, to last for a day or two.

Her painting equipment went into a smaller bag, her reticule was filled with purse and more personal things. How would she carry it all? Momentarily she wondered about getting Hoskins to drive her into town, but then decided against it. *I must be independent.* When she had an address she would send a message to Father to instruct Ruby to pack up the rest of her belongings and arrange for the carrier to bring them to her.

And then she thought of what she owed her family. Aunt Jacks should be told, but mustn't be involved in this escape, so just a note of explanation. And a letter to Father. A short, loving note, saying she hoped he would soon change his feelings about her departure. That she would write again. She wrote these letters with great concentration, addressing them and leaving them to be found in her empty bedroom tomorrow.

Dinner time and the same silence. Clearly, Father had told Stepmother about the morning's emotional confrontation. After painting in the afternoon, Hester pleaded a headache and retired early. She felt guilty, but increasingly filled with the passion that told her that it was right to go. To escape, like the butterfly, out into the blue freedom.

She slept badly, awaking with the dawn chorus. As she dressed she heard the blackbird in the pear tree, and realized she would no longer hear it in town. *Stop being sentimental. Painting is more important than birdsong. Hurry up and leave.*

Carrying her bags as well as the painting slope was difficult. She crept down the stairs and then paused on the landing, aware of the silence, until a figure stepped out from behind her and she turned quickly.

'Ruby!'

'Yes, Miss. I'll help you carry that thing. You've got enough with those bags and your reticule.' The girl took the slope, smiled and gestured Hester to precede her down the stairs.

Disconcerted, Hester reached the hall and then turned to take the slope from the girl's hands, but Ruby shook her head. 'You can't manage it all by yourself, Miss.' She paused. 'I dunno where you're going, but if I can help. . . .'

'I'm catching the omnibus in the village.' The words came out unthought. Hester couldn't think straight. Ruby was spoiling all her well-laid plans.

'Tell you what, Miss, I'll come with you to the bus stop. Carry this ole thing for you. No one'll want me yet. I'll get me coat.' She disappeared, returning with her coat done up, hiding her apron, a scarf over her hair, taking the slope from Hester's hands and unlocking the front door. 'Lovely morning,' she said. 'But you've forgotten something, Miss – your blue plant out there in the rockery.'

Hester sucked in a breath and let anger unroll itself. This girl knew too much. What was happening? She said sharply, 'Why do you think I want to take it, Ruby?'

The girl turned, and their eyes met. Ruby smiled. 'Cos I reckon you're leaving, Miss. Taking your luggage and that painting thing. Going somewhere else. And you'll miss that blue flower, won't you?'

Hester stopped, put her bag on the ground, and stared as a shutter opened in her bewildered mind. 'Ruby, you've been listening You've eavesdropped. If my father knew he would dismiss you – without a character.'

Ruby laughed, a deep-throated, confident sound that Hester stepped away from. 'He won't never do that, Miss. I'm too useful to be put off. No, I'm here now and I'm gonna stay. When you've gone I'll see to the house, give the orders, see it runs all right. And I'll look after the old folks. They can't do without me, see?'

'What do you mean? What are you saying? You're a wicked girl, I always knew it.'

Ruby's smile vanished, her little cat-face fiercely determined. 'I won't tell you why now, Hester, cos you've got enough troubles in front of you, I reckon, leaving home like this. But when you come back – if you come back – then I'll tell you. It's a secret I've kept ever since my ma died, so won't hurt to keep it a bit longer, but tell you what, Hester, you oughta be grateful I'm here to take over now you're goin' off and leaving them.'

She's calling me Hester. She's behaving as if she were a girl of my own class. I don't understand. She had no words; only jumbled thoughts which she couldn't express.

In silence they continued, reaching the village and the main road.

Hooves in the distance approached. 'Jest in time,' said Ruby brightly. 'Hope you get on all right. Send me a message if I can help.' When the bus halted beside them, she waited for Hester to climb aboard and then handed up the painting slope.

Her smile was friendly and bemused, Hester thought the words carried a loving message. How ridiculous: Ruby was a servant. But, even so, she had helped, carrying the wretched slope up that long hill. 'Goodbye,' Hester said faintly. 'And – thank you. . . .'

The omnibus rumbled away and Hester saw Ruby waiting, waving farewell before she turned, running down the lane, back to Oak House.

She's going home. And I've just left it. Hester sat in thought as the omnibus jolted along, soon reaching Newton Abbot and depositing her by the market. The Globe Hotel had a room to let, so she paid a deposit, leaving her baggage before ordering coffee and toast in the dining room. Realism hit her. This breakfast might well be a meal that must last – where would she find her luncheon? The money in her purse would not last long and Father would, of course, stop her allowance. So the jewels must be sold. But first she must start painting Mr Hayward's flowers.

Thinking bravely, clutching the painting slope and her reticule, she headed for the Hayward Nursery. Walking along, she banished the temptation to feel nervous, to wonder if she was doing the right thing after all. She must remember Emily Watson's words, grab this opportunity, and greet Mr Hayward and – she caught her breath – Nicholas with a confident smile.

Behave like Emily and I'll be successful. I will – I will.

Ruby took morning tea up to Mrs Redding's room and then hot water to Mr Redding's dressing room with a huge smile on her face. 'Good morning, Madam,' she said, and then, less exuberantly, 'Good morning, Sir.' Oh, what a shock they were going to have!

Back in the kitchen she told Mrs Caunter that Miss Hester had left home.

'No!' shrieked Mrs Caunter, almost dropping her mug of tea. 'You're making it up!'

'No, I'm not. I helped her carry her stuff up the hill to the bus.

She's gone, all right. But the Mistress and Master don't know – not yet. I dessay she left a note or something – I'll go up and look.' Ruby preened herself, thinking of the new responsibilities which were bound to be offered her now. 'If she didn't then I s'pose I shall have to tell them meself. . . .' She flounced out of the room and ran up the stairs and into Hester's bedroom.

'Well, I never.' Mrs Caunter's ageing mind tried to work out why Miss Hester had gone. And then she wondered about Ruby, getting so much above herself, almost like trying to run the household. 'Somethin's up,' Mrs Caunter muttered. 'Always thought she were a bad lot.' But it was time to start the breakfast, so she creaked to her feet and reached for pans and pots.

Ruby felt the emptiness of Hester's room hit her as she came to an abrupt stop just inside the door. The bed was crumpled, as if last night had been a restless one. No painting things inside the studio. She looked around. The jewel box was open and empty, but on the dressing table were two envelopes, sealed and addressed.

Mrs Jacquetta Hirst.

Arthur Redding, Esquire.

Ruby's uneasy sense of something painful left her. She was right – here were the notes. She picked them up, turned them over, felt the seals but realized she couldn't open them. *Don't matter, I'll be there when Master opens his – I'll see what she says.*

She waited until Master and Mistress were in the dining room, safely sitting down, opening the newspaper, unfolding napkins, before she produced the two envelopes. Didn't want them to fall down with shock, did she?

'Found these in Miss Hester's room, Master,' she said, her face expressionless.

'What?' He took them, looking up at her. 'Where is Miss Hester? She's late coming down.'

'Don't know, sir,' lied Ruby, close to his elbow.

His eyes were narrow, mouth tightly pursed. With his knife, he ripped open the envelope addressed to him, pulled out a sheet of paper and read it.

Ruby heard his breathing quicken as she edged nearer. She made out the first words, *Dear Father*, but suddenly Arthur Redding threw down the letter, tried to stand up, and then sank back in his chair. 'Gone,' he muttered. And then, louder and explosive, 'Gone! My daughter, my Hester. I didn't think. . . .'

'What, dear?' Mrs Redding stared down the table. 'What has Hester done? I don't understand. . . .'

Ruby looked at the pale, disturbed face and wanted to comfort her mistress, but there was no time. Master drooped in his chair, face suddenly grey and twisted, left hand collapsing by his side, one leg outstretched but seemingly lifeless. He tried to speak but she couldn't make out the words, although they sounded like 'my fault . . . too late . . . Hester – Hest—' and then his head fell to one side, body crumpling like a rag doll.

Mistress screamed and wept but Ruby had no time to help her. She raced from the room, down the stairs and into the garden. 'Hoskins! Hoskins! Come 'ere!'

He appeared, giving her his usual surly frown. 'No need to shout – what d'you want?'

Ruby's heart raced. She didn't know she cared so much. 'Master's ill. Go and get the doctor – quick, quick. . . .'

Hester walked through the town, reaching Hayward Nursery a few minutes before the clock in St Leonard's Tower, a quarter of a mile away, struck nine. The painting slope was heavy and she paused at the entrance, smoothing her crumpled sleeve where it had lain, straightening her shoulders, and taking a long, deep breath.

The door to the house was open but she stopped, uncertain. 'Good morning,' she said hesitantly, hoping someone inside would hear her. Nicholas, perhaps? Or his father? Or was there a housekeeper? No answer. She repeated the words, louder this time and took a step over the threshold. There was the office, straight ahead of her. Should she go in, uninvited? Thoughts raced. Abruptly she realized she had no idea of how working women behaved, or of the relationship between employer and employee. This was harder than she thought, and she'd only just started.

'Miss Redding.'

Twisting around, she let the slope fall to the floor. Confused, she looked into Nicholas Thorne's face and knew a blissful second of reassurance as he smiled, his straightforward gaze friendly.

'You keep dropping things, Hester.' Bending, he picked up the slope.

His amusement helped to banish the shyness. 'I do, don't I? So silly of me.' And then she heard herself add, 'A good thing you're always near to retrieve them, Nicholas.' No – what was she saying? He must think her flirtatious, shallow. Why couldn't she behave properly?

'Come into the office and see your table. I've cleared things up a bit. Will this do? You said you wanted to be near the window.' Gesturing her to go ahead, he followed her into the little room.

She looked around, suddenly grateful to be here, to see where she would work, to know that in a minute the familiar painting things would be around her, the feel of the brush in her hands, the dividers open and measuring, variations of colours running around her mind, Mr Hayward's flowers calling out to be painted. She looked at him and smiled, allowing her feelings to show. 'Thank you, Nicholas. It's lovely. I shall be happy here.' She felt herself again, Hester Redding, on her way to becoming a botanical artist, no longer the foolish young woman, so nervous and unsure of the new world around her.

His eyes were as bright as the gentian she had left at home as he returned her smile, and his deep voice a touch lighter when he said quietly, 'And we're happy to have you, Hester. Now—' He paused at the door, a tall, powerful figure, a gardener dressed in a brown suit with patches on the elbows of the jacket and stains darkening the creased trousers. 'If it's not too personal a question, have you had any breakfast? I don't want you to work on an empty stomach and Mrs Kent can always produce something if necessary.'

Mrs Kent must be the housekeeper. Relief eased an earlier ridiculous fear. So she wasn't alone here with two – perhaps more – men in the nursery, a solitary woman. She took off her hat, put it on a few empty inches of packed bookshelf, and started unpacking her bag.

'Yes, I have, thank you. I had it at The Globe, where I shall stay.'

He stood very still. 'You mean you're not going home after your work here?'

Hester's newfound serenity vanished. 'No. I shall look for a room

– or something – this afternoon. I mean, I suppose I shall only work for your father for a few hours, and then . . . and then. . . .'

And then what? Sell her jewels. Tramp the streets finding somewhere to live. Have her evening meal alone and then pack up again, ready to move into the room which as yet she had not found. She would be alone. Free, yes, but alone. She hadn't thought of this until now and it was a dark shadow abruptly overwhelming the joy of this longed-for moment.

Then footsteps broke the silence stretching between them, and Edward Hayward's wheezy voice said, 'Ah, Miss Redding. You're on time. Let's get working, shall we?'

And then the painting took over. Hester had no more time to think about where she was to live, for a primula in a pot was brought and put on the nearby desk, together with a scrap of cardboard carrying its seeds, Edward having pushed aside papers, inkwell and piles of catalogues to make room. 'This is the one I want you to paint first. *Primula farinosa*, a pretty thing, eh? Brought back from Europe several years ago, and already a favourite with garden people. It's also called the little bird's eye primula. Well. . . .' He was standing in front of her table. 'What do you think? Can you paint it?'

'Yes, Mr Hayward.' She could smile now, setting out the painting paraphernalia, thoughts happily settled on the work ahead of her. 'It's lovely. I shall enjoy trying to capture those little pink petals, and the rosettes of leaves . . . and those tiny seeds.'

'Yes. Well, anything you want?'

'Some water, please.'

'I'll tell Martha to bring it to you.' He walked to the door, giving her a final smile. 'Martha Kent is my housekeeper. I'll tell her to include you in the break for tea at eleven o'clock.'

'Thank you, Mr Hayward.' Already she was inspecting the small flower, opening out the dividers, stretching the clean sheet of paper, smoothing it, getting the brushes ready for the first wash. A sigh of relief, of gratitude, of hope, and then she was lost in her craft, watching the faint lines become perfect copies of the flowers in front of her, knowing that this was the fulfilment of all those dreams. This was freedom.

Oak House was in ferment. Ruby hovered outside the drawing room where Master had, at Dr Winters' orders, been carried by Hoskins and a passing farm boy. Arthur Redding lay on the chesterfield, comatose, a grey heap of a figure now collapsed and incoherent. Emma sat in her usual chair staring at him, white handkerchief dabbing her eyes, her unsteady voice whispering his name. 'Arthur. Oh, Arthur. . . .'

Ruby brought her mistress a cup of strong, sweet tea, and a small glass of brandy.

'Drink this, Mistress – 'twill give you strength.' She smiled into the red-rimmed eyes and produced a clean handkerchief.

'Thank you. Oh dear, poor Arthur. . . .'

Realizing that no orders were to be given, Ruby took matters into her own hands. Blatantly, she read Hester's letter to her father, now dropped and forgotten on the dining room carpet. Then she took the letter addressed to Mrs Hirst and thought hard before going down and telling Mrs Caunter she'd be away for a while. 'Delivering the letter, see? Mrs Hirst must know about the Master. Don't shout at me – I know what I'm doing.'

'But what about luncheon? All those vegetables waiting. . . .'

'Let 'em wait. We won't be having no proper luncheon today.'

She walked very fast down to Brook Cottage and found Mrs Hirst sitting in her rose bower, writing something. She looked askance as Ruby suddenly appeared.

'Ruby, isn't it? What do you want?'

No reply was needed as the letter was handed over. Jacquetta Hirst read it quickly then looked up into Ruby's face. 'Thank you for bringing this.' She was silent and then muttered, 'So she's got the job at the nursery, well, that's good, but leaving home?' She stopped, aware of Ruby's eyes, wide and full of something that alarmed her. 'Why do you look like that? Is there something else?'

'It's Master. Mr Redding. He's ill. The doctor's with him. I thought you oughta know.'

Jacquetta got to her feet. 'How ill? Is he conscious?' She tutted. Would the girl understand? 'Is he awake?'

'No. Can't speak. His face is all funny.' Ruby swallowed. She hadn't imagined that Master's illness could be such a shock.

'Come with me.' Jacquetta didn't stop to fetch a coat or a shawl, just pulled her gardening hat further down her head as she led the way to the stables. Ruby had to help harness Duchess and then climb into the trap beside the driver. They trotted up the lane and reached Oak House in four minutes.

'Tell Hoskins to tether the pony.' Jacquetta disappeared into the house in one swift movement and Ruby was left looking at Duchess and wondering what to do next. Hester must be told about her father's illness. Ruby knew Hayward Nursery, and that's where Hester's letter to the Master had said she was going.

'Here,' she said to Hoskins as he waited beside the pony. 'Take me into town. I gotta tell Miss Hester.'

He stared at her. 'You can't do that, not without orders.'

Ruby climbed into the trap. 'I'm giving the orders. What you waitin' fer, eh?'

'But—'

'Oh, damn you and yer buts! Get in and drive – or do you want me to do it meself?'

Grumbling, he got up, waved the whip and clicked to Duchess to start off. 'So what if I gets me notice for this, then? Tell 'em it's all your fault, I shall.'

Ruby sat straight and surveyed the road ahead. 'Shut up and make this bloody horse go faster, can't you?'

They reached Newton Abbot in record time. Hoskins cursed at wagons delivering beer, at farmers chatting in the middle of the road, but finally trotted up Wolborough Street, towards Hayward Nursery.

He glanced at his companion. 'Sure she's there, are you?'

'No,' said Ruby, 'but I reckon she is. I gotta find her. I gotta tell her about the Master.'

Hoskins sucked his teeth. 'Why you? Mrs Hirst's the one who—'

Truth hit Ruby like a lightning strike. 'No. It's gotta be me. I'm the one who's gonna tell her. To see that she's all right.' Something was pricking behind her eyes. Her throat was dry, her pulses raced. Funny, she never thought she would care so much about Hester. But she knew she did.

'There, that big gate on the right. Go on, drive in.'

Duchess snorted at the pull on the reins, then walked into the wasteland beside the nursery. Ruby didn't wait. She was down and running towards the house before Hoskins could say anything.

She had to see Hester and tell her the awful news. She had to be there, with her, didn't she?

CHAPTER FOURTEEN

A man with bright blue eyes and a suntanned face met her as she raced towards the house. 'Can I help?'

Ruby stopped. 'I gotta see Miss Redding.'

He frowned. 'She's very busy. Why do you want to see her?'

He was trying to stop her seeing Hester. 'Oh, get outta my way!' Ruby pushed him but he didn't move. She glared at him. 'Her father's took ill, she must get home, to be with him. . . .'

'Come with me.' Suddenly the man had his hand under her elbow, taking her into the half light of the house. 'Stay there. I'll tell her.' The dark passage smelled of cigar smoke and musty old things. Ruby pulled a face. This was no place for anyone as particular as Hester, brought up in a lovely house which was cleaned regular. She heard voices and stepped nearer the half-open door.

'Hester, I'm afraid I have bad news.' Such a lovely voice, sort of deep and soft like velvet. Sounded as if he cared, didn't want to frighten her. 'A girl has come with a message. Your father is ill.' Suddenly, a sucked-in breath, a chair scraping back, a rapid movement and then Hester's voice, unsteady. 'Who is it? Ruby, I expect. Nicholas, I must go to him.'

She appeared in the doorway, eyes worried, hands outstretched as if in search of comfort. Ruby had never seen Hester look so fearful, so less than confident. She took one of the searching hands. 'He's at home, miss, got the doctor with him. Thought I'd come and fetch you. Don't look like that, he's still alive.'

'Thank God. Is Hoskins outside?' She whirled around, hands to her face. 'Let me think – I must explain to Mr Hayward. What shall I do about the painting?'

Then the man's voice again, standing behind her in the doorway. 'Don't worry about that, Hester, my father will understand. And I'll take care of the painting.'

Ruby saw Hester turn and look at him. She saw an expression that she'd never seen before, a soft look that made her weak smile surely mean much more. Oh, thought Ruby, so he's the one, is he? And I thought as it was that Mr Hugh.

But no time then for anything but climbing into the trap, tucking herself beside Miss Hester and hoping that Master would still be alive when they got back to Oak House.

Hester jumped down before the trap stopped. She rushed into the house and then halted. There were voices upstairs, footsteps coming down; looking up she saw Aunt Jacks, followed by Dr Winters. 'How is he?' Her heart was racing. 'I came as quickly as I could. . . .'

Dr Winters said gruffly, 'Don't distress yourself, Miss Hester. Your father is conscious now. I have left medicine for him and given your aunt instructions as to his treatment. I will come again tomorrow to make sure he makes the good progress that I anticipate. Try and calm yourself – your stepmother is in need of your care and support. Now, good day to you, and to you, Mrs Hirst.' He bowed, collected his hat and went out, to where Hoskins waited with the trap.

Ruby was at Hester's side. 'Go on up, Miss – I'll see to Mrs Redding.' She disappeared into the drawing room and Hester looked into Aunt Jacks' taut face. 'You've seen him – will he be all right? The doctor seems to think so, but—'

Aunt Jacks took Hester's hands in her own and said, 'Stop worrying. It won't do any good. Go and talk to your father. Be cheerful, don't let him see you're upset. And Hester—' She frowned. 'Tell him that you haven't gone away. Your father needs you here. You must forget the painting until he recovers.'

They stared at each other, Hester's face drooping as the truth hit her, and then Jacks added, 'It's your duty, child. You can paint later, when all this is over.'

Hester breathed very deeply. Her dreams were shattering, falling in small pieces all around her as duty called again. Now she could no longer neglect it – she knew she must answer the call. Wretchedly she nodded. 'Yes, Aunt, I know. I'll do my best for Father.'

A long, shared moment of understanding. Then Jacks said, 'I shall return this afternoon. If you need any errands run, send Ruby. She seems sensible enough.' A last smile, an encouraging nod, and she walked towards the open front door.

Hester watched her aunt leave. Then, slowly, she climbed the stairs, mind full of one thought, which like a doom-laden bell reverberated around her head, clanging the terrible knowledge that her departure had almost certainly been the reason for Father's seizure.

Nicholas stood in the office; suddenly it was empty. Hester had only been here for a short time but already she had made a difference to the feel of the room. Her painting equipment was spread on the table, the jar of coloured water awaited her return, and her hat perched on the end of the bookshelf. Her reticule lay on the floor.

Frowning, he pondered. A difference to his life? Ridiculous. Hester was a lady, he was a gardener, an adventurer. She could have no time for him, no feelings, no wish to extend their tenuous acquaintanceship. And yet he knew there was something within him recalling the importance of her smile, the way he thought he saw her when she wasn't there.

He strode out into the nursery. *Good God, this is sheer imagination, get on with your work.* And yet. She seemed to be walking beside him, her smile warming his heart. It became vital to clear his mind. Finding his father in the far glasshouse, he explained that she had gone home.

Edward pursed thin lips, frowned, removed his hat, put it on again. 'And my painting?'

'It's safe. I've put it where no sun will reach it, no hungry mice . . . don't worry.' Nicholas forced a smile. 'I don't imagine she'll return – not until her father's recovered. So you may have to find another artist. Will that Flynn fellow help again?'

Edward huffed noisily. 'It's infuriating. She was so good. She put life into her painting . . . well, I'll think about it. So annoying.' He stormed out and Nicholas returned to the office with a sense of having to do something but not quite knowing what it was. Then he saw the hat, the reticule, and immediately knew. He must return these two items to her. She would wonder where they were. She might need her purse. He must see her.

Telling the apprentice he would be out for a while, he packed both items into a small haversack and left the nursery. The walk to Chudleigh would do him good, thinking as he walked. Deciding what to say to her, to Hester, to the girl who had suddenly become far too important in his life; who even appeared to be banishing the cold, dark guilt that he still felt about Jonathon West.

Hester sat beside her father's bed, looking down at his drained face, seeing the ageing lines that had become so much deeper, listening to his breathing, praying that he would recover. After a while she moved to the window, staring into the garden, trying to find comfort somewhere.

Out in the May sunshine flowers filled the long borders which Aunt Jacks had introduced, growing in single clumps, in drifts and great bushes. Delphiniums, tall and darker than the cerulean blue in her paintbox, luring bees under their hoods; all the garish red, white, blue and yellow bedding that her father admired; blowsy roses billowing up the arches and pergolas that stretched away from the house; and her favourite cottage pinks, white with picotee edges, handsome laced purples, maroon centred doubles, dancing in the breeze, all crowding the beds. She smiled, imagining that she could smell the sweet clove fragrance up here.

And there, in the scree garden, was the gentian Nicholas had given her, uplifted blue flowers reminding her of his eyes. Something arose in her mind then and she felt a lessening of the pain that grasped her body, but she knew that the deep abyss of guilt would never go.

Turning, she looked at the still figure on the bed, and then returned to the bedside. 'Father?' An eyelid flickered, one hand twitched. She leant over him, her hand on his forehead. 'Father, it's Hester. I'm here, Father.'

Slowly – so slowly – his eyes opened, closed, opened again, flickered and widened. His tongue licked dry lips. He saw her, and the unafflicted hand made the slightest upward move.

Guilt, love, something buried deep inside her, erupted; she felt near collapse but slowly she gathered the courage to stop the threatening tears. She smiled, took his cold hand in both hers, chafing him, and said, very quietly, 'You're better, Father, thank goodness. Just lie there and rest. I'll sit with you.' She pulled the chair nearer the bed. 'Is there anything you want? A drink? Some broth? Tell me. . . .'

His mouth opened slowly and muttered words that didn't reach her. She leant nearer, listening, trying to understand what he found so hard to tell her.

'Hester.' A long pause, a lick of the lips again, an endeavour to move his head from the pillow, and the hint of a smile around the thin, dry mouth. 'You're here. All. . . .' A gasp for breath, and then, 'All I need. Dear girl.'

Her heart was bursting. She swallowed the tears and the pain and bent to kiss his hand. 'Dear Father. Yes, I'm here. I'll never leave you. Never.'

The smile stayed on his racked face as he slowly turned his head into the pillow. She watched his eyelids close, heard his breathing become slow and knew he slept. Only then did she put her head into her hands and allow her shattered dreams to fill her mind.

The hours passed. Ruby came, offering to take Hester's place at the Master's bedside while she went down to Emma, still weeping in the drawing room. Hester sat with her stepmother, trying to help her understand that Father was alive and conscious, with a definite hope of recovery. She held Emma's hands and realized, with dismaying truth, that this was what her future held. Domesticity, comfort and caring for the sick and the old.

When the front doorbell sounded, knowing Ruby was upstairs, she went to answer it. 'Nicholas—'

He stood motionless, looking down at her. 'I've brought back your hat and your reticule. I knew you would need them. And I thought I would offer my services. Hester, is there anything I can do to help?' Opening the haversack, he took out her hat and purse.

She took them silently, thoughts crowding in. He must have walked in from town; no gig or trap in the drive. That meant he cared. Mustering her manners, she said, 'Thank you. Come in. Perhaps you'd like a drink? It's so hot today. I'll go down to the kitchen and fetch some lemonade.'

'No, I don't want to trouble you. I'll be on my way again. But—' His eyes were very dark, his voice gentle, and she felt herself longing to tell him how awful everything was. She hardly heard him add, 'How is your father?'

Footsteps behind her, Ruby coming down the stairs, pausing on the last one, looking at the visitor. Hester turned, suddenly in command of the situation. 'Ruby, can you sit with Mrs Redding for a short while?'

'O' course, Miss Hester.' The green eyes were wide.

Hester smiled back. 'Thank you,' she said. Perhaps she should explain. 'I have to discuss several things with Mr Thorne.'

'I see.' Ruby nodded, and disappeared into the drawing room.

Uneasily, wondering if Ruby saw too much, Hester looked back at Nicholas. He was waiting. 'Come into the garden.' She held out her hand.

Slowly, he took it, turned to put down the haversack, and stood aside while she led the way out of the dark house into the light and comfort of the garden, wondering what she was doing, what she meant to do, what she would say when they were alone. But now the sadness had gone and she was floating in warmth and a sense of something so lovely that she was able to smile quite freely, leading him down the long borders, towards the privacy of the summerhouse, already anticipating the joy of being alone with him.

The summerhouse was warm, the sun's brightness deflected by the oak tree growing at the side of the small wooden building. Hester went in, turned, watched Nicholas stop in the doorway. His body blocked the light and for a second she thought. This is wrong. We shouldn't be here, together, in this intimate space. But then deeper feelings swamped the conventions. He was someone she could talk to.

'Nicholas.' She looked into his eyes; they were darker, filled with something that excited yet alarmed her. 'My father had a seizure, and it's my fault. I left a note for him, saying I was leaving home. He must have read it and – and – collapsed.' Her voice died away, as the awful truth returned. She sank into a cane chair, hiding her face in her hands. 'I – I feel so guilty. . . .'

The words were low and uneven. She was on the verge of tears but knew that she must contain them. Where was her strength, her resolution and passion? Sniffing, she fumbled for a handkerchief, only to have one put into her hand.

Nicholas stood beside her, his face expressing what she sensed was pain. 'Guilt,' he echoed, staring at her, and then blinking, as if to hide the dark shadows veiling his eyes. And then, suddenly, he knelt on the dusty floor, close beside her, saying, 'Hester, cry if you want to. I understand. But guilt is a curse you must get rid of. Don't let it grow any stronger.' He stopped, then added, 'We're safe here. You can tell me anything you want.'

A pause while she dealt with the threatening tears, and then looked up into his face, a hand's span away from hers.

'You do trust me, Hester?' Rapid, low words, warm and comforting.

She was too close to him, yet full of an extraordinary feeling of rightness; they were together and talking freely. Relief filled her. 'Yes, I trust you, Nicholas. Of course I do.'

He put an arm around her, lowering her further back into the chair, his other hand lifting her face. He looked deep into her swimming eyes. 'This is all wrong.' There was tautness in his voice and she guessed he was trying to check the words which needed to come out. He said, very low, 'You know I admire you.'

She nodded, mesmerized by the light in his eyes, by the touch of his hard fingers on her face, the sound of his voice. 'Do you?'

'I could love you, Hester, if I allowed myself that great privilege.' The words were quiet, his voice very deep.

She watched the generous mouth tighten, saw a shadow creep over his face, and knew the moment had gone; now he was closing the barrier, and her heart jumped a beat.

'Love?' Her breathing quickened and he smiled, stroking her cheek, saying, almost whimsically, 'Love. Something I never thought to find. And here it is, whenever I see you, think of you, long for you. . . .'

If only the dreaming moment could go on for ever. Being loved, being admired, being wanted. But there was a sound in the garden, voices, Ruby calling to Hoskins, his gravelly, irate reply, and she knew the dream had flown. Carefully she pushed away his hand, rose and slipped past him into the sunny entrance of the summerhouse. 'I think we had better go.' But she wanted to stay.

He was beside her, his smile polite and ordinary as he said, 'Of course. Please forgive me. I took a liberty. Summer scents, and a lovely woman – all too much for any man to contend with.' His voice was amused, self-mocking.

She winced. 'No, Nicholas, you didn't take a liberty. I was to blame, bringing you here.' It was all spoilt. She stepped away, walking up the grass path towards the house, he following behind her. By the front door she turned; he would go now. What could she say?

Nicholas resolved the problem. 'Forgive me,' he said, almost casually now, 'but you told me this morning that you were to spend the night at The Globe Hotel and I suppose you have left some luggage there. Am I right?'

She had quite forgotten. 'Yes. A valise.'

'Have I your permission to collect it? It would be no trouble.'

Her heart pounded. He sounded as if nothing had happened in the summerhouse. He was just a servant offering to do something beyond the expected duty. He looked at her as if she were anyone, not the Hester he admired, could love. . . .

'Thank you, that would be very kind.' She kept her eyes down.

'Not at all. And also – about the painting.'

'Yes?' She had to look at him again. The painting, the commission, Mr Hayward's book. The old passion had a greater hold on her now, thundering through her veins, followed by the bleak truth that it had all come to an end.

Perhaps he saw her thoughts revealing all this. He took her hands in his and the impersonal expression softened as he said, 'Stop worrying, Hester. I'll bring your painting things back and perhaps you can continue here, in your home. I'll arrange it with my father. And another thing—'

'Yes?'

He smiled, and his voiced lightened as if, she thought, he intended the next words to be unimportant and easy, yet knew they could never be. 'Please forget what I said – in the summerhouse.' His eyes were dark.

For a couple of seconds they looked at each other, until Hester despairingly nodded, accepting his unexpected wisdom. 'Yes,' she said again. 'If that's what you want, Nicholas.' She stopped, swallowed, and tried to find words to bring this painful moment to its end. 'You've been. . . .' Inside her the knot tightened. She added lamely, 'So helpful.'

He nodded. 'If I can do anything more, send a message. I will leave your valise and your painting things with Mrs Hirst.' His voice lowered. 'I won't come here again.'

No, he was right. They mustn't meet again unless it was in the company of someone else, and anyway he obviously didn't want to see her. But if they did happen to meet – she caught her breath – at Aunt Jacks', they would be merely polite to each other. No more personal, extraordinary exchanges of words and feelings. Just a warm feeling of friendship. It was the most she could hope for. She nodded.

'Goodbye, Hester.' He held out his hand and she took it, knowing that this was goodbye. 'I hope to hear good news of your father's recovery before too long.'

'Thank you. Goodbye, Nicholas.' She forced herself to let the hard fingers slip away, then watched him reach for the haversack, and then walk away down the drive. He strode out of the entrance and round the corner. He was gone.

Hester went into the house and returned to the reality of life. Luncheon, she thought numbly. Would there be any today? How was Stepmother feeling? And she must return to Father's side. This afternoon Aunt Jacks was coming and she would mention a possible visit from Nicholas with her luggage.

It was all a bad dream, but even in this wilderness of desperation, she kept the promise of one gleaming star. Nicholas had said he could love her.

CHAPTER FIFTEEN

Leaving madam dozing, Ruby had spied it all from Hester's bedroom window. Away from the kitchen for a while, she was spending the afternoon sitting beside poor Master and then peeping into Madam's bedroom to make sure she was sleeping. But she had heard the doorbell, and voices, and couldn't stop herself running into Hester's room, hiding behind the curtain and watching the big man and Hester walking down the garden.

Where were they going? she wondered, with a grin. But suddenly Madam was awake, calling, sitting up in bed with her grey hair awry and her hands clasped as if in prayer and Ruby had come running.

'Ruby! We must let Mr Marchant know about the Master. Tell Hoskins to take a message that we need to see Mr Marchant as soon as possible. Miss Hester needs someone to help her take charge of the house – can you remember that? Oh dear, and Mrs Hirst will be here soon – go and tell Hoskins and then come back. I must get dressed. And tell Cook we shall need tea when Jacks is here. . . .'

Ruby offered her a drink of lemon barley water, a clean wrapper, and then seated her by the window in the comfy buttoned chair. 'I'll be back in a minute, Madam. Don't worry, everything's gonna be all right.'

In the garden she ordered Hoskins to convey the message to the Marchant household. 'And bring back an answer, else Madam'll be going on about it. . . .' She watched him grumpily walk towards the coach house and then stayed for a moment in the garden. It was lovely here, warm and full of green things and butterflies and some bees in the herb bed. She wondered again about Miss Hester and that big man who were now in the summerhouse. What was going on between them?

Back indoors, telling Cook that a cake would be needed and then going upstairs to Madam again, Ruby hoped that the meeting in the summerhouse was a happy one. Miss Hester had looked as if she needed cheering up, so terribly unhappy when Ruby saw her in Master's room. A queer feeling made Ruby's head spin; she wanted to do something to show Miss Hester how sorry she felt for her. Suddenly, climbing the stairs to go and help Madam dress, she stopped. Was this the time to tell Hester the secret? To offer her—

On the staircase, with the Redding portraits staring down at her, Ruby took a long, breath, and let the next word come out from where it had been hiding all along.

To offer Hester her *love*?

After an awkward luncheon which helped neither her nor her stepmother, Hester went to see how her father was. He slept and his expression was peaceful. She knew that until Dr Winters called tomorrow little could be done, except for watching, feeding, keeping him clean, quiet and as cheerful as possible. Ruby had been helpful, and Aunt Jacks would be here this afternoon. Perhaps there would be a moment when she could escape to her bedroom; her studio; the garden . . . somewhere.

When the time came, with Aunt Jacks sitting upstairs and Stepmother dozing in the drawing room, Hester found sanctuary in the garden. Now she could relive that strange and wonderful time in the summerhouse when Nicholas had said he admired, could love her. When he had awoken new, amazing feelings which she would never forget. But he had apologized for those words and had left with never a backward look.

She knew that he would not come again to Oak House. Her valise and painting equipment would go to Brook Cottage, and she would probably never see him again. She walked the length of the border and then stopped at the scree garden. The gentian flowers were still open and she remembered the blue of his eyes.

Reality shadowed her once-happy thoughts. She picked a single bloom of the trumpet shaped flower, held it for a moment, and then carefully picked it to pieces. Petals, sepals, anthers, stigma, stem, leaves. These tiny organs would never now become part of her painting. Their deaths were reflected in her own inner thoughts. Joy, ambition, hope, delight and amusement – all gone, along with that overwhelming excitement at hearing Nicholas talk about his love for her.

She dropped the gentian parts and knew that, like her dreams, they must be forgotten. She would not become a botanical artist now, for Father would need her for the rest of his life, and she could never leave him again. The world turned dark, despite the brilliant sunshine, and the garden fragrance was merely a haunting reminder of the summerhouse's smell of mustiness and the earthy scent on Nicholas's dun-coloured jacket. The flaunting palette of colours held no more importance. Flowers were merely an inconsequential part of a tragic summer day, which would be forever engraved on her memory.

Turning back to the house, she was appalled at her sad thoughts. Was there nothing good to find in this challenging disaster? Nicholas had suggested she continue painting at home. Well, there might be the odd hour when she could leave her two invalid parents and think about flowers, colours and paints, but the joy at the heart of that idea was coldly listless and quite unreal.

Knowing she must awaken Stepmother for tea, and call Aunt Jacks down to the drawing room, Hester returned to the house. Routine. Duty. Going on for ever. She shivered and tried to stop thinking.

When Ruby came up from the kitchen with a smile on her face, saying, 'Good news, Miss, Hoskins brought back a message—' Hester looked at her blindly.

'Where has Hoskins been? What message?'

Ruby put down the tray and looked warily at her. 'Madam told him to go to the Marchants' and ask Mr Hugh to come as soon as he could.'

'*What?*' Hester felt her legs suddenly weaken.

Ruby said over her shoulder, 'An' Hoskins said as how Mrs Marchant was sorry 'bout the Master, and she'd ask Mr Hugh to come later today.'

Hester's head spun. She sat down, trying to put these muddling thoughts into an understandable whole. She certainly didn't want to see Hugh Marchant today – or tomorrow. Anger grew. Why had Stepmother taken it upon herself to inform him? To ask him to come? As if she needed him!

Aunt Jacks came into the room. 'Hester, what's the matter? You look worried.' Her voice, calm as ever, brought sense into Hester's raging thoughts.

'Stepmother sent a message to the Marchants, Aunt – and Hugh is coming here this evening. I wish she hadn't done so.'

They looked at each other. Then Jacks said quietly, 'No doubt Emma thought she was being helpful. And perhaps you do need a man at this difficult time, child.'

'I don't. I just want to help Father to recover and I don't want Hugh or anyone coming to tell me what to do!' Hester heard her voice grow shrill and knew she was behaving in just the way Hugh might expect, like a hysterical child in need of masculine authority and assistance. And then, the words echoing in her mind, she saw in her aunt's astute eyes a hint of amusement and was able to laugh.

'Sorry, Aunt. I'm sure Hugh will have helpful suggestions which I will politely turn aside. I won't shout at him. And I won't blame Stepmother—'

'Of course you won't. Put the bad things behind you, Hester, and concentrate on what is happening now.'

Calmness spread through Hester's mind. She held out her hand. 'You're the only help I want, Aunt Jacks. And what is happening now is that it's teatime. Come in and let's cheer up poor Stepmother.'

Hugh Marchant arrived in the early evening. Stocky, well dressed, almost but not quite handsome, with pale sandy lashes above observant eyes, Hester thought he was no longer a welcome friend but the villain of the piece, sent to stir up her already overwhelming emotions.

'My dear Hester, Mrs Redding, I'm so sorry – you must let me do all I can to help in this sad situation.' He bowed to Hester, crossed the drawing room, kissed Emma's hand and then took up an authoritative stance in front of the empty fireplace. Hester thought crossly that he seemed to think he was the master of the house.

But Emma was grateful. 'So good of you, Hugh – but I knew poor Arthur would want you to know and to come and help us to deal with this tragedy.'

'Of course, Mrs Redding. After all, I'm almost one of the family, aren't I?'

Such arrogance. Hester sat up very straight, staring at him. 'Not quite, Hugh.'

Quickly he came to her chair, bending down, taking her hands and holding them in his own. 'My dear Hester, you're upset, of course, you are.'

How dare he treat her like a child? She frowned but he continued in the same soothing voice. 'I suggest that we sit down together and have a chat and see what can be done to help you and your stepmother to weather this unhappy storm.'

She pulled her hands away. 'Stop talking like a bad novelist, Hugh. It isn't a storm, it's an illness, and already Father is recovering. Stepmother and I can manage perfectly well, thank you. Everything is running smoothly. In fact, I think you have rushed over to see us quite unnecessarily.'

'Oh, Hester, – how unkind! Hugh is only doing what any newly affianced man would do.' Emma was pink with emotion, waving her hands and shaking her head.

'Affianced?' The word erupted like a thunderclap. 'He's not we're not – really, Stepmother, I think Father's illness has affected your memory.' Hester was on her feet. 'I told you both that I am not going to marry Hugh. As I also told him.' She turned sharply, finding herself close to him, staring into his face, seeing the frowning brows grow deeper and darker, knowing she was handling it all very badly, but not caring.

His hand was on her shoulder and she shook it off, pushing back her rage. 'I'm sorry, Hugh, but you know my feelings. And certainly let's sit down – we'll have a glass of sherry. And will you stay for dinner? Yes? Excuse me while I go and tell Cook.'

She left the room in a whirlwind of annoyance, but in the kitchen common sense returned and she smiled weakly at Mrs Caunter and Ruby, busily filling trays for dinner.

'Ruby, please bring three glasses and the sherry decanter to the drawing room, and Mrs Caunter, can you stretch the meal to include another place? Mr Marchant will join us for dinner.'

The meal was a tedious period of trivial chatter and Hester was thankful when it was over. As soon as Emma was settled in the drawing room, Hugh said forcefully, 'You and I must talk, Hester. Somewhere private – in the garden?'

She knew it was inevitable, and might help clear the air. 'All right. But I can't be long – I must make Father comfortable for the night.'

She led him out of the French windows onto the terrace and then down towards the orchard. The fresh air was a respite from the overheated house and she felt herself growing calmer. When he offered his arm, she slipped her own into the crook of his elbow and smiled. 'Sorry, Hugh, I know I've been rude and unpleasant. Forgive me. Everything is . . . difficult.' But it was the wrong word. Difficult would give him the chance to lay out his plans. And at once he did so.

'Hester, I understand how you feel. Such a shock, and it's all too much for you. No, don't argue – just listen. I know exactly what we must do.'

We was his mistake. Hester stopped in mid-step and stared at him. She must explain. 'Since we last talked, Hugh, something momentous has happened.' His eyes narrowed. 'After an argument with Father I decided to leave home. I had received a painting commission and there was no other way of taking it on other than living on my own. I left him a note saying I was going and then he had this seizure – and so I came back.' Her voice trailed away into the quiet country night sounds. 'And now I'm here again.'

He snatched his breath and his arm tightened about hers. 'You did what? My God, Hester, you really are impossible. How could you possibly live on your own? And where? What rubbish! Thank heavens Mrs Redding sent for me. Of course you'll do no such thing – in fact, I can see that your father's illness, shocking as it is, has come at the right time to stop all this nonsense.'

Hester pulled away, turned and faced him. She was shaking with renewed anger but her voice remained steady. 'It's not nonsense. I still want to leave, to go out into the world, and earn my living as a painter. I know I must wait until Father has recovered, but then—'

He stepped closer, pulled her into his arms, and held her. His voice was rougher, unrecognizable. Instinct made her try and free herself, but she was unable to do so. 'Hester, my dear, stupid girl, you're quite a rebel! I had no idea you had such passion! Let's sample it, shall we?'

She struggled again, but he held her tighter still. She felt the heat of his body, smelt the pomade on his hair, and knew with all her being that she hated every moment of this embrace.

He said, very low, into her ear, 'Come to your senses, Hester. We must plan to marry as soon as possible. I need you – I want you.' His voice became firmer. 'I have my eye on a suitable house just outside Bovey, not too far from the business, and we will install a nurse here to look after your father. Of course you will visit him and Mrs Redding quite often – you could come by trap or landau – and no doubt you will find time, once the house is furnished and everything is comfortable, for some painting. A hobby is a good thing that every woman should apply herself to.'

Shocked, Hester could only stare into his eyes. He must be mad to make such plans without even asking her! Her thoughts circled and she was totally unprepared for the tightening of his arms and his voice suddenly quietening, deepening. 'But until then, my darling, let's seal our agreement, shall we?'

At first his lips were warm and soft and she was so taken aback that she didn't demur. But then they hardened, and she felt her anger swell until she found the strength to push him away. 'Stop it! Leave me alone, Hugh. You just don't understand. I don't want your kisses or your selfish plans – I can manage my life without your interference. *How dare you* !' She pulled herself away from him, seeing in his eyes an anger that surely matched her own.

'I shan't give up, Hester. You're upset today and that's only natural. I'll come again later in the week and I feel sure you'll have different thoughts by then.' She heard a warning in his lowered voice before he stepped back, watching her, and then, very slowly, as if playing a part, began to smile in the old friendly manner that she remembered from their childhood. 'You know you must marry me,' he said very quietly, but with an underlying persistence that she also remembered. Hugh, as a small boy, had never given up.

'No,' she said hoarsely. 'No, I won't.'

'I think you will. It's the only way you can come to terms with the shock you must have caused your parents. The only way to make up for it, doing what they both want. After all, you know that leaving home was the reason for your father's illness, wasn't it?'

A shiver ran through her. 'Yes.' Her voice was so low that he leaned forward to hear the one word.

'And you must feel so guilty, Hester. So think about my plan and see how well it would all work out. Your parents relieved, you free of your guilt – and you and I being together, a new life for both of us. Marriage, and then children, and surely that's all any woman really wants?'

'No,' she said again, with a sob in her voice. 'No!' she ran back into the house, leaving him alone on the terrace, watching her, nodding his head as if pleased with the evening's work. Then a second later he went towards the stables and found Hoskins waiting to put the cob into the trap, ready for the homeward journey.

Somehow Hester survived the remainder of the evening, making excuses for Hugh's sudden departure and finally ensuring that both parents were comfortably asleep and the house quiet enough for her to think through all that had happened during the day.

She found it impossible to keep still so wandered again through the fragrant garden, watching the bats and the moths and hearing a nightingale somewhere far off making magical music.

Ruby came out to find her. 'You there, Miss Hester? Anything I can get for you before I go up?'

Hester turned, looked through the half light at the green eyes watching her so intently, and said wearily, 'No, Ruby, thank you. I just needed some fresh air. I'll lock up when I come in.'

'Very well, Miss.'

Why did the girl hesitate for a moment before turning away and going back into the house? It was almost too dark to see details but Hester thought she had seen an unexpected look of something – pity? – on the small, pretty face. The idea made her smile tightly, made herself a strong promise to be brighter in the morning, and then slowly go to her bedroom, after a last look at her father. She undressed with a feeling of relief and longed-for sleep.

144

Perhaps it was the aftermath of all the disturbances that had overwhelmed her during the long day – Father, Nicholas, Hugh – but, as she got into bed and felt the cool comfort of the pillow, tears suddenly came, streaming down her cheeks, choking her breathing, making her sit up and rock to and fro, utterly at the mercy of emotions that were too painful, too powerful for her to even try and control.

She didn't at once hear the soft knock on the door until it was repeated, and Ruby's whisper reached her. 'Are you all right, Miss Hester?' she was unable to answer.

Another scratching little knock and the door opened a crack. Ruby peered in, her face lit by the candle she carried, saw her, and said, 'Oh, Miss, whatever's the matter?'

Hester could only shake her head and hold a handkerchief to her streaming eyes.

This was terrible, humiliating, quite awful – to let a servant see how upset she was, how she couldn't stop crying. Still she choked. with sobs racking her body. *She must stop. She must.*

Ruby put down the candlestick and sat on the bed, arms around Hester's shoulders.

Her whispers were gentle and comforting. 'Never mind, Miss, it'll all be better soon. No wonder you're crying – what a day you've had, going off like that and then having to come back when poor Master was took bad . . . but never mind, I'll help you deal with everything. You just lie back and dry your tears and try to sleep. I'll sit here till you do.'

And then, as Hester stared aghast and tried to speak, she smiled, a big warm grin that took away all thought of words and persuaded Hester to drop back against the pillow, staring into the bright green eyes that looked so cheerful and unbelievably friendly. 'Yes, really, Hester. I wants to help you. After all, it's what I'm here for, only you don't know, do you?' Ruby pulled the eiderdown over Hester's shoulders and tucked her arms beneath it.

She sat there, still smiling, and then, very quietly, tried to explain. 'You see, when my ma was ill and knew she was going, she fished out this bit o' paper and give it me. "Your birth certificate," she said. "And look, there's no father's name cos you was born illegitimate, but see,

145

I've pencilled in his name just here – look – can you read it?" '

Ruby paused and slowly her smile disappeared. 'An' I could,' she went on. 'An' that's why I come here, Hester, to find you – and the Master – cos I wanted to find my own real place in the world. And, you see, I have . . . haven't I?'

CHAPTER SIXTEEN

A sob ceased in mid breath as Hester gasped. Somehow she pulled herself up, staring at Ruby's triumphant face. Her mind chased around like a merry-go-round, her breath quietening as those words filled her mind. What did Ruby mean?

In the silence binding them she looked into the wide green eyes and was amazed at what she saw there: familiarity, amusement, and then a look of something much more shocking. Power. 'Go on,' she said unsteadily. 'Tell me what you read – what it means.'

Like a torn cloth, the words ripped out. 'Your pa's my pa.'

Hester sucked in a huge breath, gaining the strength to consider this preposterous tale. She didn't believe it, of course not. Ruby was making up a story for her own ends. Father would *never.* . . . Surely, after Mother died, his need had not been so great? Hester's face tightened distastefully. Great enough to take advantage of a servant? She frowned, thinking back into her childhood and the name of the maid who was in the house then. Ruby was not yet seventeen, so it was easy, according to the date on the certificate, to work out that she herself had been four years of age at the time. *Think back to when Mother was alive. Mrs Caunter was here, but who was the housemaid?*

It came in a flash of memory. Ellen, a rather dumpy woman, a maid who was quick on her feet and always running around but who suffered with her breathing. Yes, she could still hear that wheeziness.

A terrible image struck Hester. Could Father really have crept up the attic stairs into snuffly Ellen's bed? The idea grew, pushing aside the disbelief. Had he fathered a child by Ellen? Impossible. But then more memories came, searing her mind: Ellen had suddenly left. Was

147

Ruby telling the truth, or was this just a wicked lie, intended to dig herself more firmly into the household?

Hester's chest grew tight. Was it a shameful ploy which would make Ruby a daughter of the Redding family, with all the benefits that such a position entailed?

My sister? She can't be. I don't believe a word of it.

Anger was a welcome relief. She glared at the small, triumphant face, and said harshly, 'You're lying. You're not my father's daughter, you're not my sister—'

'Half-sister,' Ruby cut in, cat-smile never fading. 'Ma said I'm your half-sister. The same pa, see, different mothers.'

Hester had no reply. She sat up very straight. For a moment neither of them moved, until slowly Ruby got off the bed, picked up her candlestick, and moved towards the door. She turned, looking back at Hester.

'Sorry you're upset. I heard you crying and I come down to comfort you – I mean, we're sisters. But you don't feel like that, do you?'

'No.' Hester spat out the word and watched Ruby's reaction. She expected sharpness and was unprepared for the self-satisfied smile which came instead.

'P'raps you'll think different in the morning. I hope you sleep all right. Good night, Hester.' Ruby slipped out of the room, firmly closing the door behind her.

Hester lay back, staring at the outline of the window. Outside a waxing moon shone brightly, and a breeze flapped the curtains. She heard an owl in the distance. Thoughts came racing; past memories, present shocks, future anxieties. Sleep eluded her for some time, but finally she drifted off, only to dream of spoiled gardens and ravaged flowers and creatures with gleaming eyes hunting her through the greenery.

Waking early, abruptly she faced the nonsense that Ruby had insisted was the truth. Was she Father's illegitimate daughter? His bastard child? Her sister? Ruby's words echoed, and she frowned; the girl had been so sure.

Sitting up in bed, something caught her eye: a crumpled sheet of what looked like a well-used official document on the bedside table.

Picking it up, knowledge came, sickening and sour. Ruby had come down again last night while she was asleep and put her birth certificate here.

She read it. Ellen Jones's name was clear and so was Ruby's. The mother's address was a back street in the poor part of Newton Abbot. Father's name? Not here – at least, not written in ink in the registrar's own forward sloping hand. No, just a couple of scribbled, pencilled words, misspelt, giving the vital information.

Arther Reding.

Hope filtered through Hester's dismay. This was surely added after the birth had been registered but was it legal? Suddenly she knew exactly what to do: take the document to Hugh and ask his professional advice. Dressing, she paused. He mustn't know exactly why she was asking – she certainly wouldn't show it to him. Think of the shame, of the social reactions if he said it were true. But it wasn't. Even so, she must have Hugh's advice. And if he said this pencilled scribble was illegal, then Ruby's cock-and-bull story could be thrown out of the window.

Heartened, Hester's spirits rose as she went about the morning duties of seeing to Father, helping Stepmother downstairs and waiting for breakfast to finish, at the same time avoiding Ruby's questioning glances and keeping her own eyes fixed on her plate.

When the household was settled, Hester put on her hat and told Stepmother she would be out for an hour. 'Stepmother, please tell Ruby to look after Father until I return. And I expect Dr Winters will be here soon. I shan't be long.'

She forced Hoskins to race the pony down the lanes, and once in Bovey Tracey she ran down the high street and into the Marchant, Marchant & Forrester offices.

'I must see Mr Hugh Marchant at once. . . .' The command in her voice was enough to open all doors, and Hugh quickly appeared.

His voice was friendly, his grin as easy as ever. 'Why, Hester, this is a very pleasant surprise. Taking me out to luncheon, perhaps? Or planning an afternoon's ramble on the moor? Luckily I'm not too busy at the moment. Come in and sit down.'

She whirled into his room and confronted him across the leather-topped desk.

'Hugh, I'm not here for any of those reasons. I need your advice.'

The smile faded slowly. 'Ask away. You know I'll do anything I can to help you, Hester. What's happened? Not bad news about your father, I trust?'

'No.' For a second she paused. Of course, it might well be bad news – but then she forced herself to think more positively. 'Is it legal to add a pencilled name to a birth certificate? A name that clearly hasn't been written by the registrar? Yes or no, Hugh.'

She held her breath and stared into his unblinking brown eyes.

He frowned and then said shortly, 'No, it's not legal.' The frown deepened as he leaned over the desk. 'What's all this about, Hester? I can't help unless you tell me the details.'

But she was up, running around the desk, throwing her arms around him, kissing his rather scratchy cheek and then heading for the door. 'Bless you, Hugh, you're wonderful. What would I have done without you? No, don't try and stop me, I have to rush back.' She gave him a last exuberant smile as he followed her to the door and watched her fly up the street, calling over her shoulder, 'Dr Winters is coming to see Father and I must be there. Goodbye.'

What a relief! Thank goodness! The shadows fell off her shoulders as she climbed into the trap and told Hoskins to hurry home. Now she could face that evil Ruby and tell her just what she thought of her. Hester smiled into the morning sunlight as the pony trotted down the lanes; she tightened her lips and planned to tell Ruby to leave. At once and without a character. *I can't wait to do so.*

Dr Winters was at Arthur Redding's bedside, his long face unsmiling as he turned to acknowledge Hester's arrival.

'I'm sorry I'm late, Doctor—'

'Your maid was here, Miss Redding. She had the good sense to bring Mrs Redding to sit with your father when he became restless. He's quieter now.' One hand on the invalid's pulse, Dr Winters consulted his watch, put it away and then gestured Hester towards the window. He stood, looking at her gravely. 'Your father is making rather slow progress, Miss Redding. I advise complete rest, and as much nourishing food as he will take, although I fear it may be difficult for him to swallow. Don't disturb him in any way and try to be cheerful when you are with him. Indeed, any scraps of good news you have would be beneficial. And a few gentle exercises to get the strength back into his arm and leg.'

She nodded, uneasily hearing a mournful warrant for her future in those words, but tried to add a note of optimism into her voice as she said, 'Yes, Doctor, I'll do all you say.'

'Don't bother to see me out. Perhaps you could sit with him for a short while. He wakes periodically and needs reassuring.' Another nod, and then a more cheery tone. 'Good morning, Miss Redding. I'll call again in a few days. But send me a message, should it be necessary.'

Hester let the warning run around her mind as the door closed and she was left alone with her father. Was he going to recover? Her thoughts circled, becoming personal. Forget Father – what about her own life? So much for leaving home, for starting a professional career, for exploring the world. Sitting on the bedside chair she looked at the pale, lined face lying on the pillow, and knew that she must be thankful for this chance to make up for her wickedness in causing Father's seizure.

Perhaps there might sometimes be a few spare minutes in which to think about painting, to sit down with a brush, her paintbox and some flowers, but then reality stepped in, and she knew that all her time was going to be filled. For there was Stepmother to care for as well as Father. The house must be run, the meals carefully organized. No time for flowers or painting them. She must forget that joyous and hopeful passion which had brought such plans, such dreams.

She sighed. And what about Ruby? She shook her head. All that mattered was that Father should recover, which meant that Ruby's horrible little plan must never be divulged. So how should she deal with the matter?

Downstairs the hall clock struck noon, and she got to her feet. Time to consult Mrs Caunter about a meal for the invalid. Time for sherry with Stepmother, while trying to make light of the terrible situation. Hester lifted her head, straightened her shoulders and felt a shift of thinking; time must be found today to have a stern talk with Ruby.

A showdown, that was what was needed. A few well-chosen words, piercing the evil bubble the girl had blown; then an apology would be demanded, and after that the inevitable dismissal. Hester was smiling as she went downstairs to the kitchen to suggest some beef broth or possibly steamed fish for Father.

And after luncheon – Ruby.

It was mid afternoon before the opportunity came to order the girl into the summerhouse, after ensuring that Father was asleep, that Stepmother was resting, and that nothing of any event would happen in the house for the next half hour or so. She met Ruby coming up from the kitchen, on her way to her bedroom to change into her teatime dress, apron and cap, and said briskly, 'Come with me, please, Ruby. I have something very important to say to you.'

Not waiting for a response, she led the way into the garden and then to the summerhouse, turning and facing the girl as she entered behind her.

'Now, about this birth certificate and the ridiculous idea that you are my father's natural daughter.' She saw Ruby's eyes widen, watched the small, bow-shaped mouth lose its attraction and become sharper, and realized this was not going to be the plain sailing she had envisaged. She hardened her voice. 'Ruby, the pencilled name of my father on your certificate does not' – she paused, and then repeated the word, louder – 'does *not* mean that there is any truth in your mother's claim about him being your father. It is not legal to add a name to a document. I have consulted a solicitor and verified the fact.'

Ruby gasped. And then came the words, rapid, unsteady, aggressive, the country burr more evident than usual. 'I don't believe it! You'm making it up. Just cos you'm a lady and I'm on'y a workin' girl you think you can get rid of me, well, you won't. I'm gonna tell everybody who I am. I don't care what your solicitor said, my ma said he was my pa, and that's what I believe. . . .'

Green fire shone out of her eyes and the small face set in a hard mask. Hester stared, shocked. She was unsure how to react, but then Ruby took a step nearer, so close that she was just a breath away.

'I'm gonna tell your pa – and your stepma – who I am,' she hissed. 'They'll believe me, even if you don't. You never liked me, always had

that high 'n' mighty sound in yer voice – Ruby this, Ruby that.' The
last words were shrill and ugly, and Hester shrank, stepping away
further into the summerhouse.

'I'm yer sister, I tell you, and you're gonna have to treat me
different.' Ruby's voice suddenly quietened, her smile triumphant.

They looked at each other, Hester open mouthed and searching for
words. Outside, in the garden, Hoskins passed, his wheelbarrow
squeaking, and Ruby glanced aside. 'Needs oiling that does. I'll tell
him – I shall give orders now.'

A shutter clicked open in Hester's bewildered mind, and abruptly
she knew exactly how to deal with this extraordinary situation.
'Ruby,' she said quickly, 'listen to me. We have to understand one
another. Yes, I know what you think of me, but you must see things
from my point of view, too. Now. . . .'

She eased herself into a chair and nodded at Ruby to do the same.
Slowly the girl obeyed, sitting straight and tense, eyes never leaving
Hester's face.

'I am telling you again that your mother's claim about my father is
illegal – it has no truth. This is hard for you, as obviously you've
dreamed of becoming his daughter.'

She paused. Ruby's face was drooping as her dreams slowly
shattered. The moment grew longer.

I know about shattered dreams. Hester softened her voice. 'Tell me
about your life before you came here.'

The girl stared. 'Why should I? You don't want to know, you on'y
wants to get rid of me.' But she leaned back, picking at her apron with
restless fingers.

Hester waited. 'Tell me, Ruby. Perhaps it will help me understand
why you were so ready to believe your mother's claim.'

'Well. . . .' A moment's pause and then, in a rush – 'I wasn't
schooled proper, like you was, but I can read and write. And I loved
my ma.' Ruby's eyes took on a faraway look and her voice grew
quieter. 'We was very poor, and we shared a room with another
family. And he, Mr Stevens, the man, was horrid. He frightened me.
He were like an animal. . . .' Stopping, she shook her head and stared
down at the dusty floor. Then, looking up, she met Hester's eyes. She
sniffed. A tear rolled down her cheek, she put up a hand and wiped it

153

away, gulped in a big breath, and sighed.

'Then Ma took ill and was going to be sent to the workhouse cos the landlord didn't want her dying there. That's when she give me the paper, and said as how I was his daughter an' if I come here I'd be made fer life.' The words died into a choking sob. 'An' I believed her.' Tears fell openly now.

Hester sat silently, her mind full of images, of pain-filled voices and of a young girl's dreams which would turn a sad, dreary life into a near-paradise. She found a handkerchief and passed it to Ruby.

Slowly she realized that this was a turning point in both their lives. No longer was there anger and resentment churning deep down, but a new sense of understanding. Perhaps she could take a step nearer to this girl, whose background had been so hard. 'Ruby,' she said, leaning forward in her chair and taking one of the girl's hands in her own. 'Thank you for telling me. I can see how you hoped to make a better life for yourself—'

Ruby pulled her hand away, folded the damp handkerchief into a neat parcel, and then looked at her. Hester saw surprise and a softening of the bitterness that moments before had made the small face so hard and unlikeable. There was a new note in the girl's voice as she whispered, 'That was it, I was taking a step away from all that nasty stuff in town – I was coming into a new world. An' I like it here, you see. Like the Master and Mistress. Why—' Suddenly a bright, almost saucy grin lifted the tear-stained face. 'Even Mrs Caunter's not so bad when you gets used to her. An' I want to stay here, learn to run the house, learn a few ladylike things from you, Miss, sewing and stuff, but now—' Ruby sighed, slowly stood up, looking down with a bleak frown. 'Now you wants to put me off, don't you?'

A moment of inner truth, of rapid decision and of new hope. 'No, Ruby, I want you to stay. Sit down again, listen to me. . . .'

They sat in silence, looking at each other while Hester's mind began to outline the way ahead. 'Dr Winters has told me, Ruby, that my father must not be disturbed in any way. He is still very ill. So it's important – very important – that you don't upset him by telling him what you believed. Can you imagine how much worse he might become if you did tell him?'

Ruby nodded and in Hester's busy mind a flickering light showed itself. She went on. 'I need you here, Ruby, because I have to do too much, all by myself – look after my father, care for my stepmother, as well as running the house and making sure that my father has every possible opportunity to recover.' She stopped, thoughts awhirl. If Ruby could spend time sitting with Father, talking cheerfully to Stepmother, might there not be a few hours in which painting could be returned to? Her voice was firm. 'Yes, I want you to stay, but, Ruby, you must promise me – and it will last for ever – that you will keep secret all this business about the birth certificate and what your mother believed.'

Her hands locked as tension grew. She knew that what she was planning was right. Indeed, it was the only way out of the extraordinary situation. *Father must never know – and everything depends on Ruby.*

It seemed for ever but was really only a moment before Ruby answered, reluctantly, Hester thought, but in a voice growing stronger with each word. 'All right, Miss. I promise. I don't want poor Master – or Mistress – to get worse, you see.' She raised her head and Hester saw a hint of the old familiar assured look come back into her eyes. 'But I wants to be a bit freer, Miss. Like being able to do things to make life easier in this ole house. Do things my own way. And the dumb waiter – the lift? Now that really would be a big help.'

A bargain. So that was it. Hester found a smile: was it amusement or cynical acceptance? What had she expected? Certainly not this, but then why not? The practical side of her character came to the fore as she assessed the possible situation. Ruby was sensible, a good worker and she was showing fondness for her employers. Build on this, said her instinct, so she allowed her smile to grow warmer. 'Very well, Ruby, I agree to that. I'll let you have a freer hand with the housework. But remember your promise and let's both pray for my father's complete recovery.'

She stood up, looking into Ruby's now grinning face, wondering if there could possibly be any sign of her father's familiar features. Surely not . . . but she knew that there would always be an unfounded doubt in her mind. Smothering a sigh, she said, 'It must be time for tea. Hurry up and change, Ruby, while I see if my father needs anything. And then we'll have tea in the drawing room, if you please.'

She could only wonder at the way things had turned out. Was she really right in allowing Ruby to stay? But they had agreed, and it was too late now to change her mind.

Ruby stepped out of the summerhouse. 'Yes, Miss Hester,' she said, walking away towards the house and not looking back.

CHAPTER SEVENTEEN

The days were wearisome, slow-moving copies of each other. Hester watched her father's symptoms, trying to decide if he was deteriorating or improving. Dr Winters visited and said it was a matter of time, but gave no idea of whether time would bring good health or permanent weakness.

And then there was the still almost unbelievable business of Ruby and her growing self-confidence. 'I'll watch the Master this morning, Miss.' Ruby never gave Hester her full title now. 'I s'pec you'd like to spend time with poor Mistress. She's got friends calling this afternoon.' Ruby's eyes were full of new, unsettling authority. 'You'll be there, o' course, won't you?'

Hester found herself nodding in agreement and then redeeming black humour allowed her to smile, and she went into the garden for five easing minutes to look at the early summer flowers; especially to admire the gentian, now producing buds and seeming to be a bluer blue than she could ever describe in words or painting shades. Cerulean blue, Madonna blue, perhaps? And then she remembered Nicholas Thorne and his brilliant eyes, until she told herself that there was no time to stand and dream, no time and no hope. Duty called and she could only obey. So back to the house and the next dreary, time-consuming task.

But one night, Hester rebelled. In the quiet house, suddenly her thoughts struck out, firing sharp resentment. Where was her youth? She needed brightness and adventure and fun. *I feel old, old before my time*. Alive with self-pity she walked down to Brook Cottage as the evening sun began to set. The hedges were full, with grasses brushing her side and trees casting heavy shadows on the lane ahead of her. She became calmer with every step, as scents, sounds and the joy of being in the fresh air infiltrated her weary and tense body.

She had slipped out of the house after dinner; Stepmother was drowsing in the drawing room and Ruby promised to keep an eye on her. Father had eaten very little for his supper, but was now sleeping. Since his seizure he had had small but regular moments of consciousness, and whenever he saw Hester at his side had managed a stiff smile. Gentle exercises seemed to be strengthening his limbs and once he had even tried to sit up.

Hester tried to block out the anguish of his illness, telling herself that it was imperative to recoup some of her energy and strength which the emotional, tiring days drained from her. She looked forward to being with Aunt Jacks, perhaps to be stimulated into a more positive mood. Her aunt was not one for moping, and just being with her helped so much.

She tried to become more sanguine about the future. As she walked she looked at the long lines of Dartmoor in the distance, fading into purple shadows as the sun set, the lower stretches of green landscape slipping into bosky half light.

She paused at the gate, feeling suddenly free, uplifted and young again until she felt again the shock and despair of the last few days. The extraordinary conversation with Ruby echoed, and once more she felt herself slipping back into anxiety, but the evening scents, Dartmoor's wild presence etched against the western sky, and the wonder of the flowers in Aunt Jacks' garden brought a gift of new hope. She smiled. Father would recover. And she would come to terms with the end of her dreams. Then, as she opened the gate, her mind struck a new bargain: *I'm doing what I know I must do but I will find time to paint. Somehow. . . .*

Aunt Jacks was talking in the kitchen. Hester called, 'May I come in?' The voices ceased, the kitchen door opened and Nicholas Thorne stood there.

A moment of silence. 'Nicholas,' she said unsteadily, 'I didn't expect to find you here.'

No longer the untidy, earth-stained gardener in the familiar dun clothes, now he wore a dark suit; his shirt was white and the stiff collar crept up his tanned throat, emphasizing the deep-cut features of his lean face and the brilliance of his eyes.

'I have business with your aunt.' He smiled, held out a hand and drew her into the kitchen. She relished the hardness of the long fingers, the warmth that rocketed through her, bringing relief and the ending of all the recent worries and shocks.

Her breath quickened. This was a sudden magical moment, and she sensed they shared something warm and intimate – until Aunt Jacks broke the silence. 'Hester, I was hoping you might come around. But you still look very pale. I shall get you a glass of my cowslip wine – that should perk you up a bit. Come and sit down.' She got to her feet and looked back. 'Nicholas, find some glasses in the dresser, will you, please?'

Hester watched her disappear into the big larder, leaving them alone for a few precious moments. She must let him know what his presence meant to her. What could she say? No words came; her mind was just full of this huge, blissful happiness. She pressed his hand and he drew her close.

'Hester.' His voice was quiet. 'What can I do to help you? Anything – anything at all.'

She smiled, allowing the feeling of freedom to blossom even further. 'No one can do anything, Nicholas, thank you. We just wait and hope.' She paused while he collected glasses and put them on the table. He looked at her again, and she said, her joy only half concealed, 'It's good to see you again.'

And then Aunt Jacks was back, pouring out the wine and holding up her glass. 'To happier days. To your poor father, Hester, and to you, Nicholas, on your new expedition.'

Hester sipped her wine, feeling her happiness somehow diminished. What expedition was this? Carefully, she asked, 'Where are you going, Nicholas?'

He put down his glass. 'Nothing is certain yet, but Miss Watson – you remember her?'

Hester nodded. She would never forget the formidable woman and her inspiring advice.

'Miss Watson has asked if I would accompany her on her next trip. June this year is a possibility, but it could be later.' He avoided her gaze and looked at Aunt Jacks. 'Which is why I'm here, to ask Mrs Jacks' advice about finding someone to help in the nursery while I'm away.' He looked back at Hester. 'I can't leave my father on his own, with just an apprentice, and because Mrs Jacks knows so many people I've come for her advice.'

'I see.' Disappointment coursed through her. He hadn't come in the hope of seeing her – she should be ashamed for even thinking such a thing. He was a businessman, a professional gardener; he had so much to fill his life, it was amazing that he remembered her at all. She took another sip of the wine and managed a hard, bright smile. 'I'm sure whoever my aunt suggests will be right for you and your father.'

He was watching her. 'Thank you. There should be no problem. Mrs Jacks' reputation will ensure that.' A pause, then he added, 'My father is anxious that you should continue painting his flowers. Is there any hope that you might return to the nursery?'

She took a breath, trying to sort out the thoughts going round and round. 'I should love to continue. Please tell your father and thank him for his trust in me – but life is difficult at the moment.'

Aunt Jacks cut in very firmly. 'Even so, you need some time to yourself, child. Surely an hour during the day could be managed? Get that servant of yours – Ruby – to take over some of your tasks. She seems a reliable girl and she can keep an eye on your father. Get back to your work, Hester, you really must.'

Hester sat back in her chair, thoughts racing. A few hours a day to paint at home or – her heart leaped – to go to the nursery, where Mr Hayward and Nicholas would welcome her back. Ruby would be with Father, Stepmother might hopefully be resting – could she do it?

'Yes.' Her smile blossomed. 'I'll arrange it somehow, Aunt.'

Nicholas was looking at her, his eyes darkening. She turned to him. 'I might manage to come for a short while.'

'Whatever time you can find would be very welcome.' The words were formal, but Hester saw the glow of warmth illuminating his face. He waited, smiled and added, very quietly, 'We will look forward to seeing you again soon, Miss Hester.'

Then, abruptly, he got to his feet. 'Time I was off. Thank you, Mrs Jacks. I'll tell my father that you'll be sending him some suggestions shortly. Miss Hester—' He looked down at her. 'May I escort you home? Or is your groom coming to collect you later?'

'No, I shall walk back. Thank you.' Hester rose, excitement surging. They would be together, alone, for that short walk up the lane. She smiled at her aunt. 'Dear Aunt, thank you for the wine and the advice, and I'm sorry I can't stay longer. But I'll come again soon.'

'Far more important to spend your free time painting, my dear,' said Aunt Jacks firmly. 'Well, goodbye, and my love to your father and your stepmother. Tell them I'll visit when I can – but the garden keeps me busy these days.'

Hester and Nicholas set out into the twilight, closing the gate of Brook Cottage behind them, and heading up the lane towards Oak House. Shadows abounded, and all around the evocative night scents drifted in great wafts of perfume. They didn't speak, but Hester felt a bond between them and wasn't surprised when Nicholas stopped beside a field gate, stretched up and picked a spray of golden honeysuckle.

Silent, she waited, suddenly aware that since their first meeting they had been instinctively waiting for each other and now, for this one brief moment, they were together.

He took her hand, drew it to his mouth, opened the warm, willing palm and kissed it before pressing the flower into her fingers. 'For you, Hester,' he whispered. 'I don't know whether we shall ever meet again – possibly not, because I understand your family duties are so many – but my house is lonely without you and I look forward to the day when you can return and finish the paintings you started for my father.'

She looked at the flower, then leaned her head against his chest. What he had done and said was so wonderful that she could make no response, except to look up at him, putting all her heart into her smile.

Their kiss was tentative, Nicholas just brushing his warm lips against hers, but then, as she leaned closer, it became stronger, his mouth passionate, making demands which she felt herself responding to. The moment stretched but she ended it, stepping away, wanting more, but knowing it must not be so.

He was looking at her, eyes as dark as lapis lazuli, she thought, no longer the untroubled blue of summer skies; his hands were warm and strong around her body. 'Hester?' A low, almost inaudible question which she couldn't – mustn't – answer.

From deep inside she found the strength to return to reality, forcing her voice to be firm and steady. 'Thank you for the honeysuckle. You're always giving me flowers. First the bastard balm, then the gentian and now this.'

Perhaps he recognized the finality in her voice. He stepped back. 'Is the gentian growing?'

They were back to normal friendship. Hester began walking away and heard him follow. Over her shoulder she said, 'Very well. It's a beautiful plant.' Why was she behaving like this? They had kissed, he had said he missed her, but he had also said they might never meet again. What did it all mean?

'Gentians,' he said, in a firmer voice, 'are very attractive plants. And perhaps, somewhere, there might even be a double one.'

'How splendid that would be.' It was all over, that magical moment of shared pleasure, and now she was back in her dreary life. At the entrance to Oak House he suddenly, almost roughly, took her hand. 'Hester, we must meet again – somehow.'

She turned, saw a longing in his eyes that touched her heart, but had no idea how to reply. And then, abruptly, it was finished. Horses' hoofs were trotting down the lane, a trap was reined in, and Hugh Marchant stared down at them.

'Hester? What are you doing out here? And who the hell are you, sir?'

She heard the arrogance, the rising anger, and said sharply, 'Hugh, this is Nicholas Thorne, who has escorted me home from Aunt Jacks' cottage.' She turned. 'Nicholas, this is my friend, Hugh Marchant.'

There was a charged silence while the two men appraised each other. Then, grudgingly, Hugh said, 'Good of you, Thorne, to bring her home. But I'll take her into the house now – no need to delay you any further.'

Hester said nothing. She watched Nicholas smile wryly, nod his acknowledgement, then bade her a cool good night, turning and walking rapidly away, disappearing into the shadows, his footsteps the last memory of his presence.

'What do you want, Hugh?' she asked wearily, climbing up on to the seat beside him.

'To see you, of course. To ask after your father.' He paused. Then, curtly, 'Hester, you shouldn't be out at this time of night, alone. And ought I to know that fellow?'

Driving up to the entrance of the house, she smiled wryly. 'No, Hugh, you wouldn't know him. He's a plantsman, a professional nurseryman.'

'A gardener? Good God! The impudence of the man, being out here, alone with you at this time of night.'

She was too tired, too full of emotion, to argue. 'Never mind. Now come in and sit down. I suppose you want to talk?'

He handed her down from the trap as if, she thought resentfully, he imagined he already possessed her. He smiled. 'Of course I do, dear Hester. And you know what I'm going to talk about, don't you?'

She did. The subject was always the same. How proper it would be, how wonderful, for them to marry. He would look after her, relieve her burdens, give her prosperity and affection. Her father would be pleased: indeed, their engagement might help his recovery. Again and again, he asked, would she marry him? And although she always gave the same answer – *thank you, Hugh, but no* – her tired mind was slowly accepting that perhaps one day, with life controlling her instead of the other way around, she might be well advised to say yes instead.

Nicholas Thorne walked back to town very fast, his thoughts racing. So that was the man whom local gossip linked with Hester. The new boy, joining the old, well-established law firm. Of course, what could be more suitable than that Hester should marry this Hugh Marchant? He had everything to offer: excellent prospects, family connections and a good lifestyle. She would be foolish not to accept him.

His footsteps slowed as he entered the nursery garden. All was quiet, only Mrs Kent's cat emerging from the shadows to rub against his legs as he walked to the front door. He entered the still house, his thoughts unfocused, and then went into the office. A moon nearly at its full shone cold light through the uncurtained window and immediately his eyes looked at the table in the curve of the bay. He had removed Hester's painting and taken her equipment back to

Brook Cottage, but still something of her remained. Her breath. Her smile.

He lingered by the window, wondering what was happening to him. Those moments alone with her had been rare and precious. The sweet fragrance of the honeysuckle crushed in her warm hand would now always haunt him. And her uplifted, beautiful face, turned to him, inviting, welcoming. He would never forget, never be free of the memory of their kiss.

But he must. A plantsman, a professional nurseryman, yes, that was all he was. No model for the husband of a girl brought up in a higher echelon of life. He stared through the window, thoughts circling in great painful drifts as he tried to come to terms with what he knew he must do.

Go away. Leave her to live her own life while he continued his plant collecting. Contact Emily Watson and ask for details of the expedition. She had mentioned the possibility of going in June, this year. Well, returning to the mountains would take him back to the debt he knew he owed Jonathon West. And perhaps those hard trails through valleys and up dangerous crags with their enticing new plants would relieve the pain that trying to forget Hester was causing.

Tomorrow he would write to Emily. In the morning, his thoughts would be calmer and the words would come. He went up to his bed, aware of a presence following him up the stairs, standing by the window, looking into the garden, and then, just as sleep hit him, turned and looked back at him.

Closing his eyes, he muttered, *Let me be, Hester. For both our sakes I must forget you. Just let me be. . . .*

In the morning the sunlight showed a small room with a bed, a table, a chair and a washbasin. No haunting shadow by the window. No welcoming, arousing smile. He washed and dressed quickly, went downstairs and out into the garden. The nursery beds needed attention, young Jim had scamped the weeding. And he must talk to his father about the next expedition. His father would complain, of course, but Mrs Jacks would suggest a suitable man to take his place. He bent over the alpine rockery and stared at the row of gentians, before turning away and moving on to the next task.

There was so much to do, and thank God for it.

164

The post came early but already Nicholas was at work in the nursery beds, inspecting, nurturing, assessing and almost, but not quite, lost in his concentration. The click of the closing gate alerted him to the postal delivery, and something made him stride back into the house. Perhaps there would be word from Emily Watson. He knew now, clear and plain, that he must leave Newton as soon as possible.

A couple of business letters, some early autumn catalogues, and a large packet with a London postmark. Curiously, he opened it first, realizing at once that this was some of the dried foliage of recorded plants occasionally sent to him by his contact at the Royal Botanic Gardens at Kew. He had met young Alan Meacham last time he was in London, before setting out on the expedition to the Dolomites, and Alan had promised to inform him of the new plants which collectors were regularly bringing back to Kew. As well as seeds, they brought with them the dried plants for storage in the herbarium, to be sorted out and recorded in large books. Alan Meacham had said that sometimes unusual plant foliage found its way into the material being recorded, and if there were any alpines which might interest the nursery, he would send examples.

His note was brief. 'Thought you would be interested to see this. It came back a few months ago with some new plants from the Dolomites. Looks like a different form of gentian. I know there is talk of doubles, but I doubt if this is what they are thinking of. Anyway, I'm sure you'll enjoy having a look at it. Look me up next time you're in London.'

Nicholas let the note slip out of his fingers. His eyes fixed on the anonymous beige straw-like foliage that slid out of its encompassing envelope. Yes, it was a gentian, no doubt about it. But – a double? For a second his heartbeat increased, but then the professional side of his nature took over. *Don't get too excited. There are only tales about doubles, nothing of any proof. This may well look like a double but. . . .*

He turned it over in his hands, found a magnifier with which to inspect any tiny verification of double growth, and then put the dried-up material back in its container. Nothing there to prove it was anything but a slightly offbeat gentian; perhaps a throwback to an old ancestor, long since extinct, with no future to it.

But. . . .

Again his heart raced. And suddenly, all the old guilt about Jon's death, the pain of knowing he and Hester could never be together, left him. He was a new man with a new future. He would go with Emily on the next expedition; she had mentioned June, which meant they could be there in July, which was the time a double gentian would bloom. *If there was one.*

Hurriedly, he pushed aside the rest of the unopened post, took a pen and began a letter to Emily.

Dear Miss Watson

I am in receipt of some important new information about the possibility of finding the legendary double gentian in the northern Italian mountains. Of course it may mean nothing, but I hope to find definite proof or not of its possible existence. Therefore, as before, I offer you my services in the expedition you are planning, and hope to travel to London to make final arrangements with you very soon.

I trust you keep well, and look forward to seeing you again.

Yours sincerely, Nicholas Thorne

He rose, sealed the envelope, walked out of the house and posted the letter. Suddenly the world was new and he felt as if a miracle had remade his life. Yes, from now on he would be forever lonely, but perhaps that was what destiny had in store for him. To plough his solitary path, and ignore this burning, yet hopeless, need for Hester's love.

CHAPTER EIGHTEEN

Ruby looked around her small bedroom and pursed determined lips. She was at the top of one of the two turreted gables of the house which, although certainly handsome seen from outside, were cramped, stuffy and extremely uncomfortable. Look at those sloping ceilings – she had often knocked her head when leaning down to make the bed. Stand up straight and – bash.

The high window offered a slight consolation, looking down into the vegetable garden, but the chimney stack at the side of the window had a very unfriendly appearance. Dirty bricks, bird droppings all over it, and those old jackdaws forever clacking away.

She had made the room as pretty as she could. Rain still seeped through worn lime wash, making stains under the window, but she had some nice things to look at. The patchwork cushion, recently finished, and admired by Mistress, decorated her little iron bedstead. Miss Hester's picture was pinned on the wall and gave Ruby a lesson in determination every time she looked at it. The dandelion stood erect, its mind clearly on its next step. Nothing could impede the growth of that flower. What had Miss Hester said? Affinity. It was a word Ruby liked and she wondered if it applied to her and the dandelion. And that moth creature on the stem – that suggested something growing and finally flying away. Just like her, really.

She knew that stepping out into the future was important, but where and when? Since Master's seizure last week, and that horrid conversation with Miss Hester, her plans had gone awry. So she wasn't Master's daughter after all. Grudgingly, she supposed a lawyer had to be right. And Ma had spelled Master's name wrong on the paper, which hadn't helped. But Ma had been very funny in her last days.

So that left her just where she was, housemaid with no prospects. Slowly, Ruby grinned. Ah, but she would make some. Looking around, she came to a vital decision. She wouldn't stay here, perched up beside Mrs Caunter's equally miserable room, from which every trumpeting snore disturbed her own sleep. Ruby nodded her head. There was an empty guest room downstairs. It was time to make a move.

Even in her worst moments, she had always seen the light at the end of the tunnel. Very well, if she couldn't be the new daughter of the household, she'd be something else. Her smile flowered, imagining herself as Mistress's companion. A step up into a better life. More freedom, more enjoyment, fewer orders and hard work.

Sitting on her bed, Ruby saw herself dressed in new clothes. A companion was higher than a house servant and would always be with Mistress, meeting new people, watching how they lived and behaved and dressed, hearing how they talked. She might even meet a nice young man. Not that she was keen to marry – the marriages she had seen mostly ended in drink and rough houses, with children growing up neglected and miserable.

No, she'd be happy to settle down here, running the household, giving orders to Mrs Caunter and the new maid who would take her own place downstairs, and, yes, all this while she would be sitting with Mistress, doing her sewing and generally behaving like a lady.

Like a lady. But she'd never be like Hester, would she? Hester was so pretty, elegant and strong-minded, and these days, since the business of the birth certificate, seemed to be more friendly. She admired Hester but had doubts about her future. Would she marry Hugh Marchant? But what about the gardener, the big man with the lovely voice?

Ruby got up, saw that her dark afternoon dress was tidy, her apron and white starched cap was straight. She admired herself in the cracked mirror and then went down the wooden stairs to Master's bedroom, where she knocked, then entered and sat by his bedside for five minutes before going to the kitchen and getting the tea ready.

She liked these easy, caring duties. At the beginning she had planned to tell him about the birth certificate, to watch his face when she said who she was, but that wasn't possible now. Firstly, she had promised Hester she would keep silent; secondly, her feelings for this pale figure lying beneath unmoving bedclothes had become warmer, even if he wasn't the father she had hoped to confront. Now the idea of shocking and hurting him had quite gone.

She sat by his bedside, planning the new wardrobe a companion would require. When Mr Redding suddenly opened his eyes, looked up at her and frowned, it was a surprise. She bent over him. 'Can I get you something, Master?'

His face moved, cracked lips trying to open and close until finally he said in a faint voice, 'Miss Hester. Where's Miss Hester?'

'In her room, painting. Shall I get her?' A weak nod. She got up, dampened his lips with a cloth wrung out from the bowl of water on the table, and then left the room, knocking at Hester's door and saying urgently, 'Master wants you, Miss. He's awake, talking. Shall I bring him a cup of tea?'

Hester roused from deep concentration, brush poised over the flower she was painting. A newly picked gentian had replaced the one she destroyed; its petals were coloured in, bluest of blue, and she was painting the tiny figure of a caterpillar nibbling one of the green fleshy leaves below the flower. It was necessary to work hard, denying other unhappy, resentful thoughts and instead focusing on the painting.

During the days since she had last seen Nicholas, her mind had taken in, considered and finally, very painfully, accepted the new plan of her life. She would not continue painting at the nursery; it would be agony to see him again. She must forget she had ever met him. Difficult, but instead she must be grateful for Hugh's interest and his help during these awful days of Father's illness.

Would marrying Hugh be so awful? They would honeymoon in the south of France, he had said, where she could find wild flowers; he would make her a studio in the house he contemplated buying and there would be a groom and a trap for visiting Father every day. She frowned and the dreams grew darker. Everything depended on Father's recovery; she could not leave him and so she had written to

Mr Hayward explaining that she could not spare time to continue painting for him. He had responded with a scribbled note saying: *All right, I expect Flynn can find someone else. Hope your father gets better soon.*

That had brought disappointment and spoiled pride; would someone else be as good as she was? But flower painting was a popular hobby. Of course he would find someone else. But then anger rose. *But I'm not just a flower painter – I'm a botanical artist.*

The decision taken, she now managed short spells of time in the afternoons painting. The flora was no longer attractive, but when, this morning, she saw another gentian in the garden, memory had forced her to pick it without further thought. This painting would hold all her love and her shattered dreams. She was devoting her attention, her technical knowledge and all her creative instinct to making this a painting that would stay with her for the rest of her life.

When Ruby knocked, she didn't, for a few seconds, understand. But then the demands of everyday life returned and she put down her brush. 'Yes, Ruby, bring up some tea. I'll go to Father.'

He was looking at the door with new interest in his eyes, and a patch of colour on pale cheeks. 'Hester. I must talk to you.'

'I don't think you should do too much, Father. Dr Winters said you needed rest.'

'Winters is an old fool.' There was a familiar rasp in the breathless voice. 'I'm not going to lie here and die – things to do. Help me sit up.'

With an arm around his shoulders, she arranged an extra pillow and held his shaking hand. 'What do you want to talk about, Father?'

'About you. And me.' He looked at her with a feverish intensity that scared her.

'Please, don't force yourself.'

Shaking his head, he closed his eyes, sucked in a breath and kept looking at her. 'I've been away – I've learned a lot. Lying here, thinking, I know I was wrong. I've denied you all you asked for. Freedom, happiness. My dear daughter, you are a blessing to me. I'm fortunate to have you. But. . . .' The breath ran out and he panted, lying back, eyes closed.

Ruby knocked and brought in a tray of tea. She exchanged glances with Hester and said, 'Pour out, shall I, and bring a cup over to Master?'

Hester nodded. Her father's apparent relapse into overwhelming weakness worried her. She took the cup Ruby offered, and gently helped her father drink. 'Sip this, Father. I'll hold the cup steady.'

It was a slow business, but when Ruby brought over a plate with a slice of Victoria sponge, topped with cream and jam, the patient nodded and managed a mouthful or two before lying back again, eyes closed, breath abruptly rattling in his chest.

Anxiously, Ruby came to Hester's side. 'Shall I tell Hoskins to get the doctor?'

Hester said a slow no, but suddenly Arthur Redding opened his eyes, stared from face to face, and said in a stronger voice, 'Tell the maid to go. We must talk.'

Hester looked at Ruby and nodded. 'Give Mrs Redding her tea, please, Ruby. I'll stay here.' She was encouraged at the warmth in the girl's eyes, and smiled as she left the room.

'What is it you want to say, Father?'

'I would be happy . . . for you . . . to continue painting, Hester.' His eyes were fixed on her face. 'I've been away – seems like years. Empty and frightening. Made me understand how one needs a busy life – a satisfactory life. And if I can't have that myself, I want you to have one. You must paint, Hester. Express your passion, use your talent. And if you can't do so at home, then I'll help you to go wherever you choose.' The words died away, his eyes closed and sleep descended on his still body. Hester held his hand. There were tears in her eyes, and her mind was in turmoil.

What had he meant? Where had he been? Fearfully, she imagined the black depths his collapse had taken him to, and despair racked her, but then his words echoed in her head, and the true meaning of all he had so painfully forced himself to say became clearer.

At last Father was showing his love and his new understanding of what she longed to do with her life. He was encouraging her to renew her shattered dreams. For a second her breath stopped; now she could become an artist after all. As he drifted into deeper sleep, she sat beside him, new thoughts creating ideas, plans and hopes. Could she go back to Mr Hayward? And then the nightmare of loving yet losing

Nicholas thundered in; no, she must not do that. She would paint here, working as hard as the household's demands allowed her. She would be with Father, watch him slowly recover until he was downstairs again, shifting his old papers in the library and giving her his approval as she brought down the day's work to be assessed, even perhaps admired.

She was smiling, building this new world, when Ruby knocked at the door and said, 'Mrs Redding's in a state – can you come down, Miss?' And then, again, all the old fears and anxieties rushed in. She looked at her father, sleeping quietly, put his hand, which she had been holding, beneath the covers, and left the room.

Another worry. Another problem to be resolved. When would it all end?

Stepmother certainly was in a state. In her usual chair, she was a trembling bundle of tears and sobs. She had spilt her tea down her lap and, despite Ruby's vigorous drying and rubbing of the maroon silk dress, was sitting there looking for all the world, thought Hester, like a girl she'd once seen in the doorway of the workhouse.

'Come along, Stepmother, come upstairs and change your dress. Give me your arm. . . .' Hester raised an eyebrow at Ruby, hovering beside the chair, and together they managed to raise the small woman, take her out of the drawing room and up the curving staircase.

Ruby glanced at Hester. 'Wish the new lift went all the way upstairs,' she murmured dryly. 'Madam would like that.'

Hester was too busy sorting out her thoughts to reply, but she registered the change in Ruby's tone. She was even more familiar these days. Yet, as they reached the top stair, she admitted that life without Ruby would be extremely hard. She was always there, offering help, sometimes muttering unwelcome advice, but ready to assist in any way asked, and so good with Stepmother.

As if sharing her thoughts, Emma leaned against Ruby as they entered the bedroom, looking up at the girl's bright young face. 'Dear Ruby, what would I do without you?' she murmured.

Ruby smiled, and Hester saw the green eyes suddenly widen and shine as if the sun had touched them. But then they were both busy undressing Emma, and the moment was filled with unlacing corsets, removing camisoles, enclosing Emma in her wrapper and consigning the sodden dress to the floor. Ruby glanced at it. 'I specs it'll wash out. I'll see to it later.' She helped Emma lie down on her bed, folding the eiderdown over her, and said, 'You rest there for a bit, Madam, before dinner and I'll get you a nice drink that'll help you sleep. I'll be back in a minute.'

Hester, folding cast-off clothes onto a chair, watched the interplay of expressions between her stepmother and the maid. Emma smiled, her eyes following Ruby's every movement. When the door closed behind her, Emma turned her watery smile onto Hester, whispering, 'Such a good girl. She looks after me, you know.'

And so do I. But the sharp comment was unspoken. Hester said quietly, 'Shall I sit with you, Stepmother?'

Emma nodded, her eyes drooping. 'Until Ruby comes back.'

Sitting there, Hester thought over her father's change of heart. She felt calmer than usual, but knew there were still obstacles to overcome. Should she tell Emma what he had said? Would the nervous little woman really want to know? It seemed, thought Hester, wryly, that all Emma needed in life was to have Ruby running around caring for her. So she watched silently until Emma's face relaxed into peace of mind, and she dozed.

Even when Ruby appeared with a tall glass of pale liquid, Emma slept on.

'What's in that?' Hester asked, gesturing at the drink.

'Chamomile tea. Hoskins told me 'tis good for calming you down, so I thought that Mistress might try it.'

Ruby put down the glass, staying at the bedside, watching Emma's drowsy face, and Hester wondered at the idea that had suddenly slipped into her mind. 'Come outside, Ruby,' she said, 'there's something I want to ask you.'

The girl hesitated. 'But Madam—'

'It will only take a few minutes.' Hester paused. 'Have you time to sit with her after tea, Ruby? She's quieter when you're there.'

'Yes, o' course. And, well, Miss, I did wonder. . . .' Ruby bit her lip, but her expression was sharper than words and Hester wondered if they were sharing the same thought.

Outside the bedroom, on the landing, they looked at each other with veiled expressions.

'I suggest you should be Mrs Redding's own maid, Ruby – which would mean we must get someone else for the rest of the work. What do you think?'

Even as she said it, Hester was astounded at herself for offering Ruby a better situation. Was it really such a good idea? But the expression on Ruby's face banished the doubts. 'It's jest what I been hoping for, Miss. I'm that fond of Madam – and Master, too – and if I could have the time to really look after her . . . oh yes, be her companion, well, yes please, Miss!' The high voice was joyous and Hester felt her own sad thoughts flying upwards to share such lightheartedness.

'Very well. I know you'll care for her as well as you can, Ruby. Being a companion means, of course, that you must be with her at any time that she wants you.'

'I know. And I'll be there. But, Miss, I don't want to be up in that hot ole attic any more – not now that I've got such a better situation. What about me moving down into the guest room? It'd be more like the room for a companion, don't you think?'

'Moving down?' Hester found it hard to keep up with this rushing outburst of new ideas. *Yes, she will need to be near Stepmother's bedroom, and we don't often have guests these days.* 'All right, Ruby. I'll see about it. When the man has finished working on the lift he can come and help rearrange the furniture in the second guest room.'

Ruby's face was flushed, her smile enormous. 'Oh, and Miss, I can't wear this ole stuff when I'm a companion – I'll need a nice new dress and things. I mean, I've gotta look tidy and smart if I'm to be with Madam and her friends.'

This is getting out of control, thought Hester, but she felt part of Ruby's excitement. Youth demanded this sort of passion, as she knew only too well. She felt it herself, so often. And how wonderful that Stepmother would be looked after, leaving the time usually spent with her to be given to her painting.

'Very well, Ruby. I'll see to all these things. But I think you should spend one more evening helping Mrs Caunter with the dinner and tomorrow I'll go to the agency in town and engage a new maid.'

They looked at each very directly, and Hester felt something new had grown between them. In a flash, she wondered if Ruby really was her sister. But commonsense returned. That was all behind them. What mattered now was that Ruby would be more responsible for looking after Stepmother, which meant she would have time to paint. She closed her eyes, blinking away the hot tears of excitement which threatened. And then opened them again. Ruby was staring at her, face full of understanding.

'Miss,' Ruby whispered, 'are you all right? You look – well, sort of . . . funny.'

Hester was laughing – so good to laugh – and wiping her eyes, then lifting her hands as if to embrace Ruby, but then stopped and let them drop down. 'I know – I feel funny! I feel . . . oh, I can't describe how I feel, but I know I can get back to painting now, and it's wonderful.'

Ruby's expression brightened. 'Of course you can. And, Miss, I've got another idea – why don't you have your studio out there, in the summerhouse? Roger, the lift man, he could do some work there, make it nice for you. What d'you think?'

Amazed, Hester drew in a breath. Where did Ruby get all these ideas from? She smiled, laughed again and nodded. 'I think that would be splendid. I'll talk to him tomorrow. And now – why, it's nearly dinner time. Please ask Mrs Caunter to give my father something tempting tonight; he was seeming so much better earlier this afternoon, and we must feed him up.'

Hester was changing her dress prior to having dinner with Stepmother when Ruby knocked at her door. 'Mr Hugh's here, Miss,' she said. 'Wants to see you – just for a moment he said. Won't stay. . . .' The grin on her face made Hester wonder exactly how much Ruby knew about her private life. She said sharply, 'Thank you. Ask him to wait in the drawing room – I'll be down in a few minutes. Perhaps he would like to share a drink with Mrs Redding – offer him one, please, Ruby.' She turned away quickly, as it struck her uneasily that if the girl was to become Stepmother's companion, then everything in the household would change. Conversations would no longer be private – Ruby would be listening. But did it really matter? asked the wry, small voice of intuition.

Hugh was chatting to Emma in the drawing room, and rose as

Hester entered. 'I called in for just a moment, Hester, to give you a message. Mrs Wellington is having a party at Court Hill House next week to celebrate Fanny's eighteenth birthday, and asked me to pass on an invitation from her. Of course you'll get a proper note, but I said I was calling and would mention it to you. It's to be next Tuesday, in a marquee on the lawn. You'll come, won't you? I can take you there and bring you home afterwards.' He took her hand and looked into her eyes. 'You could do with a bit of fun in your life, you know. All work and no play. We'll have a good time, Hester, plenty of people we know, champagne, no doubt, and we'll dance the night away.' He was smiling, eyes warm and inviting. 'You'll come, of course, won't you?'

She resisted but only for a second. Did she want to be seen publicly in Hugh's company? Would he ask her again to marry him? And if he did, what would be her answer now? With a chill, she knew that things had changed, but then Emma Redding's weak voice broke in on her thoughts.

'It will do you good, Hester, to have some fun. You've spent too much time lately nursing us. And Hugh will look after you. I do hope you'll accept the invitation.'

An evening out. Dressing up, meeting friends. Dancing . . . *having fun.*

Hester's sudden smile was radiant. 'Yes, I'd love to go. I'll write a note of acceptance to Fanny's mother tomorrow. And now, Hugh, will you have another glass of sherry before you leave?'

He nodded and she felt his eyes following her as she went to the table holding the decanter. He was clearly admiring her. She turned, returned his smile and suddenly realized that he loved her.

Wasn't that what she longed for? Someone to love her? It couldn't be Nicholas, she knew, but perhaps it might be Hugh. And yet it was to Nicholas she had given her heart. She banished these difficult thoughts while Hugh drank his sherry, chatting to him in the usual friendly way, and then had a quiet dinner with Stepmother. But as the evening ended, those doubts returned and she faced them with a new realizm and maturity.

Yes, she thought she loved Nicholas, but was it possibly just a passing attraction? She imagined that all young girls thought they had lost their hearts, and perhaps, like her, to unsuitable men, a sort of rite of passage, really. So forget. Enjoy the moment. Go to the birthday party with Hugh and – what had he said? 'Dance the night away.'

What would she wear? The blue, off-the-shoulder silk with those beautiful puffed sleeves? Or the white muslin with the high neck and golden sash? Quite an important decision to make.

CHAPTER NINETEEN

It had to be the pale blue silk with the puffed sleeves and small train. Mother's pearls looked wonderful around her neck, echoing the tiny seed pearls decorating the bodice and the wide sash. When Hugh arrived to collect her, Hester felt at her best and determined to enjoy the evening.

It promised to be a joyful celebration. Champagne flowed, the setting sun shone on the colourful gardens of Court Hill House, and Hester decided that Fanny's birthday party was really splendid. As she and Hugh met friends, chattered and laughed, Hester felt her frustrations and shattered dreams vanish into the warm, scented air. Recently, in the anxious ambience of Oak House, she had missed this easy, youthful friendship, with its banter and shared laughter.

In the marquee a buffet supper of vol au vents, cold meats, pies, salads, potatoes in various guises, salmon and game tarts, followed by raspberries and clotted cream, jellies, fruits of all kinds, thick custard and ice cream, was eaten with relish, washed down with fruit cordials and chilled white wine.

When later the orchestra, half hidden behind potted palms in the upstairs ballroom of the house, began to play, Hester drifted around the floor in Hugh's arms feeling slightly up in the air – too much champagne, perhaps – but happy. The air was vibrant with the warmth of dancing bodies releasing perfume from floral corsages, and the atmosphere had become free and increasingly sensuous. Eyes met in intimate glances and entwining limbs became closer in the passion of the dance. She was enjoying it, and now, waltzing, with Hugh's gloved hand warm on her back, she was glad she had accepted the invitation.

But there had been an awkward moment on arrival, when Fanny, looking like a coloured fruit sweet wrapped in pale pink muslin decorated with a striped sash of pale green and with a magenta pink rose in her fair hair, had said, 'Thank you for your present, Hester – well, it's from Hugh too, isn't it? Now that you're engaged. . . .'

Sharply Hester said, 'No, we're not, Fanny. That's untrue. Why do you say that?'

Fanny coloured, put a hand to her mouth and whispered contritely, 'But people are talking. I heard it in the coffee shop in town – that you and Hugh. . . .'

'Well, just forget what you heard. Hugh and I are definitely not engaged.'

'Yet. . . .' Hugh sounded amiable, but when Hester looked at him, she saw the determined gleam in his eyes, and was annoyed.

Taking his arm, she led him towards the garden. 'I think we should allow Fanny to greet her other guests – shall we go and look at the long borders?'

As they wandered, pausing at the end beneath a pergola covered in pale roses with a subtle scent, she said slowly, 'We must stop this silly talk, Hugh. Perhaps we should part company until the gossip dies down. What do you think?' It was a foolish question and she knew it, even as the words came out.

'Certainly not. I shall keep courting you until you say yes. Damn the gossip, that's what I think.' His voice was sharp, his arm abruptly drawing her closer to his side, and his expression very decisive.

Taken aback, Hester changed the subject but now, dancing among the other couples, she felt differently. Hugh held her too closely, his breath was warm on her face as they circled the floor, and her mind floated in a happier world than usual. When, at the end of the waltz, he led her onto one of the balconies overlooking the twilit garden, she realized that she was in no mood for any more arguments.

She lifted her hand, brushing her cheeks. 'It's so hot. Shall we go outside for a breather?' Instinctively, she knew it was a mistake. But this evening nothing seemed very serious, nothing could go wrong. She and Hugh were enjoying themselves – let it go on, she thought dreamily.

The darkening garden was lit by small lamps hanging on tree branches and among shrubs. A full moon shone down, highlighting white flowers and turning them into gleaming, eye-catching delights. Standing within the pergola, Hester fingered a bloom that drifted down her shoulder; soft, warm petals, the shape enticingly persuasive. A perfect flower to paint. Yes, when her studio had been moved into the summerhouse at home, she would choose a rose for her next subject. The images slowly took shape. Perhaps Father, very slowly recovering, might even sit at his window and see her working below. Their love for each other would reach through the garden and if – *if* – she became engaged to Hugh, she knew that Father would be glad and perhaps feel all the better. She would be the daughter he longed for, the wife of a good man, a busy, social housewife who occasionally found time to indulge her hobby of painting.

And then the dream broke. She turned to Hugh, sober and free of the foolish hopes and ideas that had filled her mind as they danced.

'I can't possibly marry you.' She felt his hand tighten beneath her arm. 'Don't ask me again. Let's go back to the house. We can't stay here – it's getting dark and people will talk even more.'

He drew her close. 'Stop talking rubbish, dear Hester.' She tried to step away, but his hold was too powerful. His voice lowered. 'You shouldn't have worn that revealing dress if you didn't want me to admire it.' His fingers ran down her shoulders, and she shivered. 'You know as well as I do that we must marry,' he said tersely. 'Your father expects it, so do my parents. I've found a splendid house and you'll have time to paint – although I want a family. A boy first, and then perhaps a couple of girls.'

Again she tried to pull away but he held her. Opening her mouth to argue, she found his lips coming down on hers. They were hard and tasted of wine and cigars. Into her mind flew the memory of Nicholas's kiss, which had been so different, which had sent waves of pleasure through her whole body, which had made it almost impossible to pull away.

But this was different; no pleasure in this embrace, just a panicky feeling that she must escape. Until slowly, guiltily, she began to enjoy both his kiss and the closeness of his body. Fear and resistance vanished. This was what she longed for, a man's love, and if she couldn't share that love with Nicholas, then Hugh would be the next best thing.

They parted breathlessly, and she said, unsteadily, but knowing what she was saying, 'I'm fond of you, Hugh, but before I decide to marry you, please let me have a little more time.' She eased herself away, laughing nervously. 'I think the champagne has gone to my head – I must be quite sober before I say yes.'

His arms dropped and he said nothing. And then he nodded. 'Well, I suppose that's something. All right, I'll wait – but don't keep me waiting too long.' He reached out, stroked her cheek. 'I want you, Hester. Very badly.'

Her mouth was dry, her cheeks too hot. She needed to go home before he kissed her again. With enormous relief and a feeling of escape, she left him, running back to the house to say good night to her hostess and to collect her cloak.

By the time the trap appeared at the front entrance, and Hugh had also said his farewell to Mrs Wellington and Fanny, Hester had recovered and was in control of herself.

She knew she had been foolish, giving way to the emotional impact of Hugh's love-making, but her mind was clear now. She had half promised herself to him, but there was still a hope of escape. Surely a few days could go on indefinitely?

During the next week she painted in the newly established summerhouse studio. Thoughts of Hugh's proposal and of that intimate embrace were still in her mind, but the creative passion had returned, more demanding than ever, and perhaps because Nicholas's presence lived on in the small, warm room, they were happy hours in that good light, fingers returning to brushes, eyes constantly focused, watching the pictures grow. One afternoon, as teatime neared, she was working on the gentian picture, hoping to finish it before the light failed, when Ruby ran down the path.

'Miss Redding—' Ruby, now Stepmother's companion, spoke with less dialect and paid more attention to manners.

Hester paused, reluctant to stop working, but hearing in her spoken name something disturbing. When the girl came to a halt just inside the doorway, she saw fear in the wide green eyes.

'What is it?' Her voice rose.

'The Master. He – he—' Ruby's face was distraught. 'I don't know . . . you'd better come. . . .'

For a second they stared at each other. Hester's heart jumped and her mouth dried. 'Yes.' She dropped the brush, got up, pushing past Ruby, running rapidly back into the house.

He had gone by the time they reached the bedroom, lying seemingly at peace in the white bed. Hester took one look at the grey face and the open, sightless eyes. She knelt by the bed. 'Send Hoskins for Dr Winters. Quickly, Ruby. . . .'

'Starvation, of course, the usual end.' Dr Winters closed Arthur Redding's eyes and ushered Hester from the bedroom. 'Seizures generally end like this, I fear. Of course you and your cook did your best, offering him nutritious food but that restricted breathing, the tensing of the swallowing process, and so on, caused effort, which brought on a second seizure. Were you with him?'

'No.' Hester's voice was cracked. She couldn't believe that Father had been smiling at her only half an hour ago, when she had told him she would be in the summerhouse, painting, and at teatime she would be with him again. And now – gone.

Dr Winters put an arm around her shoulders and shut the door behind him. 'We must go and tell Mrs Redding, Miss Hester. I need you to be there. I have some sedatives with me, just in case.'

Through her shock and all the disturbed thoughts churning up her mind, she became aware of Ruby, following them downstairs. The once over-familiar and chatty housemaid was a silent figure, offering unexpected strength and help. It was Ruby who comforted Stepmother when the news of Father's death was broken; Ruby who, after Dr Winters had left, said quietly, in a sure voice, 'Leave Mrs Redding to me, Miss Redding. I'll be with her while you see to everything else. And I'll send Hoskins with a message to Mr Hugh. He'll need to know – to help you with the arrangements.'

Hester looked into calm eyes, and after a pause, muttered unsteadily, 'Yes. Thank you, Ruby. Thank you.'

Ruby put out a hand, very gently touching Hester's shoulder. 'He might have been my father, too.' She sighed. 'I know that lawyer said he wasn't, but I shall always wonder.'

Hester nodded and wiped the last tears from her eyes. 'No,' she said chokingly. 'We shall never really know.'

The funeral was well attended and Aunt Jacks and Hugh were the twin rocks of support that Hester gratefully accepted. Her father's death had been a great shock, but there were joyful moments of recalling how their love had freed itself and she was thankful for it. She was glad of Hugh's help in taking upon himself so many of the necessary arrangements and slowly felt her strength returning.

After the interment in St Mary's church in Newton Abbot, the mourners – family, friends and colleagues – returned to Oak House. Somehow Hester kept smiling while kindly wishes were given until eventually the last carriage and trap rolled out of the drive, leaving the house sadly empty and almost unnaturally quiet.

At her side, Hugh put his arm around her. 'You've done well, Hester. Your father would be proud of you. You've been strong, but I do feel you need to rest now.'

Suddenly she felt the truth of his words. Her body ached, her mind was weary and she longed for the peace of her bedroom where sleep could work wonders. She smiled, seeing the concern on his face, and nodded. 'Yes, I'll rest now. I can't thank you enough for your help, Hugh, for being with me in this difficult time.'

His arms tightened, but his voice was gently undemanding. 'I'll call again tomorrow and perhaps by then you'll feel able to talk about our future. But don't even think about it now – go and rest.' He turned her towards the staircase and stood in the hall, watching as she dragged herself up, finally smiling down at him before going into her room and collapsing on the bed.

She slept, dreams forgotten when she awoke several hours later, feeling an insurge of new strength, of more vital thoughts, of fresh physical lightness and the ability to get up, change, and then go downstairs to sit with Stepmother.

After dinner, when Ruby had taken Emma upstairs at bedtime, Hester wandered in the garden, finding the solitude and beauty wonderfully comforting. As she sat in the summerhouse, looking at her painting equipment spread on the table in front of her, she became newly aware of a growth of unexpected commonsense, which helped revitalise her even further. It built on the fact of her father's passing; of Ruby caring so well for Stepmother. And of her own need for love growing ever more urgent as day followed day.

Walking back to the house, she knew now that she would accept Hugh's proposal of marriage. What a steadfast friend he had proved himself, offering help and affection. She smiled then, wondering at this new vision of life. Without doubt he would be a good husband. She and Hugh, in that new house, living their new lives. Yes, when he called again, she would take him into the quietness of the garden, and say, 'Dear Hugh, I would like to marry you. And as soon as you like.'

But next morning that comforting world crashed. Nicholas's letter came as a disturbing breakdown of her sensible plans of the previous evening. She took the letter upstairs to her bedroom, opening it with trembling hands.

'*Dear Miss Redding.*'

For a second she was distraught; what had she expected? Not this formal, cold address. Confusion raced through her mind: she was going to marry Hugh so why should she feel like this because Nicholas had written what was most certainly just a note of condolence, and nothing more?

Trying unsuccessfully to quieten her mind, she read on.

Hester, I write this note to offer you my sympathy on losing your father. I send you my loving thoughts, although I know they are not acceptable. You will now, doubtless, engage on a new life which I pray will be happy and fruitful. I am leaving shortly on a further expedition which will give me, also, a new direction in life. Because we won't meet again, I must tell you that I will always remember you, continue to love you and hope you will find success with your God-given talent for painting.

184

Beloved Hester, you stay in my thoughts and dreams. Your smile, your beauty and the memory of that one precious moment of our coming together. Forgive me for this, but I will always love you. Dear Hester, goodbye.
    Nicholas Thorne.

She sat there for a long time, tears falling and then drying on her cheeks as she looked at the strong, slanting handwriting, hearing his resonant voice, feeling again the joy of that intimate embrace, and wondering how life could so suddenly turn on its axis, sending her from comfortable commonsense into emotional chaos.

Only when Ruby appeared at her door was she able to control her thoughts and wearily return to the routine of domestic duties. She looked in the mirror, wiped her face, glanced back at Ruby. 'Thank you for what you're doing. I couldn't have managed the last few weeks without you.' She watched as Ruby nodded, went to the open window and rearranged the curtains.

'Me and Mr Hugh.' Ruby's voice was calm, more mature, and reassuring.

Hester smoothed her hair, sighed and tried to hide the ever-returning expression of grief, but knew Ruby understood. 'Yes,' she said. 'We mustn't forget Mr Hugh. He'll be coming around this evening. We have a lot to talk about.'

They looked at each other, then Ruby nodded. 'I'll take Mrs Redding upstairs. You can be alone in the drawing room.'

'Thank you.'

Ruby stood by the door before turning, smiling and saying very quietly, 'I hope you'll be happy with him, Miss Redding.'

A hint of doubt, Hester thought. She was silent, and then she sighed. So Ruby knew about Nicholas, did she? Of course, every young girl always dreamed of romantic love; she and Ruby were of one mind. But it wasn't to be.

'If not happy, Ruby, at least I'll know that I've done the right thing. Father would be pleased.'

They went downstairs together and parted in the hall, Ruby heading for the kitchen and Hester going to find Stepmother and continue the seemingly everlasting business of comforting her.

185

So this was what life was about. Dreams, joys, nightmares, and the ongoing reality of trying to find the right way. One thing sustained her, trying to push aside the pain of Nicholas's last letter. He loved her. And like him, she would never forget.

CHAPTER TWENTY

Aunt Jacks' brisk voice soared through the hallway. 'Hester, are you there? I have a message for you.'

Hester came down from her stepmother's bedroom, now becoming a cosy boudoir. Ruby had suggested this and so Hoskins and the lift man were arranging the furniture around the new day bed.

'Wait a minute, Aunt Jacks – I'll come down.'

'No, I'll come up.'

They smiled at each other, meeting on the upstairs landing, and Jacks opened her arms. Hester flew into them. Comfort was very important now, with Father gone, Stepmother in a constant tizzy of tears, Nicholas forever at the back of her mind and the next meeting with Hugh an uneasy shadow. 'Lovely to see you, Aunt. Come downstairs and we'll have a cup of coffee. And you must see the new lift – it's going to be so helpful.' She laughed. 'All thanks to Ruby, whose ideas seem to go on for ever. Now she's suggested we get an invalid carriage for Stepmother so that she can be wheeled around the garden.'

'A good idea. She's turning out to be a most unusual girl. And Emma's companion now? Well, well! But such a blessing to you, I'm sure. Now, never mind that. . . .' Jacks set off down the stairs. 'No coffee, thanks, I can't stay, dear child. Off to Hayward Nursery to get something colourful for the garden because the slugs have demolished all the delphiniums. Yes, I know we're in mourning, and I really shouldn't be out and about like this, but life has to go on. And I've got my rose day in a week or so and must have the June borders looking their best. But I have something to tell you.'

187

Hester took her aunt's arm. 'Come into the morning room where it's sunny.'

Sitting down, she looked at her aunt's shrewd eyes and sensed excitement. 'So what is this message?'

'Well. . . .' Jacks produced a folded letter from one pocket and fumbled for her spectacles in the other one. 'Emily has written. You remember Emily Watson?'

'Of course I do. The painting lady. She inspired me.'

Jacks chuckled as she opened the letter. 'Well, it seems that you must have made an impact on *her*, if not actually inspiring her, dear child! She writes that she is a judge for the Kew Painting Competition and has come across an entry which is a watercolour of a flower, and she thinks it could possibly be yours.'

Hester frowned. 'But I have never entered a competition. Is there a name on the painting? Surely that would tell her.'

'This is what she says.' And Jacks adjusted her spectacles. ' "*This entry reminds me of your niece's work because of the true colours, the grace of the composition and the nice touch of the little grub climbing up the stem. Some painters do this, but not many. Please ask your niece about this. I am not writing to her personally as I imagine she has many letters of condolence to answer at this sad time. My sympathies to her, please, Jacks. And let me know as soon as possible.*" '

Silently, they looked at each other. Aunt Jacks put away her spectacles. 'What do you think, Hester?'

'I have no idea. It's a mystery. No one has any of my paintings.' She thought. 'Except Ruby, and that's in her new bedroom.' She laughed. 'The dandelion – she took it with her when she moved down. No, it's not that one. And no one else has one.'

A memory touched her indistinctly, slowly growing in reality. The art room in Newton Abbot. The tutor with his black coat and outlandish hat. 'But yes, I offered Mr Flynn one of my paintings because he'd so kindly arranged for me to meet Mr Hayward. I let him choose it from my portfolio.'

Aunt Jacks tutted. 'Did you sign it?'

'No, should I have done?' Hester looked askance at her aunt, who was getting to her feet.

'If the painting really is yours, then clearly he's played a disgusting trick on you, entering it as his own. Go and see him immediately and demand an explanation.'

'But—'

'My dear girl, be sensible. It's possible that this man is cheating you, so you must do something about it. When I'm in town I'll telegraph to Emily, tell her that you will see this man and then be going to London to sort it all out.' Aunt Jacks walked briskly to the door, turning to look back at Hester who sat on, eyes wide with surprise.

'But I can't just go to London—'

'Whyever not? The train only takes three or four hours to reach Paddington and then you can get a cab to Emily's house in Kensington. Here's her letter so that you can see her address. I'm sure she would be delighted to give you a bed for the night. Go to the bank when you're seeing this Flynn man and make sure you have enough money.'

'Yes, of course, I suppose I could, but. . . .'

Aunt Jacks heaved a sigh. 'Hester, really! Do you need a nursemaid to help you live your life? Surely you understand that women can do anything these days?' She threw the letter onto the table. 'Dear child, just go. Sort out this muddle and then come home again. It's as simple as that. Now I must dash. Let me know when you come back, won't you?'

Hester followed her aunt out of the room. 'Yes, of course, Aunt.'

'Goodbye, then.'

'Goodbye.'

The front door opened, Aunt Jacks climbed into the trap and Hester began to laugh as excitement raced through her.

Yes, she would go to London. But first she must find Mr Flynn. Her shock had gone now, and she felt a heated anger rising in its place. If he really had stolen her painting, then how dare he? And if Emily Watson, one of the judges of the competition, thought her entry was good – surely that meant her talent might be recognized.

Passion mounted. So she was back to painting. Colours – cerulean blue, smoky ochre, all the crimsons – and flowers; the slow build-up of form on white paper; the instinctive knowledge of how to do it.

189

Those timeless moments of creativity when she was in a different world. It was all coming back. This was what she was meant to do. Never mind Hugh and his imminent proposal, never mind worrying about Stepmother and how to run dreary Oak House, her muse was calling her, demanding full attention now. She must sort out her dreams and ambitions and take this new, wonderful step forward.

And then, out of the blue, came another thought, sharp and joyous even though it was tinged with sadness: she wished Nicholas could know about her return to painting.

Upstairs, she put on her veiled black hat, flung on a black coat, picked up her reticule and went down into the hall, calling for Ruby as she went.

'What is it, Miss Redding?' Ruby, also in black, but with her brilliant hair lightening the sombre dress, came out of the glass pantry, a list in her hand.

'Please ask Hoskins to get the trap ready, I have to go into town.'

Ruby's eyes widened. 'Of course. I'll tell him straightaway.' At the top of the kitchen stairs she paused and looked back to where Hester was standing by the hall mirror, adjusting her hat. 'Is there anything I can do, Miss Redding? What's happened?'

The familiar curiosity made Hester smile. 'Yes, something has come up. And I may have to go away for a night—' She stopped, thoughts whirling. 'A few days – I don't know, it all depends.' She met Ruby's eyes. 'I can't tell you what all this is about, but I will, when I know myself.' Conscience struck then and her voice grew tight. 'One other thing, Ruby. If Mr Hugh calls this evening, please just tell him that I've been called away urgently.' They looked at each other. 'On business. That's all he needs to know.'

Ruby said unexpectedly, 'He won't like it, Miss, will he?'

'No, he won't. But I have to go.'

'Yes, Miss.'

Hester turned away. 'And Ruby, please pack my valise, will you? And don't tell Mrs Redding anything – she'll worry too much.'

Disappearing, Ruby said, 'Leave it to me. I'll see that everything's all right.'

Waiting for Hoskins to bring around the trap, Hester, on an impulse, went down to the summerhouse and looked at her painting things, still lying where she had left them on the day of Father's death.

In the gentian picture, she had been painting the last infinitesimal antenna of the blue butterfly on the point of flying off the page. How strange, she thought, Father passing on and the butterfly ready to fly.

She wrapped the picture carefully before returning to the house and putting it in the hall. It could come to London with her. She was uncertain why, but perhaps Emily Watson would like to compare the two works.

In the trap, Hester looked at the countryside all around her as they trotted down the lanes. The hedges were full and starred with wild roses, while Farmer Bartley's fields grew green and rich as summer continued. In the distance Dartmoor shone under a brilliant sun, its age-old history punctuated by dramatic hills and tors. Passing the gate of Brook Cottage, she caught a glimpse of a foam of flowers, and by the gate where Nicholas had given her a spray of honeysuckle, the memories were almost too strong to face. She sighed, then, bravely, thought ahead. Yes, London would be so different.

In town, she went from the bank to the Reading Room. No one knew where Mr Flynn was, so she ordered Hoskins to take her to his house. Outside the small, rather dilapidated cottage where she had studied with him, she said, 'I shan't be long, Hoskins,' and heard new authority in her voice.

No reply to her knock at the door. She knocked again, then walked around the side of the cottage and rapped on the shut back door. Only when she was returning to the trap did a man's head appear, looking over the hedge separating the two gardens, saying, 'The Flynnses is gone. Went a week or so ago. Never said – don't know where.' He nodded. 'Funny lot, anyway. Didn't pay their bills, so I 'eard. Best be rid o' them, eh?'

Hester thanked him. The mystery was deepening but she felt excitement and readiness for what came next. The trip to London. It was an adventure and one that she suddenly knew she was ready for. As Aunt Jacks had said, women could do anything these days. Well, she would prove that to herself – and to anybody else who thought that she was just a country girl, bred to domesticity and a dull marriage. And that brought her back to Hugh. He would have to wait a few days longer for her answer; a sense of guilty relief filled her at the thought.

After luncheon Ruby waited in Hester's bedroom, the valise half packed. 'Only put a few things in, Miss Redding. Your nightdress, toilet things, wrapper, and a dinner dress; don't know where you're going to stay, or for how long. Will this be enough?'

'I think so. I'm not sure when I shall be back.'

Ruby neatly folded a paisley shawl, putting it into the valise before closing it. 'You might need this – they say London's colder than down here.' She met Hester's eyes. 'I hope everything goes all right, Miss Redding.'

A moment of unexpected intimacy, and Hester suddenly wished she and Ruby could talk more openly. It would be good to have someone to confide in – if the girl really had been her sister, things would be different. Then she remembered the scribbled name on the birth certificate and banished the thought, but her voice was warm as she said, 'Thank you, Ruby. You're being very helpful.'

'I'm pleased to be able to do so, Miss Redding, and don't worry – I'll look after everything while you're gone.'

Hester felt unexpected emotion pricking behind her eyelids and turned away. 'I must go. The train leaves Newton at 2.20,' she said, and hurried downstairs.

London was certainly different. Here, in the metropolis, with seeming millions of people bustling all around her, Hester felt out of her element. Standing outside the station, trying to summon a hansom cab, she wished she were back in safe Oak House, with Alice, the new maid, bringing up the tea, and she and Stepmother and Ruby in the drawing room, trying to find cheerful topics of conversation to while away the long hours.

And then she saw something bright, almost garish, on the pavement just ahead of her; a chalk picture of a country scene, tall trees crowned with unlikely-shaped leaves, a blue river flowing past, and a group of colourful children playing tag. Something deep inside her leaped and she felt the old passion ignite, hot and thrusting as it seared her mind. She approached the artist, a bedraggled young man with thin cheeks and a skeletal figure, bending over the pavement, putting finishing touches to his picture. She put some silver in the cap lying on the kerb. 'Keep drawing,' she said, voice firm, and had the pleasure of watching him smile as he put a finger to his forehead. 'Thank 'ee, lady. I will.'

A cab stopped then and she ran for it. 'Campden Hill Road, Kensington, please. Number twenty.' And then she felt in the right place, and at home in this new world where art welcomed her, even there, in the street.

Emily Watson's smile offered a warm welcome. 'Come in, Hester. I had your aunt's telegram and we have a room prepared for you. Are you ready for a meal? Take off your coat, my dear, and come and sit down. That's it. You look tired – well, now you can rest.' She went to the stairwell and called down to the kitchen. 'Tea, please, Sally, and that lemon cake you made yesterday.' Returning, she took Hester into the drawing room, a pleasant room elegantly furnished and with a homely atmosphere. 'We have a lot to talk about, Hester.'

They talked late into the evening after dinner served in the dining room at the back of the house, overlooking a long, green, shaded garden. New life surged through Hester once she was fed and rested, and she listened, fascinated, as Emily talked about her latest project – the book that she was completing – and the imminent expedition to the Dolomites to return to a site and check a particular painting she had made, which must be included in the book.

'We go as a party,' Emily told her, sitting by the fireplace in the drawing room. 'I pick my friends very carefully, and have a reliable courier to organize our accommodation as we travel. Last year it worked well and I have every faith in it being a good experience this time.'

Hester said, 'It sounds wonderful. Makes me almost want to come with you.'

Emily smiled as she sipped her brandy. 'You would be very welcome, and I'm sure you'd enjoy finding new plants and painting them.' Her tone grew firmer. 'But now we must discuss the entry into the painting competition, which I know your aunt has told you about. It was sent under the name of Joseph Flynn, but—' She paused. 'But,

193

when looking at it at Kew, I recalled seeing your work at Jacks' garden day in the spring, and something made me wonder about this particular painting. The tiny grub working its way up the stem, for instance, heading for the newly opened leaves, touched a chord of memory.' She laughed. 'An original idea, and I remember that the painting you showed me then had a similar creature climbing around the flower.'

'Yes, Miss Watson, I don't know why, but I like to put a beetle, or a moth, or a butterfly in my pictures. It gives vitality and life, I think.' She hesitated. 'I have brought my latest picture for you to see, in case you wish to compare it with the other entry. Shall I fetch it?'

'Please do.'

Emily took one look at the gentian and the blue butterfly and said, 'Yes, of course, I recognize your work. And it is very clearly the same artist who has painted the competition entry.' She looked across at Hester. 'Do you know this Flynn man?'

'He was my tutor.'

'How shocking. Have you seen him, demanded an explanation?'

'He's no longer around. I was told he has left the district.'

Emily pursed her lips. 'In London, seeking his fortune, and trying to become this year's competition winner, I shouldn't wonder.' She gave the painting back to Hester. 'We must clear up this annoying muddle. Tomorrow we'll go to Kew and get it sorted out.'

Standing up, she reached out her hand and drew Hester from her chair. 'I think you should go to bed. We shall need our wits about us in the morning if we're to bring that rogue Mr Flynn to his just deserts.' She smiled. 'Come now, my dear, let me take you upstairs.'

The Royal Botanic Gardens at Kew were wonders of beauty and fascination that Hester could never have imagined. She longed to wander through the trees and explore the vast glasshouses, but Emily briskly led her to a large building and left her at the entrance, saying, 'I will leave you here for a while. There are various people I must see and I daresay you can amuse yourself looking around.' She paused briefly. 'This is the herbarium where all the plants are recorded. I shall talk with the resident botanical artist, and discuss your painting and that of Joseph Flynn. Then I'll be back – shall we meet in about an hour? Is that all right, Hester?'

'Yes, Miss Watson. There's so much to see – and I want to visit the Marianne North Gallery of Botanic Art. I've read about it.'

'Yes, of course.' Emily smiled approvingly. 'All those paintings of the plants she discovered when travelling. You'll learn a lot from them, my dear.'

Alone, Hester looked around her. The gardens stretched on and on, but she knew exactly where she must go, and easily found the long, low building of the gallery opposite the famous Temperate House. Inside, she caught her breath. So many paintings. Leaflets informed her that there were 832 of them, all the work of Marianne North, who had travelled alone to North and South America, South Africa and many parts of Asia, searching out the native plants, setting up her easel and then painting them. Before her death she had bequeathed this gallery to Kew, together with the paintings contained in it.

She had died, Hester noted sadly, just a year ago. If only she had had been able to meet her, to find out about painting the world's unknown plant life. Looking at these paintings, by a middle aged lady who had travelled alone among hardship and danger to fulfil her passion for birds and butterflies, Hester found her own passion mounting. If only she could do what this intrepid artist had done.

If only. . . .

Something urgent began to burn inside her. Father had died. Nicholas had said they must never meet again. She supposed she was going to marry Hugh. Yes, life was plagued with difficulties, sadness and regret, but if she had nothing else, she had her painting. And Emily Watson thought highly of her talent. And perhaps something might come of this muddle over the painting competition.

I will paint. I will make a career for myself, out here, in the world. Women can do anything – everything. And so will I, even if, as Hugh's wife I have only a few spare hours a week.

And then another surprising thought crept into her mind. *IF I marry Hugh. . . .*

She gave a last look at Marianne North's amazing output of work and then turned and left the gallery. Outside the fresh air reinvigorated her thoughts and her resolve. She started walking towards the herbarium to meet Emily Watson, for the hour was nearly up.

And then, in the distance, coming down the path ahead of her, a figure caught her eye. Tall, unmistakable, the gait and strength so clearly revealing someone she knew. Someone she loved. *Nicholas.*

She waited, heart racing, and saw him stop a stone's throw away, removing his hat, eyes intent on her. Slowly, he came nearer. She saw wonder in his eyes, warmth suffusing his face, and knew that this was a moment when she must be strong. She should turn away at once, for only pain and longing could result from this accidental meeting. But he was looking at her, holding out his hands. Indecision wracked her. What could she do?

She was lost. 'Nicholas!' She ran forward to meet him, smiling up into his astonished face. 'Oh, Nicholas!'

'What are you doing here, Hester? Of all places – I thought you safe at home in Devon.' His hands were strong, his voice low, full of pleasure and surprise.

Stumbling, she explained about Emily Watson and the painting competition. 'I am going home tomorrow,' she said, 'but why are you here?'

'Making final arrangements with a colleague here in the Gardens about Emily's expedition – we leave next Friday.' They stood, gazing at each other, hands clasped. Hester knew her heart was in her face and her voice as she said, unevenly, hesitantly, 'Your letter, Nicholas. When you said we must never meet again – did you really mean it?'

At once his face hardened and he let fall her hands, but slowly, as if he couldn't bear to abandon them. 'Yes, I did mean it. I have nothing to offer you, Hester. I'm just a plantsman – someone with a mind full of guilt, and a ridiculous sense of ambition which will never achieve anything. Believe me, it's best that we part.'

Slowly, painfully, her radiant smile died. His words were hard, his eyes had become steely blue and determined. She felt as if he had struck her. Was there no love left in him? Not even enough to hope and plan for a future they could somehow share?

But then, mercifully, pride came to ease the pain and dictate the next step. She lifted her head, forcing her voice to be casual. 'I see. Well, it's been nice to meet you again, and I wish you well on the expedition. Perhaps you'll find that wonderful gentian you told me about.'

'Perhaps.' One cold word, putting an end to the meeting.

Their eyes clung, but the moment had passed. He nodded, replaced his hat and seemed only to be waiting for her departure. Hester turned away, tears masking her vision, but then Emily's voice called from the herbarium entrance.

'Over here, Hester – time we went home, I think. And I have some news for you.'

It was hard, leaving him standing there, feeling his longing and his wretchedness reaching out for her as she walked away, thankful to have somewhere to go, to have a reason for putting all the pain and regret out of her mind.

'I'm coming, Miss Watson.' She hurried on and by the time she reached the herbarium steps the tears had vanished. And the thought of Nicholas, still standing there, watching, was just a torturing image which would of course return, but which, for the moment, she could thankfully replace with a more positive, exciting thought.

Painting, she told herself determinedly. All I've got left is painting.

CHAPTER TWENTY-ONE

Returning to Kensington, Emily told Hester the result of her talk with the botanical artist working in the herbarium. 'Miss Smith will try to trace Mr Flynn – his note enclosing the entry has a London address – and will tell him he is not eligible for entry.' Beaming, she went on. 'And yours will go forward for judging. A decision will be made in a day or two, so let's keep hoping that you at least earn a good recommendation, shall we?'

Hester fought to keep Nicholas out of her mind. 'Yes,' she said. 'Thank you for sorting it all out for me, Miss Watson.'

Emily's smile vanished. 'Is something wrong, my dear? You look disturbed.' Her glance was sharp. 'Was that Nicholas Thorne I saw you talking to?'

'Yes.' But she must not think about him.

'I suppose he was at Kew meeting his colleague who works in the herbarium. And no doubt he's busy making arrangements to join my party when we leave next week.' Frowning, Emily added, 'I believe Nicholas has a fondness for you. my dear. How well do you know him? Nothing about his troubled background, perhaps?'

Hester tensed, waiting for control to return. 'I only know that he has hopes of finding a double gentian.'

'Oh, that!' Emily laughed. 'Of course, all collectors believe they can find something rare – even non-existent. But perhaps I should tell you about the accident that happened last year when we were in the Dolomites, and for which Nicholas believes himself to be responsible.'

'He feels guilty?' A shutter in Hester's mind opened painfully. Memories struck. Nicholas had said he knew about guilt. She looked at Emily. 'Please tell me.'

But the cab slowed, and Emily looked out of the window. 'We're nearly home. I'll tell you the rest indoors.' The cabbie reined in and they got out, going into the house and removing their wraps and hats.

And then it was time for Emily to work on her book and after luncheon Hester went upstairs to repack her valise and think about going home.

Looking out of the window, hearing the traffic in the high street and half longing to be back in the peace of the country, she began thinking uncomfortably about Emily's information. Did she really want to know why Nicholas felt guilty? How much better it would be to erase all the memories of him. She reminded herself that she was taking a new step forward in life. She would marry Hugh, become the highly social wife he demanded, but – here she frowned and pursed her lips – she would insist on a few hours a week for her painting. Perhaps she might even gain a commission or two, although no doubt Hugh would take exception to her becoming a working woman.

She sighed. It wasn't going to be easy, but the old passion remained. Painting would be her life, come what may.

Later, over tea, she listened to Emily's tales of exploration and discovery, of Jon's accident, and at the same time learned fascinating facts about painting in difficult conditions.

Early next morning she was ready to take a cab to Paddington station. Emily kissed her goodbye. 'I've been delighted to have you, Hester – you must come again.'

They smiled at one another and then she added, 'I hope you have a good journey home and—' Delving into her pocket, she produced a small book. 'Nicholas's journal may pass the time for you. He left it with me so that I could check details of last year's expedition. I've finished with it now and I expect he's forgotten all about it.' She smiled. 'He's so busy I don't suppose he'll remember that he gave it to me. You can return it when we meet again.' She embraced Hester. 'Goodbye, my dear, and keep painting, won't you?'

*

The journal, a pale blue scuffed leather book, burned a hole in Hester's pocket as the train steamed out of London, gaining pace and then racing towards the West Country and home. She didn't want to look at it. Yes, she did. And so, reading with increasing interest and shock, she learned the details of Jonathon West's fatal accident among those dangerous mountains and treacherous rivers. The last paragraph, in Nicholas's strong handwriting, made her catch her breath.

I shall go back and try and fulfil Jon's mission by taking the same track where he slipped and fell and then going on up into the higher peaks. If I can find that damned plant I know my mind will clear. But until then I am at the mercy of burning guilt and restlessness. I look forward to the new expedition with sad memories, yet with a fierce hope of something positive redeeming them. All I can do now is to take this step into the blue. Who knows what I shall find?

Hester wiped away her tears and spent the rest of the journey staring out of the window. The countryside passed in all its beauty – roses winding through the hedges, trees shading the stock grazing lush green fields – but she hardly saw any of it. Her mind was refilled with a new determination and resolve.

There were signs of change at Oak House. Ruby answered the front door as Hester arrived. 'Welcome home, Miss Redding.'

Hester heard the newly acquired gentility slip as Ruby added, 'We haven't half missed you.'

'Thank you.' So someone had warm thoughts of her. With Ruby in attendance with the valise, she went upstairs.

'Everything's going along nicely, Miss Redding. Madam is pleased that I can wheel her around the garden in the new invalid carriage and, do you know, she even suggested we take a stroll down to Mrs Hirst's cottage? We're going later this afternoon.' Ruby stood in the bedroom doorway while Hester removed her coat and hat and went to the washbasin.

'I'll leave you to tidy up, Miss Redding, and then I expect you'll be ready for luncheon. A sherry beforehand, perhaps?' And she went downstairs, leaving Hester smiling. What a change; what a well-mannered, thoughtful girl Ruby had become. And, drying her hands and smoothing her hair, she thought how surprisingly well this new responsible and warm-hearted persona was fitting into the jigsaw puzzle she was trying so hard, and so daringly, to put together.

It was afternoon before she had a chance to talk to Ruby alone. Luncheon was full of Emma's questions about Kew and the more than likely discomfort of rail travel, followed by yawns and then being helped upstairs for the afternoon nap.

Hester caught Ruby in the hall. 'Come into the garden, will you? I want to talk to you.' Outside, walking down the long borders, noticing how, in her short absence, flowers had bloomed, faded and been replaced by more buds, Hester looked at the well-dressed girl beside her, thought for a second how Ruby had grown into a more mature and attractive person, and then asked warily, 'Tell me about Hugh. What did he say when he called? What did *you* say?'

Ruby looked at her with sympathetic eyes. 'I gave him your message. He shouted a bit, but then, well, he's polite, isn't he? Said he was sorry and drove away. He said he'd come and see you in a few days' time.' She laughed. 'Not too bad, was it? Maybe he'll come by this evening – well, that gives you time to think, doesn't it?'

Hester bent down, fingering a leaf of a cottage garden pink, smelling the clove scent of the white laced flowers as she did so. Ruby's words, her sensible attitude, soothed the uneasiness inside her, and she looked into the green eyes watching her, and asked slowly, 'Ruby, you don't think I should marry him, do you?'

'Not if you'd rather have that nice Mr Nicholas, Miss Redding.'

A long, thoughtful moment, and then shared smiles. Ruby's expression hinted at wry amusement and Hester felt in her bones that this was surely nothing short of a revelation. Abruptly a shaft of light chased the dark and painful shadows out of her mind as she recognized truth in Ruby's advice.

Of course she would rather have Nicholas. But he had said they must not meet again.

Thoughts swirled and fluttered in her mind. Life was hard, and ridiculous: Hugh wanted her, but Nicholas did not. Or did he? Then, as if he were close, she was aware of those past sweet moments in the summerhouse with him beside her. When he had said those magical words – *I could love you, Hester* – only to apologize for them later.

Never had she felt so bewildered, so unsure of how to resolve these muddling images and thoughts, of how to live her life, alone, if she chose not to marry Hugh. And then the beauty and solace of the garden entered into her spinning consciousness and she looked down at the flowers at her feet: she heard the heavy green oak leaves fluttering as a breeze touched them; felt the serenity of the surrounding countryside soothe and inspire her, and out of that calming moment she came back to her gift – to painting – and knew then, with an ever fiercer passion, that this was the way to go.

Returning to the moment, she saw Ruby watching her and said quietly, 'Thank you, Ruby. I needed to talk to someone. I'm going to forget both Hugh and Nicholas and live an independent life. I shall make a career for myself in painting – I'm going to be a botanical artist and nothing will stop me.'

Her words hung in the air, as they smiled like old friends. Then, matter of factly, Ruby said, 'I'm glad you've decided, Miss Redding. And if I helped, well, I'm glad about that, too. Now, I dessay you want to be alone to make your plans, so I'll tell Hoskins to get the invalid carriage ready for Madam, and then we'll be off down to Mrs Hirst for tea. We shall be home again before dinner, so if you need me, I'll be here.'

Hester watched her walk away. Ruby, who had so amazingly become more than just a servant; much more like a sister, in fact. But of course, she wasn't a sister, just Stepmother's companion. How extraordinary life was, often puzzling and painful, but also offering unexpected and joyful moments leading to an inner contentment. Really extraordinary.

Hugh did not call that evening. Hester, tense at the prospect of making an end to their so-called engagement, felt the hours pass with increasing relief. He would come tomorrow, which gave her another day to find the necessary words and strength to face him. She wished, above all, not to hurt him. She and Hugh had been friends for so long that it was dreadful to think of his certain pain at her rejection of his proposal. How good if they could return to easy friendship, but she supposed it would not be possible.

The morning brought the postman with a letter from London informing her that the judges at the Royal Botanic Gardens at Kew had decided that her entry in the competition had been chosen as the winner. Hester gasped and had to read the letter twice.

We have pleasure in awarding your painting of Melittis melissophyllum (bastard balm) the prize as we consider it to be the best one entered in the competition. We congratulate you and would be pleased to know if you can be present at the award ceremony next Tuesday.

The letter was signed by Matilda Smith, the resident botanical artist, who had added a note.

I gave Mr Flynn a piece of my mind. He apologized, said he recognized your talent and was going through a bad time financially and had acted on impulse when he sent in your painting of the bastard balm. He wishes you well and hopes you will forgive what he has neatly decided to call an aberration of his artistic conscience. All over now.

Emma Redding looked up from her toast and marmalade. 'Bad news, dear? Oh, I do hope not.'

Hester laughed joyously. 'No, Stepmother, good news for once! Don't look so worried – it really is good.' She met Ruby's enquiring eyes across the table and waved the letter at her. 'I've won a competition! My flower painting was the best entry! I have to go to London and receive my prize! I can't believe it! Oh, Ruby, mine was better than all the others – I don't know what to say!'

'That's wonderful, Miss Redding. Of course you must believe it. There in black and white, isn't it?' Ruby's smile was broad. 'Here, have some more coffee – it'll bring you down to earth!'

Perhaps it did. Hester was then able to explain to Stepmother exactly what had happened, and to tell Ruby that she would go into town after breakfast and telegraph her acceptance of the invitation. 'And I'll telegraph Miss Watson, too – I'm sure she'll let me stay with her for a few days.'

'Tell you what, Miss Redding.' Ruby was full of good advice, as usual. 'Go and buy yourself a new frock for the prize winning, something bright. I mean, you can't wear mourning for ever, you know, and I'm sure Mr Redding wouldn't mind, in the circumstances.'

Hester blinked away sudden ridiculous tears – why cry over such good news? 'How sensible you are, Ruby – I'll do that. And I'll go and tell Aunt Jacks, and Hugh—' She stopped, feeling some of the joy fade. What would Hugh think? Then commonsense returned and with it a complete feeling of new self-confidence. She would find the right words when the time came.

The morning fled past. Aunt Jacks was delighted. 'My dearest child, you deserve it. I always said you were exceptionally talented. And I'm sure Emily will allow you to stay with her again.' Those dark, astute eyes raked Hester's radiant face. 'And will this make any difference to – well – whatever plans you are making?'

'Plans?' Down to earth again, Hester knew that she was, indeed, making plans but not yet able to talk about them. Flashes of ideas, hopes, certainties . . . very soon they must formulate themselves into reality. Her smile returned. She was ready now to step out into that blue that Father had talked about. And with this award behind her, there could well be offers of commissions to encourage her, to enable her to find a new place in the world. 'Yes, Aunt Jacks, I have plans and I'll tell you about them very soon. But now I have to go into town.' Excitement grew again. 'Ruby says I must have a new dress!'

She went off in the trap with Aunt Jacks' blessing and spent a happy hour in the department store in Newton Abbot choosing a dress in good taste, becoming but not garish. Pale lavender brocade, with deeper panels, and within the boundaries of mourning still, but appealing and suitable for an occasion. Then on to the Post Office to send a message asking Emily Watson for a bed for a few nights again, and then, 'Hoskins, into Bovey Tracey, please. Quickly.'

Hugh was available at once. She sat on the hard chair opposite him and looked across the desk feeling strangely sure of herself. He had taken her hand as soon as she entered the room, then kissed her cheek, smiling and looking at her with affection. The words she needed were difficult to find, but they came, slowly, and without any tremor in her voice.

'Hugh, I have won an important painting prize, which means I have begun my career as a botanical artist.' Swallowing a dryness in her throat, she knew she mustn't stop. 'And so I have to decline your proposal of marriage.' Now her voice cracked. 'I'm sorry, Hugh, but that's what I have decided.'

He said nothing, sitting there staring at her, his brown eyes gradually losing their brightness. Then he heaved a sigh, moved in his chair, looking as if he were fighting a deep pain. 'Well,' he said, at last, getting to his feet and coming around the table to stand beside her. 'Well, of course, that's marvellous news, Hester. I congratulate you. But it's the worst possible news for me.'

She rose, standing at his side, close enough to watch him forcing a smile onto his face. What could she say? She waited. And then, slowly, putting an arm around her shoulder, he said, 'I'm not completely surprised. I know how much you need your painting. But one thing I ask, dear Hester.'

'Yes?'

'That if you are ever in need – of any sort whatever – you will come to me. We've always been friends and I hope that we may continue to be.'

Tears threatened but she resisted them. Instead she lifted her face and gently kissed his cheek. 'Such a good friend, Hugh, and I'll never forget it. I hope – so much – that you will soon find someone else, someone who will be more your model of a good wife than I am.'

He released her, smiled, even chuckled. 'Only one thing I can say now – plenty of good fish in the sea, Hester! Not quite the catch I had hoped for, but that's life for you.'

They parted fondly and Hester knew, driving back to Oak House, that this was one occasion when capricious life had bestowed one more great blessing on her. Hugh would always be her friend.

London was as noisy and grey as she remembered from the previous visit, but there was the excitement of the award ceremony, with compliments and advice given to her by both Miss Smith and other smiling dignitaries of the Gardens. Emily Watson accompanied her to the ceremony, telling her beforehand that she looked quite lovely. 'That colour suits you, and believe me, you look every inch the young artist who is on her way.'

Emily was busy with preparations for the departure of the expedition very shortly and so Hester returned home the next day. But not before she had asked, hoping that the question would only be seen as a casual one, 'And will Nicholas Thorne be going with you, Miss Watson?'

'He's already left, Hester. So much to do before I arrive – the accommodation to arrange, couriers to find and porters, and so on.' Emily smiled. 'I'll be sure to give him your good news when we meet. I expect he'll be delighted.'

'Yes. Thank you.' Hester allowed an image of Nicholas to flash into her mind: tall, suntanned face full of angle and planes, that direct gaze, the low resonant voice and those vivid eyes. He would be pleased, of course he would. *But don't think about him any more.* She must get home and make her own plans. A new career. A step out into the frightening, wonderful world – alone.

Ruby sat opposite her in the drawing room, sharing a last cup of coffee before they both retired. 'So what are you going to do? Now that you're on your way? Can't stay here, can you?'

Hester met the enquiring green gaze. 'No,' she said, and then knew this was the moment to decide exactly what she would do. 'I might go back to my original plan, before Father died.' Just for a moment they looked at each other, sharing the dark memories, and then, 'Find myself somewhere to live and work at my painting.'

Ruby nodded, waited, stirring sugar into her cup.

Hester took a deep breath. 'I've told Hugh I can't marry him.'

'That's good.' There was a light note in Ruby's voice. 'So what about that lovely Mr Nicholas?'

What about him? Hester looked away. 'He's gone abroad. He doesn't want to see me again.' Her voice was sharp.

'But that's awful.' Ruby sounded shocked. 'I mean, you want to see him, don't you?'

'I—' *The truth – face it.* 'Yes, I do.'

Ruby chuckled. 'Well, then, it's obvious – go and find him.'

'But he said—'

'That's rubbish. I saw him, I heard him. He loves you. Really, Hester, you're very silly, you know.' She frowned, leant nearer. 'Of course, he's just a gardener and you're a lady. That's what's really the matter, isn't it?'

'No!' The word was sharp. Then a whisper. 'But he thinks so.'

Ruby's voice raised. 'And here you are, planning to be one of these new liberated ladies who do whatever they want, and yet you're not doing it, are you?'

Hester couldn't think straight. Yes, she could go and find him. Tell him nothing mattered except their being together. She might even help to work out all that awful guilt. But what would he say? Would he turn her away, again?

The most important things in life. Truth. Strength. Decisions.

Suddenly she stood up, nearly overbalancing the small table holding the coffee cups, smiling at Ruby, and laughing as she said, 'I'll go! I'll ask Miss Watson if I can join her expedition. I'll find him.'

'Thank goodness that's decided,' said Ruby wryly. 'You know I'll be here looking after Mrs Redding, running the house, and now you've got rid of Mr Hugh, there's nothing stopping you, is there?' She stopped, blinked. 'And I think Mr Redding would like to think you were doing what you wanted so badly.'

'I believe he would.' Hester looked at Ruby, thoughts suddenly running backwards. 'You wanted to be Father's daughter, didn't you? But now you're Stepmother's companion instead. Are you happy, Ruby?'

Hester watched the small cat's-face grow taut, and then with an explosion of certainty, let a big smile break through. 'Yes, I am. I'm someone who matters now. Not the saucy bit who came here thinking she could teach the family a lesson and better myself.' A pause, and then, 'You see, once I was here, living with all of you and learning such a lot, I knew I could better myself without being nasty. I could take a step forward and see what life had to offer. And that's what I've done.' Ruby's face was radiant. 'I've pushed myself up in the world and I'm happy enough.' She grinned. 'Just look at me! Nice clothes, bossing the servants and calling you Hester. . . .'

A step forward. Hester nodded, her mind dancing as voices and images and hopes all met and embraced.

It's worked for Ruby so it'll work for me, too. One more step into a new life.

CHAPTER TWENTY-TWO

Emily Watson's reply to Hester's urgent telegraph message came by return.

'Delighted your suggestion. Yes come. Prepare for heat and rough walking. Bring painting materials, shady hat, stout shoes. Leaving a.m. Friday. E.W.'

So many last-minute tasks. Packing, telling Aunt Jacks she was leaving, receiving her promise to care for Stepmother while she was away. Discussing with Ruby the household chores to be dealt with; the garden and the maintenance of the cob and the trap; ensuring that Stepmother must be consulted on any details of domesticity; and then, a visit to Father's grave.

Hester carried a bunch of fragrant garden flowers, walking slowly to the newly mounded grave. She stood still, wishing Father could know about her success, that she was taking the step to freedom – like the butterfly he had pointed out, going into the blue.

I wish I could talk to him. I hope he understands. Tears came but she was calm when she joined Hoskins at the churchyard gates.

And then the goodbyes. Stepmother was in floods, Aunt Jacks smiled with great control, and Ruby came into the bedroom when Hester was packing the last items.

A shared look, and then Hester said quietly, 'Ruby, I want to thank you for everything you've done, and which I know you will go on doing. I couldn't leave if you weren't here.' She opened the jewel box on the dressing table and gestured at it. 'I want to give you something to show my gratitude – if there's anything here that you'd like, please take it.' She paused, then the last words came easily. 'With my love.'

Ruby looked at the box and took out the various pieces of jewellery. The cameo, Grandmother's earrings, the brooches, the ruby bracelet and matching pendant, the moonstone necklace. She fingered this, looked at it, then put it down again, and finally picked up the green Venetian beads. 'Please, I'd like this necklace, Miss Redding. It's lovely and I shall feel a real lady in it.'

Hester nodded. 'Good.'

Ruby held it to her neck, looked in the mirror and smiled. 'I shall think of you when I wear it. Thank you.'

Sudden overwhelming emotion made Hester turn away. She shut the valise and picked up her reticule before looking back at Ruby. The green eyes were regarding her with a new expression, to which it was impossible not to respond. A pause and then she put down the valise and bag, and held out her arms. 'Goodbye,' she whispered.

Ruby's arms closed around her. Cheek to cheek, they held tightly for a moment before parting. Then Ruby cleared her throat. 'I'll carry your bag down, Hester.' Together they descended the stairs and walked to the open doorway. Hester climbed into the trap, waving goodbye, and Ruby watched until the trap turned into the lane, when she closed the door and returned to where Mrs Redding was sitting, red eyed, demanding reassurance and comfort.

Ruby's thoughts were legion. Hester had taken that final step. Would she find Nicholas? What would happen if she did? Would she ever come back here to Oak House? And if she didn't then Ruby supposed she would be mistress here until the day when poor Mrs Redding passed along – and then where would she go? But she was an optimist; so, smiling, she arranged a shopping trip into town later in the afternoon, and decided that life was good. Perhaps not exactly as she had planned it when she first arrived but really so much better than she had ever hoped for.

Taking the Venetian beads from her pocket and holding them to her throat, she wondered, eyes shining, if there was not another step to take: not yet, but perhaps one day?

At last, here were the mountains. Hester sat in the lurching carriage as it rolled and rocked over pot-holed roads, staring at what lay ahead. Huge steep peaks of grey rock tipped with snow, thrusting up into the blue sky, formidable barriers to which there appeared to be no end. And yet, travelling further along the valley, she saw green meadows, starred with flowers, between stands of trees.

The seventy-two-hour journey from London by train, water, another train, and now this uncomfortable carriage, had been tiring but exciting as she had never travelled so far before. Emily had told her what to expect in this almost uncharted region of mountains, rivers, chasms and terrifying precipices. 'You'll enjoy it once you get used to the hardship,' she said as the train rattled along. 'We shall be travelling either by mule or on foot. I hope you've brought a good thick skirt. You'll need it – those saddles are very hard. But the flowers and the butterflies – ah, Hester, they will make up for any hardship. Believe me, you are going to love this wonderful landscape.' She smiled and then added, 'Of course, you'll spend a lot of time painting – I'm delighted you're here to record the alpines we find, because I shall have time to focus on anything larger which I didn't record last year, as well as making sure I have the details right for the painting to be included in the book. So much to see and do.'

When finally the coach came to a creaking stop in a small stone-built village surrounded by vast grey mountains, Hester was almost too tired to think what was happening. She followed Emily into the entrance of the hotel, and then, from a room at the side, saw a tall man appear. *Nicholas.* Her heart leaped.

He greeted Emily, seeming not to notice Hester, standing quietly in the shade of the doorway. Until, '*Hester. . . .*' The low voice was almost inaudible but surprised, wondering.

She could only smile, hold out her hands, and wait for his reaction. Did he still refuse to acknowledge their love? She waited, knowing this was the most important moment in her life. And then, those strong arms were holding her; she heard the racing beat of his heart, felt his hands about her, his mouth touching her cheek, her forehead, her lips, his deep voice a murmur, saying the miraculous words, 'God, how I love you, Hester – how I've missed you.'

Yet, lost in all that magical warmth and love, she waited, uncertainty clouding her joy. What if he still thought they had no place in the world together? What about his pride, his guilt, his determination?

And then, like a drop into an abyss, her fear became reality. He drew away, standing at a distance, his voice stiff. 'Forgive me, I shouldn't say this, behave like this. I apologize, Miss Redding.'

Emily, watching, said briskly, 'Nicholas, Hester has won a painting competition held by the Royal Botanic Gardens at Kew. Isn't it splendid?'

Hester watched his face lift, saw, for a second, a glow brightening his eyes, and was encouraged to say, 'I painted the bastard balm you picked for me.'

Did he remember? Was she foolishly speaking out of turn? But his flash of vivid smile reassured her. 'Congratulations, Miss Redding.' He paused. 'I always thought you had great talent.' They stood looking at each other, and she read in his face all that he could not bring himself to say. All that he felt, but was pushing away.

'Thank you.' She bowed her head, trying to control the threatening emotions. For a second she felt dizzy with pain and longing. She watched him pick up the waiting luggage and start to climb the stairs at the side of the hallway. Slowly she went up behind him, aware that Emily was watching. And then, suddenly, she knew, with brave new courage, that in spite of everything and come what may, life just went on.

At least she was here. At least he had said he loved her, had missed her. Well, they would be spending time together on the trail of new plants, and somehow – she clenched her fists, engraving the decision into her mind – somehow she would help him forget the guilt, teach him that her new life as an artist was no barrier to their possible union, nothing that he could not overcome.

Turning into the room at the top of the stairs that a waiting girl indicated, Hester knew, with a surprising sense of calm, that she had come to terms with this moment in her life. If Nicholas said no, then she would return to England, and work at her career. She would always have her painting, even if love was destined to pass her by.

And yet, looking around the barely furnished bedroom, she knew she had one more step to take, to fight for his love. A step which, even yet, might bring them together and enhance their lives. Somehow she would take it. She would return his journal, and give him the painting of the gentian and the butterfly. She would write a brief message on it – and then it would all be up to him.

Chaos filled Nicholas's mind. He had sworn that he and Hester should never meet again, but here she was. And his need, his ever-growing love for her, refused to be denied. There were days, even weeks, ahead of them when he would be seeing her, watching her, feeling his longing for her grow with every minute. How was he to behave while inwardly his body and mind were in turmoil?

That evening was spent in discussion, planning the next day with the courier who had already hired several porters. Emily was eager to trek on and find the village from which she had previously travelled to her chosen painting site. Nicholas had agreed with her decision to start after an early breakfast next day, to take sufficient provisions to give them luncheon, and then to journey on until the village and fresh accommodation was reached.

Alberto, the courier, warned of rough tracks. 'You ladies must go by mule, too hard on delicate feet to walk.' Emily had responded with a chuckle, 'And almost as hard on a mule's bony back. We must be sure to put blankets under those hard saddles.'

Making such decisions, as well as Nicholas's own plans to hunt for the flower for which Jon had been searching, were a help to his disturbed mind and he realized that from now on he must concentrate solely on the reason for his being here.

So it was in a calmer voice he said good night to the ladies after supper, but it was impossible not to watch Hester as she walked towards the stairs. He thought she looked paler than usual and there was a brightness missing from her lovely eyes. He longed to take her in his arms, to kiss away that sweet frailty and tell her he would always be at her side, caring for her, loving her. Instead, he went to the staircase and said, without any emotion, 'Good night, Miss Redding, I hope you sleep well. You need a good rest – tomorrow will be very tiring.'

Turning, she met his gaze and her voice was equally controlled. 'Thank you, Nicholas. I'm sure I shall have a good night. Yes – tomorrow is a new day.'

He heard her pause, watched her eyes widen for a second, and then saw the return of strong self-control. He bowed. 'Indeed. A new day.'

His hungry eyes followed as she went upstairs, then he heard the bedroom door close and had to turn away sharply to banish the images flashing through his mind. He longed to be there, close to her, caressing her, loving her.

Alone in her room, Hester opened the journal, put her painting between the pages, and took out her pen. What should she say? She sat on her bed for a time, trying out words and phrases that would surely banish the differences between them. Finally she wrote, '*From Hester, with my love,*' and realized that those five words said everything. Nothing else was needed. She put the journal aside, planning to wait for the right moment to give it to him. An instinct told her that she would recognize the moment when it came.

Outside the night was darkening, and Nicholas thought the massive peaks were bowing down ever nearer, encircling the village and its inhabitants. Moments of sensible thinking finally banished this nightmare, but when the dawn broke next morning, he sensed a new feeling of excitement surging through him. This was the new day when the search would begin. The day when – perhaps – he would find the legendary double gentian, and ease the guilt he still felt about Jon's death. Dressing quickly, he went outside to help Alberto organise the porters and see to the padded saddles of the mules.

Day followed day. Emily, accustomed to the hardships, encouraged Hester to make light of the tiring travelling and by the end of the first week Hester felt a new woman. Strength had returned and Emily had been right: she was in love with the landscape. Mountains, roaring rivers, dark and frightening ravines: all were forgotten as they rode through valleys green with trees and flowers enclosed by a myriad of butterflies.

She had never thought she would see such beauty, know such passion pushing up inside her, finding plants to paint. She was learning all the time, setting up her easel in suitable places and painting what she saw, often leaving Emily back in her chosen venue while she and Nicholas and the remaining porter journeyed on, resting in these lush meadows. At such times she and Nicholas conversed unemotionally. 'I expect you want to move on, Nicholas – I know you're eager to search for that flower,' she said on one occasion, opening her paintbox.

He looked surprised. 'The double gentian? You know about it?'

Hester tensed. 'You mentioned it once. And then. . . .' She took courage and continued. 'I read your journal. I know you're looking for it. And I know why—' She stopped abruptly, seeing the startled widening of his eyes.

'You read my journal?' But something in Nicholas began to flow more easily. Perhaps she understood. 'But how? I left it with Emily, she needed to check on some details.'

Putting down her brush, she turned and met his challenging gaze. Was this the time to talk about Jon? To try and ease the guilt which she knew still raged inside him? Carefully she said, 'Emily lent it to me. It's in my bag at the inn. Of course you must have it back, I'll return it this evening, but Nicholas—' Words rushed on. 'I was so glad to read it; to know how you felt about Jon's accident.'

No. He was silent, looking at her with abruptly steel-cold eyes. She flinched, seeing emotion spreading over his face, but she knew she had been right to broach the banished subject.

'So you know that I failed to save him?' His voice was hard. 'That I feel unending guilt? You know all this?'

'I do. And I sympathize, but I know that you must push away the guilt – the accident wasn't your fault.'

'Perhaps not.' The words were tight and he turned away, staring at the surrounding peaks, at the drifting mist which floated over the snow-covered tops, making the landscape a palette of pale colours and wavering images. He turned back to her, words difficult to find at first, but gradually becoming easier. 'I'm glad you know, Hester. And now you understand that my search for this probably non-existent flower is vital to my future wellbeing. Thank you.'

It was a long moment before Hester nodded, ordered her emotions to sink back into their accustomed, well-drilled places, and returned to her painting. She must change the subject; she picked up her brush. 'I love recording these little alpines. Perhaps tomorrow we can go somewhere near a river? One of Emily's books says there should be a small bell flower growing in a damp habitat. What do you think?'

Normality was restored. Nicholas nodded. 'I know a place that's likely to have it.' *The river bank where Jon slipped and fell. The bell flower is sure to be there. And while I'm there, perhaps I can work out some of my wretched guilt.*

During the late afternoon they journeyed on to the next stop, a different village, a different inn, welcoming hosts and strange food. Hester, by now used to this peripatetic living, was enjoying herself. The freedom was exhilarating. She looked at her paintings and knew that these records of new plants would be of use to the world, perhaps particularly to the Royal Botanic Gardens at Kew. Her technique was improving; her passion growing ever stronger. The only problem in her world was Nicholas, who had, once again, closed up and had nothing to say except the polite necessities. In her room, she opened the journal, and looked at her painting of the gentian and her message. When would the moment come to return it to him? *Tomorrow.*

The storm broke as Hester put her head on the pillow. It had been threatening all evening, but now its full fury raged around the village. Thunder rolled and echoed, dealing enormous, vibrating hammer blows that deafened her; lightning struck down the sulphuric skies like glittering starbursts and she shut her eyes, covered her ears. But she heard the discreet knock on the door, called out 'Who is it?' and then sat upright when Nicholas said, 'Hester, are you all right?'

A moment when she thought she could not stop herself saying, 'No, come here, I need you. . . .' but then the strength that had come during the long days on the hard wooden mule saddle, the new vision of life which this extraordinary landscape had imprinted into her mind, came to her aid. She was young and free, she was strong. Of course she could deal with the storm on her own; but if Nicholas came into her room all that would disappear. His nearness, his warmth and charisma would be a seduction she could no longer fight.

'Thank you, Nicholas, I'm quite all right.'

He made no reply, and as the storm drifted away, still rumbling around the mountains, Hester lay back in bed and thought of him. For that one moment she had been so near to him, so close to offering her love, and now, again, so far. Sleep dissolved the images and disappointments, but her dreams were coloured with lost hopes.

Setting off next morning, she was astounded yet again at the magical landscape. The storm had left its aftermath of beauty, all the trees and flowers gleaming as if touched by an expert hand bestowing an extra aura of warming sunlight. The atmosphere was crystal clear, with the huge peaks climbing inexorably into the brilliant blue sky. A surge of new energy filled her and she smiled at Nicholas and Emily as they left the inn, intent on a new day's journeying and painting.

They climbed steadily, reaching the pass between two giant peaks in time to picnic and enjoy the luncheon provisions. Then Emily said, 'I shall go on for another hour – I recall an attractive stand of larches which I would like to paint. I shall take one of the porters with me. Nicholas, I think you have something else in mind?'

He nodded. 'This is quite close to the river where Jon had his accident.' His voice was expressionless. Hester, watching, saw tautness around his mouth, and wondered what he would say next. It was a surprise.

'I'm going back there, Emily – I need to deal with what happened. And I plan to climb further up the peak, taking the track that Jon was trying to follow.'

'You're still looking for that gentian?'

'Yes,' said Nicholas, and left it at that. He turned to Hester. 'Perhaps you'd like to come with me? There's a stream feeding the river, and I believe you might well find the bell flower you want to paint.'

Hester felt an uplift of spirit. '*Melittis melissophyllum*. Yes, I'd like that,' she said. 'And you can leave me with the porter while you climb – I shall be quite safe. And even if I don't find the bell flower, I know there'll be something else exciting.'

Their eyes met but Nicholas showed no emotion. 'Very well. So let's get going, shall we?'

The stream soon appeared, bubbling through moss-laden rocks that bordered the nearby churning river. With the porter's help, Hester set up her easel, conscious that Nicholas was standing silently at the river's edge. She imagined his thoughts. Jonathon's fatal accident had happened here, causing the guilt that Nicholas feared he would never lose.

He came to her side, his eyes shadowed. 'You'll be safe here with Enrico. But don't go near those slippery rocks.' He smiled rather grimly at her. 'I have a task to do, Hester – will you be happy to wait for me, however long I am?'

'Yes, I will wait.' *However long it takes.* 'But be careful.'

She watched as he rounded the rocks at the base of the grey scarred peak and disappeared. She waited for her heart to stop racing, and then prepared her easel and her palette for the work she intended to do.

Painting for nearly an hour, she was stiff as the sun began to slip down and the crisp air freshened. The young porter, sitting nearby, yawned. He got up and stretched as he saw her rise. 'You want to walk, lady?'

'Yes, but I'm not going far. No need for you to come.'

He nodded, grinned and sat down again. 'I watch.'

Flowers of many kinds starred the damp ground. She recognized some, but had already learned that this mountain landscape was full of unknown varieties of plants of every form and colour. For a while she just stood, looking around her, marvelling at nature's diversification. And then something caught her eye – a pale blue, familiar little trumpet flower, small and half hidden, but one that she instantly knew was the bell flower.

It was further away than she had thought; her feet began to slip on the moss-covered rocky terrain, but she reached the plant. Yes, the bell flower. It would make a delicate and lovely picture, those petals daintily uplifted and so blue. Just for a few moments her awareness of the growing roughness of the little stream deserted her. She would pick just one flower, take it back to the easel and paint it straightaway.

Her foot slipped. She overbalanced, fell awkwardly, too intent on saving the flower to see where she was heading. Only when the freezing water enclosed her, sending alarm and shock through her body, did she understand. Even in her panic-stricken desperation, she knew this is what must have happened to Jon. But he had died. Terrified, she lifted her head, spat out water and tried to breathe properly. Where was Enrico? Where was help? Oh God, was she to go the same way as Jon had gone? And if so, what would Nicholas do?

But it was his arms that swept her up from the now strong current bearing the waters into the river itself. Nicholas, who was saving her. She wept, cried out, unaware of what she said or did. Her body was stiff with cold and streaming wet. The good thick skirt had matted into a heavy felted weight, pulling her down. But Nicholas had his arms around her, Nicholas was saying, 'Let go, Hester, just let go – don't fight me, my love,' and slowly, with a greater strength than ever she had imagined, he carried her out of the frothing waters, onto the bank, laying her on the ground, raising her head, pulling off his coat and wrapping it around her sodden body. 'You're safe,' he said roughly, his breath warm on her cold face. 'You're safe. Thank God. I had this feeling that I had to come back. I knew something was wrong.'

It was moments before the shock left her. Nicholas told Enrico to take the blankets from under the mule's saddle and, carefully removing her soaked dress, folded them around her. 'Now,' he said, 'I'm taking you back to the inn. You need to get warm, to have something hot to drink, to dry your hair, change your clothes.' He turned away. 'Boy, bring the mule here. And put your coat under the saddle. Hurry.'

She was shocked and cold, yet she was uplifted, and joyous, a new person. He was taking charge of her and she was thankful. So much for women's liberation, she thought wryly, sitting up and smiling. And once she was in the saddle, with Enrico taking the bridle and Nicholas walking beside her, his hand holding hers, she discovered there was something new about him too. He looked different. More upright, with a firmer gait, a happier expression on his face, usually so taut and even grim at times; now there was a comfortable ease about his eyes, his mouth, his determined jaw. When he looked up at her – often, and always with a direct and unrestrained warmth that she foolishly felt was helping to dry her out – she understood that the colour blue, now enhancing the brilliance of his eyes, can encompass many different shades, something she had known before, mixing colours on her palette, but never actually experienced. Steely and cold, icy and full of splinters; mysterious and even sinister, heavenly and infinite but now, this moment, soft and caressing. Was she imagining it all?

'Nicholas,' she said, leaning towards him, 'did you find your flower?'

He chuckled. 'Not yet,' he said. 'I had this feeling that I had to come back to you, because. . . .'

She prompted very quietly. 'Because?'

His voice was deep and full of emotion. 'Because it came into my head that Jon's accident might well be repeated; why, I'm not sure. Oh, the water, and the slippery ground after the storm, I suppose – and I knew that the most important thing in the world was that I had to save you, even though I failed to rescue him.' He stopped, and she saw a brief smile emerge. 'And saving you, dearest Hester, has made me understand that I wasn't to blame for his death. Accidents happen and no one should feel guilty.'

She said nothing, but pressed his hand. Unsteadily she said, 'Thank goodness for everything.' They shared a long look of understanding until she went on, 'But your flower – you still have to look for it, you know.' And then she knew; this evening she must give him the journal and her picture.

'Perhaps another day. When you're better. But truly, Hester, the flower isn't important any longer. Not now that I've found myself – and you.' His smile was lighthearted and she responded to it at once.

'No, you can't just say that the flower isn't important. Think – if you found it, you would be famous! The horticultural world would honour you.'

His deep voice was vibrant, and his eyes, looking into hers, were yet another blue, warm, caressing, as he said, 'All that matters is that *you* do, my darling.'

Hester was thankful to get back to the inn, to dry out, to be offered healing herbal tisanes and warm towels and then to retire to her bed, Emily having ordered her to do so.

At the top of the staircase she turned and faced Nicholas, escorting her to her room. 'Wait,' she said, huskily, 'I have something to give you.' It took only a moment to return, holding the journal in her hand and offering it to him.

In silence, he took out the picture and read the message. Then he looked up, met her gaze and let out his held breath. 'Hester,' he said, his voice so low that she hardly heard the name. But his eyes were full of passion and she sensed that the last barrier had been shattered. His arms closed about her, and for a long moment they couldn't speak. 'I mean it about finding your gentian,' she murmured, stepping back.

'Tomorrow, perhaps, we must—' But he pulled her close, kissed her again, and the rest of the sentence, like everything else around her, vanished as at last she knew she was loved and now, with Nicholas enfolding her and giving way to his feelings, it was clear that life was smiling on them both.

CHAPTER TWENTY-THREE

The next day she insisted on searching for the gentian and Nicholas could only give in to her plea. By mid-morning they were back in the valley with the stream running through it; the river, several feet away, roared and churned, but their way lay ahead, around the last thrusting peak, up and up into the rocky heights where traces of snow still lay.

As they climbed, several times Hester thought she would fall but his hand was always there, his strength sheltering her from danger. 'How much further?' she gasped, and he smiled, with laughter in his eyes. 'Stay here and get your breath back – I'll just go around that crest over there. Don't move, my love, stay safe and wait for me.'

Her thoughts ran riot; how long she had waited but still the waiting continued. Looking around at this craggy, primitive view she sent her mind back to Devon, to Oak House and to the remembered view of Dartmoor, hazy and huge, in the distance, a wilderness beyond the lush, fertile, green fields. And then into Aunt Jacks' garden with its magnificent flower borders and fragrant rose bowers. But then the cold wind, touching her face, freezing her fingers, brought her back to the mountains, and she knew a moment of dawning truth. It was here, among these vast peaks and valleys that she had found love, and the fulfilment of her passion for painting flowers.

And then Nicholas was back, sweeping her into his arms, his lips warming her chilled body. She looked into his radiant eyes and murmured, 'Nicholas, don't ever leave me again.'

'You know I won't.'

She pressed herself against him and closed her eyes to the dangers surrounding them; until, suddenly, he was releasing her, taking her hands and saying, 'Come with me. Just a step more, my darling. I'll keep you safe – don't be afraid. . . .'

A step, but one with a hungry drop beneath it. Hester sucked in her breath and let Nicholas guide her as they found their way around the crest of rock in front of them. And then he stopped; drawing her close to him, looking into her eyes and smiling.

'Look,' he said quietly, his vibrant voice rich with pleasure. 'Hester, look. . . .'

A small blue, unusually flowered plant lay furled among thick leaves touched with snowflakes. Hester drew in a quick breath then let it out slowly, its warmth misting in the freezing air. This was a blue she had never known; cerulean blue, a jewel-like lapis lazuli, Madonna blue, a summer sky – yes, she knew all those, but not this radiant, almost magical blue. Gentian blue, the wonderful colour of Nicholas's brilliant eyes, as he grabbed her, pressed her to his ice-covered jacket, and kissed her.

Hester's thoughts ranged far in that magical moment: she, Hester Redding, was here. He, Nicholas Thorne, was beside her. At their feet was a small, magnificent rarity, surely to be named *Gentiana thorneii*, an honour which would proclaim him as a hero in the horticultural world.

She smiled into his rapt eyes, knowing that at last they were together, journeying on into the blue.